DEATH ON THE GOLDEN MILE

Also by Caleb Wygal

Mytle Beach Mystery Novels
The Brass Key
Death on the Boardwalk
Death Washes Ashore
Death on the Golden Mile

Lucas Caine Novels
Moment of Impact
A Murder in Concord
Blackbeard's Lost Treasure
The Search for the Fountain of Youth

DEATH
ON THE GOLDEN MILE

A MYRTLE BEACH MYSTERY

CALEB WYGAL

FRANKLIN/KERR
KANNAPOLIS, NORTH CAROLINA

Published by Franklin/Kerr Press
Kannapolis, North Carolina 28083
www.FranklinKerr.com

Edited byLisa Borne Graves
Cover art and design by Mibl Art
Author photo by Pamela Hartle
Interior design by Jordon Greene

Printed in the United States of America

FIRST EDITION

Hardback ISBN 979-8-9860006-4-0
Paperback ISBN 979-8-9860006-3-3

Fiction: Cozy Mystery
Fiction: Amateur Sleuth
Fiction: Southern Fiction

For my Aunt Karen
Thank you for the tea and chicken
and dumplings over the years.

CHAPTER
ONE

The blue electric toothbrush was vibrating between my teeth when the charge level on Autumn's phone changed from 99% to 100%. I turned it on before getting ice water out of the refrigerator dispenser. By the time I saw the text message on her phone warning her to "stay out of it, or else," I was lying in bed.

I stared at the screen in the darkened bedroom with blood rushing through my ears. The sender was unidentified. It came from a local 843 area code, but there was no other contact information associated with the mystery phone number. I checked the number against the contacts on my phone in case I knew the sender. No luck.

My finger slid against the cool glass of the screen as I scrolled through the messages that came before the threat. There weren't many.

Apparently, Autumn didn't know who sent the messages, either.

There were seven messages in total.

You stuck your nose in something you shouldn't have.

Who is this?

You're a lowly member of the courts. Just a clerk.

You know what I'm talking about, the stranger continued.

Forget what you saw.

Autumn responded, **I can't. The authorities need to know. Stay out of it, or else.**

The messages were nearly three years old. I stared at the screen and read them half a dozen times before looking at her call log. This number did not show up on any call.

She had personal and government emails linked to her phone. The court emails ended the day after she died. The straggler was a random email from HR reminding Autumn to log in to request vacation time off. We had planned to fly to Destin, Florida, for a week that fall. A trip that never happened.

I checked her personal email. The phone took ten minutes to download emails that had collected over the years. Mostly of the promotional variety. I searched for emails around the time of her death, looking in both her main inbox and junk folder. Nothing threatening there. She had an email from a prince of a country I had never heard of, telling her the king had bequeathed her a gift of $1,000,000 dollars. All she had to do was reply with her full name, date of birth, social security number, and bank account number and they would handle the transfer. It amazed me that scam artists were still trying to collect personal information that way.

Back to the texts. The sender inferred that Autumn learned or got into something she shouldn't have. Or did she discover something someone was trying to keep hidden? As a clerk of the court, she had access to court records pertaining to cases that came into Judge Whitley's courtroom. Typically, traffic and boating violations.

The sender referred to her as a "lowly member of the courts." My gut told me that the intimidator was someone in authority or someone with money who thought highly of themselves.

So, Autumn learned something this person wanted to keep

quiet. But what? How could I find the answer?

The clock on the nightstand ticked. Soft light from the lamp beside it illuminated my side of the bed. The sound of croaking frogs on the lakeshore penetrated the bedroom window. A ceiling fan swung in lazy arcs overhead, just enough to keep the air moving in the room. These summer Carolina nights could get sticky, and the fan helped. Autumn used to run the ceiling fan on high and had another small purple fan sitting on top of a dresser at the foot of the bed, blowing at full blast.

I would have frozen every night, but the weight of three thick blankets kept me warm.

She had been warm-blooded by nature. When I'd complain about the frigid night temperature in our room, she would tell me, "Hey. You can cover up and stay warm, but you can only take off so many clothes and stay cool."

That was hard logic to argue with. When she had been happy, I was happy.

I thought back to Judge Whitley's court around the time of Autumn's death. She never told me much about the cases. Most were mundane, involving drunk drivers or boaters speeding too close to shore.

After Detective Gina Gomez told me that she thought Autumn had been murdered, I spoke to a couple of Autumn's courthouse friends. Nothing stuck out to them as being unusual. Gomez had mentioned stirrings of shady activities happening at City Hall at that time, but Autumn had nothing to do with the local government's goings-on.

I stared at the phone, considering my options. It was after midnight. I didn't care.

With my thumb, I pressed the "Call" button at the top of the screen. The message screen evaporated, replaced with the telephone keypad. The mystery phone number took up the middle of the screen. At the bottom were two green buttons. One to make a voice call, the other for a video call.

I pushed the call button. My heart pounded.

The phone rang once and clicked.

A flat female voice said, "We're sorry. You have reached a number that has been disconnected or is no longer in service. Goodbye."

CHAPTER
TWO

Early the next morning, I sat at a table in my bookstore, Myrtle Beach Reads. A half-empty cup of coffee on my left. My aging laptop glowed in front of me. The store had just opened. Humphrey lumbered about stocking the shelves and helping the few tourists who had come in to browse for a book to read on the beach. I manned the coffee bar, but no one had ordered anything yet.

I had gone down a rabbit's hole of trying to figure out who owned the number that sent those messages to Autumn and how to track unknown numbers. The number had never been registered to any person or business. I figured out that it was a cellular number and not one assigned to a landline. That wasn't good news. If a telephone company like the Horry Telephone Company, or HTC for short, assigned that number, the user would have had to fill out personal information, like name and address, to get it.

Since it was a cellular number, I had several problems. Someone could have purchased a prepaid phone without having to give personal info, used it, and thrown it in the trash when they were done. Otherwise, known as a burner phone.

Then I might be able to track the phone if it were still in use.

From what I learned, only the authorities had access to that technology. Since the number had been disconnected, this was all a moot point.

As I scrolled through a website named CellTrack, a motorcycle rumbled to a stop on the street outside. A minute later, the door opened. A bell jingled, and in strutted Chris MacInally with a leather portfolio tucked under one arm. He was wearing blue dress slacks and a white vest atop a white dress shirt. The sleeves were rolled up to his elbows, revealing thick forearms covered in tattoos. Sweat beaded on his forehead. I couldn't tell if his slicked-back hair was wet from perspiration or from grease. It was already in the low eighties outside and stuffy.

He spotted me and made a beeline for my table.

"Morning," I greeted him as he sat across from me.

"Same," he said. His Irish brogue was thick. "Ready to do this?"

I closed the computer screen. "Absolutely. Coffee?"

"Sure. Have any Bailey's behind the counter?"

"I keep a bottle in the fridge just for you."

"Then make it a double."

"Sure thing." I stood and went behind the counter. As I prepared his coffee, he unzipped the portfolio and withdrew a stack of preprinted papers.

This was a big day for me. I had met Chris while investigating the murder of Paige Whitaker. He had been a coworker of hers and fellow executive at the OceanScapes Resort. She had been the head of human resources while he specialized in business development. The owner of the resort, simply called Mr. John, had tabbed Paige to take over the business upon his impending retirement. Her death delayed that.

During the investigation, I had wrongly accused Chris of the murder. Oops. Instead of the big guy punching my teeth out, we became friends, and he had offered to help expand my business. He didn't want paid and saw it as more of a hobby. Like his collection of Harley-Davidsons.

He was an Irish immigrant with an Ivy League degree. His looks gave you the impression he was an enforcer in the Irish mob, but his easy-going personality, wit, and a willingness to help others made him one of the most interesting people I had ever met.

After months of background work and scouting out the right location, today was the day we were going to sign documents for a business loan to get the next Myrtle Beach Reads location started. It was going to be called "Garden City Reads." We found a perfect location across from the Garden City pier on Atlantic Avenue, in between Surfside Beach and Murrells Inlet, to add the new bookstore. There was already a nice coffee shop next door named Garden City Coffee Grounds, so we would not offer coffee at that location. We would rely on foot traffic to bring most of the business. I had met with the owner of the cafe, and we had discussed an arrangement where customers would save a percentage off a coffee at their place if they showed a receipt from my store and vice versa.

I handed Chris his coffee and sat.

"Thanks, laddie. You hear about that storm banging its way up the Caribbean?"

"A little."

"They say it might come this way."

I took a sip of my coffee. "If it does, it does. I'll leave if they tell me I have to evacuate. I've ridden out worse."

Like many people who live along the Grand Strand, I ride

out most hurricanes. The last time I joined the evacuation line heading inland on 501 was for Matthew in 2016. The storm caused major flooding all over the area. Luckily, my house and the store came away with no damage.

Chris had moved to the area from up north several years ago, after Matthew. Threatening storms were still a newish experience for him.

"Do you think they'll tell us to vamoose?"

"Beats me. The storm is about to hit south Florida. It'll be a few days before they can make that determination."

He stared at the table as he sipped from his mug. "Yeah, sounds about right. You ready to sign these forms?"

I rubbed my hands together. "I was born ready."

He grinned and twisted the lid off a Montblanc fountain pen and held it out to me. "Here goes. I've already filled out most of this for you. This front sheet has basic information about the business and you. The other pages go into more detail. Read it and make sure everything is correct. If it is, just sign the back page and we'll get this puppy rolling."

As I glanced over the forms, the bells jingled again, and a woman entered. She wore a light pink dress with patterned fabric, broken up by a thick black belt, and heels. The woman removed her sunglasses, revealing a set of captivating emerald eyes. She looked fortyish with a runner's build. Chris turned to see who the new entrant was. He growled like a kitty ready to stalk its prey.

She scanned the store before her eyes settled on me and headed for our table. As she approached, the aroma of a delicate, flowery perfume preceded her. Without asking, she pulled out a chair beside Chris. The legs made a dry, scratching sound on the fake wood floor. She sat.

Her appearance and the fact that she invaded our space didn't arouse my curiosity as much as the envelope she had set on the table beside her sunglasses, now under her right hand. It was brown and unmarked.

"Hello," I said.

"Hi," she returned. Her voice was soft. She paid Chris no notice.

"Can I help you?"

She cleared her throat and slid the envelope across the table. "Yes, my dad wanted me to give you this."

Chris sat back and crossed his thick arms.

I glanced at the envelope but didn't make a move for it. "What is it?"

"To be honest, I don't know. After dinner last night, he told me to bring you this first thing. He's probably inviting you to our home or something."

"Who's your dad?" I sipped my coffee.

She raised an eyebrow. "John Allen Howard."

Chris locked eyes with me.

I tilted my head to the side. "John Allen Howard? You mean the composer?"

"Yes."

"The guy who did the music for those big movies back in the 80s?"

"Yes."

"Won a bunch of Academy Awards?"

"Yes. Seven, actually."

"Wow. And he's your dad?"

"Yes."

Chris let out a low whistle. She looked his way for the first time. Frank Sinatra crooned "My Way" over the speakers.

I cradled the mug on the table with both hands. John Allen Howard worked on some of the biggest Hollywood blockbusters over the past five decades. He scored films for Spielberg, Scorsese, Peter Jackson, and James Cameron, just to name a few off the top of my head. His music was famous the world over.

"Does he still work on movies?"

Her bottom lip pooched out. "Not so much anymore. He's had some health problems and wants to take it easy. Especially after mom died."

"Oh, I'm sorry."

She held up a hand. "Don't worry about it. She passed away about ten years ago. Cancer. After she died, Dad didn't want to live in Hollywood anymore. He wanted to settle down."

"Where were you before he came here?"

"With him. I've been his personal assistant since I could answer a telephone." She laughed and looked away. "Besides, Dad met Vanna White at some Hollywood gala."

"North Myrtle Beach's most famous native," I said.

"Right. They got to talking, and she mentioned she was from here. The way she talked about Myrtle Beach stuck with Dad. When mom died, he didn't want to live in their house without her. He wanted a change. He remembered the way she talked about this area and built a house here. It was an easy transition, especially since my siblings were already here."

"Based on a conversation with Vanna White?"

"Yeah. Basically."

She had piqued my interest. I placed a hand on the envelope. The paper was cool to the touch. I tapped a finger on it. A band of clouds uncovered the still-rising sun across the street, casting the shop in hues of light orange and yellow as it shone through the windows.

"What's your name?" I asked.

"Erin Howard." She cast a sidelong glance at Chris. "Is he a friend of yours or someone you're doing business with? I apologize if I interrupted."

"No, it's fine," I said. "We had just sat down ourselves. To answer your question, he's a bit of both. Right now, we're getting the paperwork together for a business loan for a new bookstore."

"Oh? Congratulations."

"Thanks," I said.

Chris explained, "I will not be involved in the business. I'm a business developer for one of the resorts around here, and I'm just helping him out."

"That's admirable of you," she said.

Chris shrugged. "Always happy to help."

"In that case, if it's an invitation, you can come too. Dad likes to meet interesting people."

I said, "Is that why he wants to meet me? Because he thinks I might be interesting?"

"Beats me. I'd never heard of you until last night."

I had been in the news twice in the past year: first for solving the murder of Paige Whitaker and then that of Connor West. I tried to keep my name out of the press, but word still leaked out about the mild-mannered bookstore owner with a penchant for solving mysteries. Me, in this case. I don't seek murders. They had a way of finding me.

I had also signed a book deal with a smallish publisher in New York that made headlines in the local press. The modest advance would go toward funding part of the startup costs for the next bookstore. My agent presented my idea for a mystery series to various publishers, and one offered me a contract. I ghost wrote several adventure books for a big-name author but wanted to branch out on my own when I came up with the idea.

It was odd to go in the Piggly Wiggly in Surfside and have people recognize me. While word about me had spread, I was still mostly unknown. I would like to keep it that way, if possible.

I held up the envelope. "If this is an invitation, where is his estate?"

She smiled and lifted her head high. "On the Golden Mile."

CHAPTER
THREE

Even Chris, who wasn't impressed by much, arched his eyebrows. Erin cast her eyes around the store and rubbed her arms.

"Nice place you have here," she said. "I can see why you would want more. Would your next location be like this?"

"More or less," I answered. "The spot we're targeting by the Garden City Pier is smaller, but still large enough to make a profit if we sell enough books by the square foot."

The corners of her lips curled down. Her head bobbed. "Impressive."

Chris peeled off a thick forefinger from the coffee mug handle and pointed it at me. "I'm teaching the lad. He and his wife started this place without having much of a business plan. It was her dream to own a bookstore, and she and Clark opened this place when the opportunity presented itself."

"Really?" Erin said.

"Yeah," I chuckled. "We wrote our basic business plan on the back of a napkin at Villa Romana one night over an anniversary dinner."

"How lovely." She smiled and craned her neck. "And where is your wife?"

"She passed away about three years ago," I said.

Erin placed a hand over her heart. "I'm so sorry to hear that. She must have been so young."

"She was." I explained to her how she died, leaving out the murder scenario. That was a discussion for a different day.

"Such a shame." She checked the smartwatch on her wrist. "Look, I must run. I have a massage scheduled at Dolce Lusso in thirty minutes."

A massage sounds nice, I thought as I involuntarily stretched out an arm and felt the tight muscles. "Well, it was nice to meet you."

"Yeah, same," Chris said.

Erin gave a tight smile and stood. "Sure."

The bell on the door jingled as she departed. She passed by the front windows on her way to her vehicle. Erin stared straight ahead, bit her bottom lip, and crossed her arms. She didn't glance at the ocean across the street. She had done what was asked of her. Then she was gone.

Humphrey trudged over. His sandy hair, upturned nose, and blue eyes were maturing. He started here as a college student and has since graduated from the Horry-Georgetown Technical College with a degree in digital arts. He had matured in the nine months he'd worked here. He wouldn't stop playing video games on his phone when he started. I almost fired him. That served as a wake-up call. He worked hard since our conversation. He knows I have security cameras in place inside the store and can watch his every move if I wanted. Now his face looked less youthful and more experienced.

"Who was that?" he asked.

I looked up at him from my seated position. "Erin Howard."

"Wow, for an older chick, she was hot."

"Hey. That 'older chick,' as you called her, is probably close to my age. Are you calling me old?"

Chris snorted.

"Well, uh, you see," Humphrey blubbered.

I smacked him on the knee. "Just messing with you. I remember being your age." I glanced up at the window to where I last saw Ms. Howard. "But yes, I agree with you. Easy on the eyes."

"That she was."

"Get back to work. You can fantasize later."

He laughed. "Sure."

After he stalked off, I drained the last of the coffee. It had cooled during the conversation. I picked up the envelope and tapped the edge on the wood table.

My name was written in flowy script on the front. Other than that, the envelope was unadorned. I turned it over and ripped it open.

An index card was inside. That was it. The same person who wrote my name on the outside penned the message on the card. It was a masculine but elegant script. Like on documents written during the 17 and 1800s, when people cared for their penmanship.

The note read:

> *Dear Mr. Clark,*
>
> *My name is John Allen Howard. I am inviting you and a friend, if you wish to bring one, to my home this Wednesday evening at seven. There is a matter I need to discuss with you. Dinner will be served.*
>
> *My address and code to enter the gate are below.*
>
> *Cheers,*
>
> *JH Howard*

The address for the place was on North Ocean Boulevard. I punched it into the Maps application on my phone. A red pin appeared up for a place just off 43rd Avenue N. I switched to the satellite view and zoomed in. The image was from the top down. It showed a gray roof on a long house, a walkway extending out to the beach, a circular driveway inside a gate, and a fence surrounding three sides of the home. It was larger than the other homes on either side of it.

The Golden Mile is one of the most prestigious residential areas in Myrtle Beach. It is filled with some of the most expensive and grandiose private residences along the Grand Strand. It stretches from about 31st Avenue N to 52nd. Beach accesses dot the stretch, to which I've been before. The cost of getting a home there starts in the multi-millions.

While I was on my phone, Chris was on his. He gave out a long whistle.

"What is it?" I asked.

"This." He turned the phone around so I could see the screen. On one side of the screen was a picture of John Allen Howard looking resplendent in a white tux on the red carpet at the Academy Awards. The other side of the box read in big, bold letters: Net Worth $100 Million.

It was my turn to whistle.

"What does the card say?" he asked.

"It's an invitation to dinner, with a plus one. Said it could be whoever I wanted."

"Have someone in mind? Like a certain leggy detective with the MBPD?"

"Who? Gomez?"

"She's the one. How about that reporter girl, Erica?"

I glanced out the front windows and back to him. "I'll be honest. One of them crossed my mind when I read it."

"Which one?"

"I'm not telling."

"Come on. I've seen you around both. There's chemistry there. Don't deny it."

Detective Gina Gomez was the lead detective in the Myrtle Beach Police Department. I met her the morning that I discovered Paige Whitaker's body by the backdoor of this place. I wouldn't say that we worked together on that case and then again with Connor West, but we had to communicate to get both murders solved. She was dedicated to her job but also displayed care and interest to those around her, including me.

Erica Sullivan was a rising reporter who worked for WMHF. We also met during the Whitaker case. She was flirty, single, and exceptional at her job. She was also a decade younger than me. Gomez was closer to my age if I had to guess.

I had thought about both in recent months, but never to the point of asking either out on a date. Just, you know, fond thoughts on those lonely evenings without Autumn.

"I deny nothing," I said. "Want to go? You already received Erin's blessing. Who knows, maybe you sparked her interest."

Chris blushed. He was single as well. He opened his hands. "If I did, I did. Not sure what she'd see in me, though."

"Maybe she likes the roguish sort with a Scottish accent."

He sat back and drained the last of his coffee. "I wouldn't turn her down for a date and wouldn't mind seeing how the rich and famous live."

I stretched my arms above my head and blew out a breath

as I laid them back down on the table. "The rich and famous. They operate differently."

He pointed a thick finger at me. "Which you learned from looking into the whole Connor West thing."

"They had money," I said and pointed at his phone, where the picture of John Allen faded to black. "But not like that. You in?"

"Absolutely."

CHAPTER
FOUR

From the time she had formed, Hurricane Karen, like so many other Karens, couldn't make up her mind. Starting as a tropical depression fifty-seven miles east of St. Lucia, she ping-ponged her way in a ragged northwesterly direction through the Lesser Antilles, gaining strength until she became a Category 1 hurricane.

From there, she dove in a straight line through the warm waters of the Caribbean, dead set on wreaking havoc as a Category 5 on Jamaica. At the last minute, she veered eastward and laid waste to the Caymans before turning north, where Havana lay in her path. As the storm approached Cuba, a front came off the coast of Texas and pushed her east and over the Sierra Maestra Mountains, where she weakened among the rugged range.

She limped toward the Bahamas before veering west and hitting Miami as a Category 2. A low front crossing over the Appalachians kept Karen off the Atlantic Coast as she made her way north.

The forecast for Karen was to pass by the Carolina Coasts, close enough to have the double red flags raised on the Grand Strand beaches, telling residents and visitors that the water was too dangerous to enter. The waves grew aggressive. Rip currents threatened to pull swimmers deeper into the ocean.

By the time she passed Savannah to the south, she weakened to a tropical storm. She seemed content to putter her way north and out to sea, having caused millions of dollars in damage along her path.

But Karen had one more surprise in store...

* * *

Towering loblolly pines swayed in the slight breeze. The colorful row houses of Market Common sat across Farrow Parkway from us as we waited for lunch on the patio at Toffino's. I invited Detectives Gina Gomez and Phil Moody to join me. My treat.

It was the day after receiving the invitation to John Allen Howard's estate.

Moody wore a dark, rumpled sport coat. Sweat beaded on his face. Thick curly hair fell beneath a tan trilby hat. If I were a casting director, I'd hire him as a dirty cop in a heartbeat. He looked the part. I knew him to be a little rough around the edges, but he had a good heart.

Gomez wore work attire as well. She sat to the side of her chair with one long leg folded over the other. Her dark hair was tied back in a ponytail. Pearl earrings dangled from each ear.

We talked about the subject on everyone's mind at present: the storm moving past us out at sea.

"What will you do if it veers inland?" I asked.

Moody's shoulders moved up and down one inch. "Same thing I always do. Nothing."

Gomez grinned at her partner, then said to me, "I live in

Burgess. If it gets bad, I'll move to a center room in my condo. Other than that, I'll stay put. Moody and I never know when we'll be needed. A storm hits, people evacuate. Then hoodlums come in and try to raid the empty businesses and houses."

"I hadn't thought of that," I said.

A server appeared and set a salad in front of Gomez, a calzone as big as a Thanksgiving turkey in front of Moody, two slices of pizza before me, and then departed.

Gomez cocked her head to the side. "Dang, Moody. Do you have an extra stomach to store that thing in?"

He cut into the edge of the calzone with a fork and stuffed a piece into his mouth. "That's what my wife used to say."

I took a bite of pizza. Gomez dug into her salad. After her first taste, she said to me, "It's been a while since I've seen you. Looks like you've lost weight."

Sitting up straight, I patted my not-as-flabby-as-it-used-to-be stomach. "Thanks. A little more exercise and less ice cream from the shop at the end of the building." I sprinkled parmesan cheese on my slice of pizza. "I've cut back on the carbs, too."

"But not today." She smirked. Moody grunted.

"Nope. I indulge occasionally, so I still feel like a human."

It's true. I went on a diet after the Gladiator Games case. Seeing those men and women who weren't much younger than me in peak physical condition motivated me to try harder to stay in shape. That, and the fleeting thoughts of catching the attention of another woman.

After taking another bite of salad, Gomez said, "Okay, Clark. What's this about?"

"Autumn," I said.

She and Moody looked at each other. It made me wonder if this had been a subject between them. Her green eyes showed concern.

"Look, I've already told you what I know," Gomez said. "My gut tells me there was something hinky going down the night of her death, but that's just a feeling not backed up by any facts."

"Yeah. Same." Moody grunted and plunged a chunk of the calzone into his mouth.

Autumn died one evening of a heart attack at her desk at the courthouse three years ago. The lead detective at the time, Ed Banner, had Gomez come along with him when the death was called in. They went, looked around, examined the body, and found no signs of foul play. The coroner deemed the cause of death as a heart attack. Autumn had lived with a heart murmur. She had known each day could've been her last.

Gomez told me after I solved the Paige Whitaker murder that she thought Autumn had been murdered. A statement I'll remember for the rest of my life. That was something that I never considered a possibility. She explained that, on the evening of her death, Banner acted weird and wrapped the case up quickly. His actions caused her to question his motives. She explained she was still coming up in the ranks and didn't want to ruffle any feathers.

She might not have thought any more about it, except that Banner died a few months later with the same cause of death: heart attack.

There was no case. She didn't have enough evidence to open a file on Autumn's death. She stayed busy enough as it was and adding a three-year-old case that was open and shut at the time wasn't possible. Particularly because there wasn't any evidence of murder.

"Right," I said. "I get that, and I appreciate everything you've done."

"I bet you wish Gomez hadn't said anything. Ignorance is bliss and all," Moody said.

"I'll admit, life would have been simpler," I responded. "But, knowing that someone had ill intentions toward her and that she may have been murdered? I would want to know."

My statement caused them to look up from their food with bulging eyes.

"You mean you found someone who might have wanted her killed?" Gomez said.

I set my lips in a fine line. "Possibly."

"Who?"

"I don't know."

"Okay." She took a drink of sweet tea. A motorcycle roared past on Farrow Parkway, drowning out all conversation for a moment. The breeze picked up, causing the tablecloths to flutter. After the commotion died away, she said, "Explain."

I reached into my pocket and laid a phone on the table. "Autumn's phone. It sat in the bottom of a desk drawer since her death. I hadn't thought about it. I fired it up to see if I could find anything that might point to a killer."

"And you found something," Gomez stated.

"Yes," I said.

Moody grunted.

I explained the messages from the mystery sender and that the number led to a dead end.

"A threat like that," Gomez said, "isn't something to take lightly. How long after the messages did her death occur?"

"Three days."

"Whoa," Moody said. That's the most emotion I remembered seeing from him since we met.

I waved the phone in the air. "Is this enough to open an investigation?"

Gomez touched a finger to her lips. "I don't think so. Not yet at least. I have someone who can look at this. Maybe he can get more off the phone."

I had spent the morning going through Autumn's phone, trying to find more clues. The string of ominous text messages was all I could find. I handed the phone to her across the table. She slid it into a pocket.

"I'll get this to him today."

"Thanks, Gomez. I appreciate this."

"Don't mention it," she said.

"Thanks."

She held up a finger. "No, I mean it. Don't breathe a word of this to anyone. Your wife and Banner died in a close time period. Could be a coincidence, but they died in the same way. I figure for what you've done for me, for us, excuse me, this is the least I can do."

"I think we're on the same page here," I said. "Let's pretend that someone murdered Autumn and Banner. The same person. You say Banner acted strange the night of her death."

"Okay," she said. "Keep going."

I grabbed another bite of the pizza to stall while I tried to string the thoughts together that I had been pondering for months. I pointed at the phone in her pocket. "Let's say it was that person. The author of those messages acted like they carried a big stick. What if this person had something on Banner?"

"And then went and killed Banner anyway," Gomez finished the line of thought.

"Means, motive, and opportunity," I said. "You know this.

You're the trained detectives."

"We are," Gomez said, "but we can only help you to a degree."

"Then, at least be my sounding board," I said.

"When we can."

"Thank you. So, if someone had some sort of power over Banner, and Autumn learned or poked her nose into something she shouldn't, who could it be?"

Gomez held her fork straight up. "That's the million-dollar question."

Moody snorted. "There's also a million people it could have been."

"You're saying the odds are against me," I said.

"Exactly," Moody said and ate the last bite of his calzone.

I hadn't noticed that he had eaten that entire beast while we were talking. Color me impressed.

* * *

I went back to the bookstore, made a joke to my employee Karen about them naming a moody hurricane after her, then locked myself in the office. I just gave one of my last connections with Autumn away, and I wasn't sure if I would get it back. Sitting here by myself, part of me regretted the decision. I realized it was a small thing. A cell phone that sat in a drawer in my desk for three years. I hadn't given it any thought.

Now that it was gone, I missed it. Or was it that I missed that personal piece of Autumn? I told myself it was worth it if Gomez's connection resulted in getting information off that phone and helped in tracking down her killer.

If Autumn were here today, she would tell me two things:

"Let them do their work," and "Move on with your life."

I sat at my desk and rubbed a hand over my face. The two-day growth of my beard was scratchy against my palm. I had neglected shaving since I remembered her phone.

The screensaver on my computer vanished after I moved the mouse. I pulled up Google and punched in John Allen Howard. The web browser bunched together several pictures of him in a collage on the top-right part of the screen, with his name displayed in bold print underneath. There were links underneath to listen to his music on various websites. YouTube, Spotify, Pandora, etc.

The top result on the left side of the screen was a listing for Howard's Wikipedia page. I clicked on that. At the top, before you got to any biographical information about him, were four lines. One listing the instruments played (piano and French horn). One for years active (1968-present). Another for Occupations (composer, conductor). The last was for genres (Film music, television score, and contemporary classical).

He was born in 1945 in Palo Alto, California. Studied music at USC-Berkeley across the bay from where he was born and finished his schooling at Julliard in New York City. He started out as a studio pianist, performing with Hollywood composers such as Henry Mancini and Leonard Bernstein.

Allen later recorded two jazz albums. I'd have to check them out. I played jazz music on the speakers here at the bookstore.

Allen's first film composition was for a promotional film for the tourist office in Nova Scotia. His feature film work began later. After that, it was a cavalcade of big Hollywood directors for which he scored films. His music was recognized around the world.

There was no mention in the Wikipedia article about him

living in Myrtle Beach. It had been a while since anyone updated his entry.

I searched for his family. It's intrusive to find out private information about a famous person's family, but in this digital era, no one can hide everything. Howard had three children, the youngest being Erin. It listed her as a personal assistant to Mr. Howard. The oldest child was DeeDee. She was in her mid-fifties. The middle child is Cade. He was tan, handsome, and an art broker.

I could only go down that rabbit hole so far before the information trail ended. Thankfully, I didn't find any of the three in the news for committing crimes.

I checked the weather. Karen was on a slow jaunt off the Georgia coast. The current track for her was to move further offshore and not present a threat to Myrtle Beach. That's good, because the estimated time for her to pass by the Grand Strand was the same time as dinner at the Howard residence.

I hoped Karen behaved herself.

CHAPTER
FIVE

Chris and I drove up Ocean Boulevard and past the Sea Captain's House on our way to John Allen Howard's estate on the Golden Mile. Tourists went about their business as though there wasn't a storm making its way past us. They paid good money to take time off work and come here, and the desire to make the most of vacation outweighed the minimal risk Karen presented.

The endless stream of resort hotels fell away, leading us to a residential stretch. The homes were immaculate and stately on both sides of the street. We passed by a playground with a mock pirate ship for kids to climb and play on. One brave kid was out there with her parents on the deck of the ship.

The sky to the west was blue. The atmosphere out to sea and moving in our direction cast a different story. High banks of gray clouds roiled past. Palm fronds bent in the gusts. Power lines shivered. Not a sea bird was in sight. Instinct told them to take refuge.

Chris watched the scene unfold out the truck window as I stared straight ahead, searching for the address Erin provided. Despite modern amenities, I still enjoyed finding places the old-fashioned way: with my eyes and sense of direction. I had a way of surprising Autumn when we would travel before the days of GPS. She would think we were lost as she flipped through printed directions from MapQuest. I would tell her to trust me. And then, when she came close to exasperation and calling a divorce lawyer to get her away from her stubborn husband who wouldn't stop and ask for directions, we would arrive at our destination.

She would put her hand on my arm and say she should have never doubted me. I would assure her I would have eventually sought help, had we kept driving, to make her feel better. Truth be told, I guessed half the time. She never knew. I think. I learned early in our relationship to never doubt Autumn. She was smarter than me. There was never any doubt of that.

We passed a beach access, and a tall house with tan stucco walls before arriving at our destination.

A tall, wrought-iron gate with an encircled H at its center gave glimpses of the mansion that lay behind it. A silver keypad with a speaker box at window height was attached to a pole to the left side of the driveway before the gate. There was a round orange button below the speaker grate.

Chris noticed this and said, "Why would he give you the gate code if you could have just pushed the button to be let in?"

"Good question. Maybe he wanted our appearance to be a surprise."

"You mean your appearance. That invitation was intended for you. I'm an afterthought," he said, pointing at his chest.

"Meh," I muttered. I grabbed the index card with the gate code one last time. I already had it memorized, but it didn't hurt to be sure. "This is the simplest security code I've ever seen. Reminds me of Spaceballs."

Chris laughed. "Yeah, the old Mel Brooks movie. How did that scene go? 'One, two, three, four, five? Only an idiot would have that on his luggage.'"

"That's it." I smiled. "This isn't much more complex than that. Two, two, three, three."

"You're kidding?" He looked through the window at the huge beach house that lay beyond the gate. "I can't imagine it would take a hacker long to break that code."

I pointed at the top of both sides of the gate. "With those cameras there, a would-be burglar wouldn't have long before someone noticed."

"If someone is monitoring the feed."

"Yup."

I rolled down the window and punched in the code. The keypad beeped with each press. Small drops of rain sprinkled on the windshield. The gates separated. I pulled forward into a circular cobblestone driveway with a stone nautilus fountain flanked by two palm trees in the middle. The enormous house had a red-brick exterior and intricate stonework along the foundation. A Category 5 hurricane wouldn't damage this place. Palm trees swayed on either side of the house. A two-car garage was on the lower left, below a three-window bump-out. Three thin windows with closed hurricane shutters were above the protrusion.

The other half of the house was more detailed and statelier. Railings with starburst woodwork led the way up to a covered front porch, complete with rocking chairs. A turret with three blue windows bunched together was in the middle of the house above the left side of the porch. The area to the right of that held another row of tight-packed windows. From the outside, the turret gave the impression of open-air inside.

"Decent," Chris said as we climbed from the truck.

"I'll say," I replied.

I pulled behind a shiny blue Tesla at the foot of the stairs.

Two other luxury vehicles were parked in front of it.

"If these are out here, I wonder what's in the garage," Chris said.

"Maybe they'll let us have a peek."

"We'll see."

The wind whipped through my hair as I climbed the steps. Chris's hair didn't budge owing to the industrial strength hair gel he used. He walked beside me.

The porch was covered in planks of reclaimed and refinished wood. Two rocking chairs sat off to the side. A wood crafted double door greeted us as we climbed to the top of the landing. I rang the doorbell and waited.

A moment later, Erin opened the door. "Greetings," she said. "Come on in."

"Hello again," Chris said with a half bow.

"We're here," I said, not looking at her, but already glimpsing into the interior of the home.

My outside impression proved correct on the inside. A vast living area greeted us as she stood aside to let us enter. Sturdy luxury vinyl plank floors that looked like refinished driftwood spread out before us in a great, open room. The ceiling hung way overhead with stained wood beams reaching to an apex. The beams matched the other finishings throughout this level. The rooms spaced around the home had sliding barn doors.

The kitchen fit for a five-star restaurant lay to our right, featuring quartz countertops and a French door refrigerator with a touch screen embedded in the right door. A gas range and ornate hood were the focal points behind a kitchen island large enough to have its own zip code.

Bags of takeout sat atop quartz counters. The cabinets matched the stain on the wood beams in the ceiling. The island had seating for six facing the kitchen on the other side. My stomach growled as the aroma of Old Bay and seafood emanated from the counter. Dinner wasn't due to be served for another half hour. I wanted to peel a bag open and grab a roll but held off.

"The Sea Captain's House catered dinner," Erin said, as though reading my mind.

"Ooo," Chris said. "They have some of the best lobster in Myrtle Beach. Almost as good as when I lived in Boston."

"The Lobster House and Mr. Fish are pretty good as well," I said.

"Noted," Erin said. "We haven't tried them. I'll add them to our list."

"Does someone from here go get the food?" I asked.

"No, we had it delivered. The guy from the Sea Captain's House got here just before it started raining. Said they were closing their kitchen early and heading home."

"Yeah," I said, "hurricanes can spoil a nice dinner out."

"Thankfully, we're eating in," Erin said. "Dad can't wait to meet you. He's upstairs getting ready."

I had looked forward to meeting a member of Hollywood royalty since Erin's visit to the bookstore. My parents were jealous. Even my older brother, Bo, said he wished he could have come. He was on assignment in San Diego and said he'd pass on giving up the perfect weather there for a hurricane here. I hadn't invited him.

A long, hand-carved table sat against the wall in the house's corner, facing the ocean. They arranged three chairs on two sides. A bench seat bordered the other two. Windows peeked out onto a swimming pool in the rear courtyard. Dark gray clouds whirled, causing me to question my decision to come.

A stairway to the upper level branched off from the right of the foyer. It switchbacked toward the center of the home, leading to a second level. A globe chandelier hung from the ceiling from high above the landing. Shiplap walls ran up the side of the stairs. A balcony on the upper floor overlooked the great room. A man and a woman stood at it, watching the storm approach with drinks in hand. Other voices echoed from there.

Beside us, a coffee bar with a mini fridge nestled under the counter was embedded into the wall below the stairs. A Nespresso coffee machine and a rack of coffee pods sat atop the counter. A tree of assorted coffee mugs sat beside it.

"Dad loves his coffee," Erin said, waving a hand at the bar. "It's the first thing he wants when he comes in."

Chris gave me a soft backhand on the arm. "A man after your own heart."

Erin's brows drew together.

"I do love my coffee," I explained.

"Have a cup," she suggested.

"Maybe after dinner," I said.

"I'm fine, too," Chris said. "I was hoping this would be a liquor bar."

Erin pointed up. "That's upstairs."

Expansive windows spanned the opposite wall, offering panoramic views of the roiling ocean and vacant beach.

"That storm looks like it's getting closer," Chris noted.

"The latest update came in from the national weather center," she said. "The storm shifted in our direction during the past hour."

"Should we get out of here in case it comes closer?" Chris asked.

She pointed at the windows. "Those are hurricane-force windows, made to withstand winds up to two-hundred miles per hour. We have a metal roof that can withstand winds that are almost as strong."

"What about objects flying through the air?" I asked.

She pressed a finger to her lips. "Now that I'm not sure about." She turned and regarded the swirling clouds off the coast. "We should be fine. We can go down to the bottom level if it comes to it. Dad has a music studio down there that's well-insulated. Follow me."

As she turned and climbed up the stairs, I looked over at Chris and shrugged. I wasn't sure I shared her confidence.

She turned and explained, "Dad hired a guy who did some of the HGTV Dream Homes to design this house."

"It's impressive," Chris said.

"Thank you," she said. "He designed it with the thought of maximizing space. There are little cubbies and hidden storage areas everywhere."

As Chris's eyes swept around the cavernous home, I wondered how much more space a person needed. This was, by far, the largest home I'd ever been in, including Ed Moore's place. He was an actor in the Gladiator Games Dinner Show and a former Olympic fencer.

"You're a little early, but that's okay," Erin said. "The others are already here. There's a great room up here with a fireplace overlooking the rest of the house. That is where people gather to chat."

"Who else is here?"

"My brother and sister, her boyfriend, a neighbor lady, and Dad's financial advisor."

"Sounds like a ragtag crew," I said, tilting my head in the balcony's direction. "Who's that up there with the drinks?"

She turned and looked. "Louise and Preacher. She lives next door and tries to see Dad as much as possible. He's the money guy and sometimes plays music with Dad. Dad invited them this evening. My siblings are normal dinner attendees. Sometimes her boyfriend comes, like today."

"Why does Louise try to see your dad often?" I asked.

"She's widowed. Her husband passed away several years ago, and I think she's lonely and looking for a companion."

"Oh," I responded.

"Yeah."

"Is she after his money or something?"

"I don't know why. Her husband owned car dealerships in and around Indianapolis. She's loaded."

I wanted to ask if Louise was as loaded as Erin's dad but didn't think it would be prudent.

Sheets of rain cascaded off the windows. Wind whipped the palm trees into a frenzy. Pregnant sea oats bent sideways, trying to maintain a foothold amidst the gale atop the rolling sand dunes. The mounds of sand blocked our view of the beach, but the storm had sent the waves into a frothy tantrum. Inside, soft piano music played through hidden speakers.

"Looks like we got here in the nick of time," Chris commented.

"That it does," I said. "Let's hope it doesn't get bad."

"That's the truth," he muttered.

We reached the top of the stairs. Two doors, set close together, ran down a hallway in front of us. An elevator let out opposite the doors, halfway down. The corridor snaked to the left at the end, disappearing into more rooms.

A great room lay to our left. A vast airy, open space complete with comfortable seating and a fireplace. More doors lined the wall beyond that.

Erin pointed at the two doors nearest us. "That's Dad's

bedroom and office. He'll come out when he's ready."

We followed her to a plush seating arrangement with a driftwood coffee table at its center. An immaculate gray stone fireplace, with a stained wood mantle to match the other woodwork in the home, lay dormant on a wall near the sofa and chairs.

Whoever picked the furniture and decorations in the house couldn't have done a better job. Ornate paintings spaced around both levels of the home all had a nautical theme. Panoramas and ocean-going vessels.

The painting above the fireplace stood out above the rest. It didn't fit. It looked like something you would see in an Eastern European section at an art museum. The painting looked old.

Chris spoke my mind. "What's the deal with that painting?"

Erin turned to him. "Which one?"

"That one." He pointed above the fireplace. "The one where the old guy with the long, white beard looks like he's offering a blessing to a sick child."

"Oh, that one," she said. "It's newer. Well, not newer as in recently painted, but newer to the house. That's why it doesn't fit in with the rest of the decorations. My brother, Cade, discovered it for sale at a gallery in Charleston. It's called Elisha Raising the Shunammite's Son, originally painted in 1766 in London by Benjamin West."

"So, it's older than the United States," I said.

"It is," she replied as we regarded the oil painting. In it, a woman cradled a pale, sick-looking child on one side, while a man who looked like a biblical prophet stood over her with raised hands. I've heard of Elisha from the Bible but wasn't too familiar with his story. "Wait, you said 'originally painted.' What does that mean?"

"The way Cade described it," she said, "This painting is a reproduction by one of his students who went on to be a prolific painter here in the States in his own right. Antoine Le Nain."

The name meant nothing to me. "Well, it's nice whoever painted it."

I agreed, and we moved on.

A man and woman sat close together on the sofa, deep in conversation, watching the maelstrom taking place outside. Their backs were to us. Across from them was a man with a bushy beard, facing us, staring at his phone. Even from this distance, I could tell he was short. His legs had to stretch to touch the floor. He wore a pair of mesh shorts and a matching blue tank top that showed off well-defined muscles. Everyone else, including me, was dressed for a nice dinner. I still wore flip-flops, though. You can take the beach bum off the beach, but you can't take the beach out of the beach bum.

Erin led us over to the end of the table and introduced us. "Hey, this is Clark and Chris."

They looked up at us. This was our first view of the back of the house. A covered porch ran the length of it. A long infinity pool and hot tub lay between the porch and fence bordering the dunes.

"I'm DeeDee," the woman said with a smoky voice. She had big dark hair, styled in a bouffant. Her plump lips and smooth skin hinted at having a plastic surgeon on speed dial. "John Allen's oldest child."

The man half-stood to shake our hands before resuming his seat beside DeeDee. "I'm Antonio. DeeDee's boyfriend." He spoke with an Italian accent.

DeeDee elbowed him in the ribs. "Hopefully, more than that soon."

Antonio closed his eyes and smiled. "Yes, dear."

"Ah," Chris said, "do I hear wedding bells in the future?"

"I'm not so sure about wedding bells," DeeDee said. "More like waves. We've talked about getting married on the beach outside."

"Well, let me give you early congratulations," Chris said.

"It might be a very early congrats, but thank you," Antonio said, drawing the evil eye from DeeDee. That's not how I would have phrased it if I were him.

The other man said, "Hey guys, I'm Cade." He stood, waved, and resumed his seat almost as fast as he stood.

"The baby of the family," Erin said.

"Yeah, yeah, yeah," he said. "Yes, I'm the youngest and smallest, as you can see."

My first impression of him proved correct. He was short and slender. I would guess a shade over five feet.

"You also have a thick beard, very unlike a baby," I said.

He caressed the thick tuft of hair hanging off his chin. He had short, cropped hair on the side and hair high and slicked back in a Caesar style. The visual effect of the hairstyle and facial hair gave him a longer face than he had. Perhaps to make him appear taller. "One reason I grew it. Sorry about the way I'm dressed. My clothes are in the dryer in the laundry room."

"You clean your clothes here?"

"Temporarily. My washing machine is on the fritz, so I'm using Dad's."

"Gotcha," I said. "Don't worry about it. I'd dress the same way if I were home, too."

"I don't live here," he said. "Got a place up in Little River."

"Nice," I said. "What do you do for a living?"

"I'm an art dealer," he said.

"An art dealer?" I cupped an elbow and tapped my lips with an index finger. "That's interesting. Erin mentioned that you found one painting for your dad."

"Yeah," Cade said and pointed at the painting above the fireplace. "I helped Dad acquire that one and several others in the house."

"Where do they come from?" Chris said. "They're marvelous, especially the one you pointed at."

Cade explained, "When an art gallery gets a new piece or new exhibit, the old paintings must go somewhere. Many are just put into storage and collect dust. I gain access to these treasure troves and arrange for buyers. If a painting is privately owned by a family or on loan to a gallery, I see if they are interested in selling and arrange for a buyer. I have people from coast to coast who buy original artwork."

"Hmm, that's fascinating," I said. "I heard a Malcolm Gladwell podcast talking about the hordes of treasures the Metropolitan Museum of Art has sitting in warehouses."

"Right," Cade said. "These museums know how to display them and get people interested but have no idea what to do after a piece of artwork has run its course. That's where I come in."

"Do you work with any places around here?" Chris said.

"Just the Burroughs-Chapin Art Museum."

"The one down at the southern end of Ocean Boulevard in Myrtle Beach? The one that has the octopus sculpture made from recycled bottles on the corner?" I asked.

"That's the one. I have contacts from various museums across the country."

"Hmm. I've never gone into it," I said.

"You should. They have fine artwork," Cade said.

"DeeDee and Antonio live together in North Myrtle," Erin said, cutting into the conversation. "I live over there." She pointed at a barn door on the other side of the living room.

"I see," I said.

"Yeah, being Dad's personal assistant is an all-day job," she said.

"She's also here to keep an eye on Dad. Make sure he does nothing to hurt himself," DeeDee said.

"Why is that?"

DeeDee whirled an index finger around her ear. "He's getting dementia. Doesn't always know what's going on."

Cade resumed his seat. "Sit down, if you'd like."

"Not yet," Erin said. "Still need to introduce them to Louise and Preacher."

He checked the time on his phone. "We should be eating shortly."

Rain pounded against the tin roof.

Louise and Preacher walked in our direction from the edge of the balcony. She laughed at something he said. They sipped cocktails and watched the storm rage outside as they approached.

As we got there, everyone's phones trilled with the distinctive beep, beep, beep of an alert from the National Weather Center. I pulled my phone from my pocket to see what it was.

Cade saw the message first. "Uh oh. Tornado."

CHAPTER
SIX

"Tornado!" the lady against the railing shouted. "Where!?"

"Looks like Garden City, headed inland," Cade said, reading the warning. "Shouldn't pose a danger to us."

When a hurricane hits the coast, intense winds and storm surge from the ocean aren't the only dangers. They often spin up tornadoes, which cause even more damage. The joys of living near the beach.

Speaking of storm surge, one factor working for us was that it was low tide. That meant that with Karen grazing the coast instead of making landfall, the water it pushed on land would be minimal. Waves crashed against the dunes but came no closer. Wind shredded the white water of the wave caps, throwing plumes of salt water in all directions. The local meteorologists did not predict coastal flooding because of Karen, which is one reason an evacuation order wasn't given.

Louise stopped and placed a hand on the back of the sofa. Her hands shook. The bangles on her wrist clattered. Gorgeously styled silver hair bounced around her shoulders. Preacher stepped over and grasped her elbow to steady her.

"Whoa, there," he said. His voice was deep. "You okay Miss Collins?"

"The alert," she gasped, "it scared me. This is the first time I've experienced this."

Preacher smiled. "I know you haven't lived here long, Ms. Collins. I've been here a long, long time. Rode out many storms." He pointed out the windows. "Trust me, the afternoon thunder boomers we get around here on summer afternoons are scarier than Karen."

She took the hand that had been on her chest and placed it on Preacher's wrist. "Thank you, Preacher."

He leaned closer to her. "Never you worry. I'll protect you. Now come on over here and have a seat. Your boyfriend will join us in shortly."

She gave him a playful slap on the arm. "Now, now Preacher. John Allen is not my boyfriend. I'll be the first to say it."

Preacher led Louise to a vacant seat. She stooped as she walked. Her face was as smooth as the day she was born. No doubt a fan of Botox. She wore clothes that looked like something you would see in Neiman Marcus.

He looked like he stepped off a Brooks Brothers' fashion show runway, wearing crisp linen shorts and a buttoned-up blue shirt with surfboards scattered around it. He was about average height, had a paunch, and walked with a slight slouch. An earring dangled from his left ear. His facial hair was more salt than pepper, which caused it to stand out on his dark face. The gray hair was working its way into the tight curls on top of his head.

When she reached us, her eyes lit. "Well, well, well. Who are these two handsome men? Erin, did you bring them for me?"

I looked at Chris. Chris looked at me. Erin laughed. "Now, Louise, you know better." She walked up in between us and put her arms in ours. "They're for me."

Louise reached forward and gave Erin a light slap on the arm. "Now, child. Behave. Your dad is nearby. Can't have you cavorting around here with two men." She tried to stand straight and regarded Chris and me. "But in this case, I couldn't blame you. A couple of handsome fellas."

My cheeks warmed. "Thank you." I held out a hand. "Clark Thomas."

Her cold, weak hand grasped mine. "Pleasure to meet you. Who's your burly friend here?"

"Chris MacInally," he said, bowing his head and taking her hand. "The pleasure is all mine, lass."

Her mouth opened wide, and she wrapped an arm around Chris's waist. "And Scottish too. Oh, Erin, I'm in love already."

"Irish actually," he said, "but I'll forgive you. This time."

"Oh, Honey, you can narrate my life story if you'd like." She turned to Preacher. "You're off the hook. I found another man to take care of me this evening."

Everyone had a good laugh at that, except for Louise. She was serious. Preacher guided her to a seat.

After depositing her on othe sofa, he came over and shook our hands. He almost broke my finger bones with his handshake as we introduced ourselves. He and Chris should be an even match. The Irishman had the thickest hands I have ever encountered. When their hands met, they locked eyes in the way two masculine men do when they first meet. There's almost a competition between two men like these when they shake hands for the first time. A moment of eyes hardening before a respectful smile when they deem each other worthy.

My dad taught me to give a firm handshake when first meeting someone. He said you can't trust someone with a limp grip. I'm not sure why he taught me that, but I tried to give a firm grasp when shaking hands.

"Hey, fellas," Preacher said. "Nice to meet ya. What sort of business are you in?"

"The pleasure is ours," Chris said. "I work for the OceanScapes resort down near the Boardwalk."

Preacher's eyes lit. "Oh, I know the one you're talking about. Tall building with blue bricks that form a wave pattern about halfway up."

"That's the one," Chris said.

"Nice place." He turned to me. "How about you? What do you do?"

"I own the Myrtle Beach Reads bookstore blocks up the sidewalk from there."

"Ah, you're that Clark Thomas. Theresa has told me about you."

Lines formed on my forehead as my eyebrows creased. "You mean the Theresa who owns the I Heart MB Tees store?"

He smiled. "Yeah, that's the one. She's saucy."

I tilted my head. Theresa's shop was two doors down from mine in the same shopping strip. She filled her store with touristy t-shirts proclaiming love for Myrtle Beach. It was a nice shop. She was a different story. Her wardrobe comprised ten pairs of the same leopard print leggings. At least, it seemed that way. A cigarette dangled from her mouth every time I saw her outside of her shop and sometimes inside of it on slow days. She came across as ditzy, but I knew better. For a woman pushing seventy, she was sharp. And flirty, always ready with a lecherous comment when she saw me. "That she is."

Theresa recently changed the name of her store because of a trademark infringement with another similarly named area gift shop. It was now called Theresa's Tees. There was a big hullabaloo about the entire matter, but that's a story for a different time. "Me and Theresa go way back. Known her for a while."

"Small world," I said.

"You guys the guests of honor this evening?" he asked.

Chris and I shared a look. He said, "I'm not even sure I was on the original guest list. I was sitting with Clark when Erin came in and invited him. It's Clark who fits that bill."

My cheeks burned. "Guest of honor" was not a title I had ever thought would be put on me.

Erin stepped in. "He is. Dad wanted me to give him an invitation the other day for tonight."

Preacher gestured at the approaching storm out the window. "Did your dad know that was going to happen when he put this shindig together?"

"Who knows what Dad was thinking," Erin said. "You know how he is."

"Yeah, unfortunately," he replied.

"You mean the dementia DeeDee talked about?" I asked.

She looked away, trying to compose herself. A tear formed in the corner of one eye. "He's developing Alzheimer's disease. His mind is going."

"Oh no," I said.

"I'm sorry to hear that," Chris said.

"It is what it is." She wiped the tear away with a finger.

DeeDee and Antonio continued conversing. Cade had gone back to staring at his phone screen now that the tornado danger had passed. Maybe he was reading updated weather reports. My money was on the latest Hollywood gossip.

Erin explained. "Sometimes Dad will think he saw something

he didn't or accuse someone of doing something they didn't."

"Like what?"

"Dad used to like to tinker with classic cars in the garage. Let's say a saw would go missing."

"Uh-huh."

"He'd accuse someone of stealing the saw, and we'd find it a few days later in a bucket or another random place."

"And he was the one who put it there and forgot?"

"We think so," she said. "He goes down there and tinkers with his cars in the early mornings. Says it helps him clear his head before going into the recording studio beside the garage. There are other things he does I won't bore you the details with. Most people might not notice it, but Cade, DeeDee, and I do."

"It's a shame." He paused and took a breath. "I've seen it getting worse since I met him, after they built this house. One thing he hasn't lost is his love of riddles."

"Riddles?" I asked.

"Oh, yes. Riddles. Puzzles too. Does crossword and sudoku puzzles to keep his mind sharp," he said.

"He's trying," Erin said, "but it's a losing battle."

"A shame," Chris said.

"Thank you," she replied, putting a hand on his wrist. "Alzheimer's runs in the family among the men. They have new treatments for Alzheimer's we hope are going to keep him healthy for longer."

I didn't know what to say to that. Thankfully, Cade jumped up and announced that he was going downstairs to check on his clothes. Erin watched him go and turned to look at her sister. She did the same. An unspoken thought passed between them in a way only siblings can do.

DeeDee hopped up from beside Antonio. "I'm going to go check on Dad."

"Yeah," he said, "seems like it's taking him a while to get ready."

"Sometimes it does nowadays," she said. "He gets to doing something and gets distracted."

"Maybe he's still in his office," Antonio suggested.

"He probably had some music pass through his head that he wanted to get on paper before he forgot it," Erin said and turned to us. "He's always doing that."

"The most I ever did with music was try to play a recorder in sixth grade," I said. "I have no musical inclination. I can't carry a tune in the shower."

Erin cocked an eyebrow.

"I strum a guitar now and then," Chris said. "Used to play in a band when I was a youth."

"What kind of band?" Erin said.

"We just played songs by bands like U2, Thin Lizzy, and Clannad. Rock stuff."

"Were you any good?"

"No, it was rubbish," Chris said, "but we had fun doing it."

"Knowing you," I said, "I bet you did." I mimicked, raising a bottle to my lips.

He smiled. "You know me, laddie."

As DeeDee passed by us, Erin stopped her by placing a hand on her sister's arm. "I'll go check on him."

"Thanks," DeeDee said. "I know you're better with him like this."

Erin gave a weak smile. "I'm around him every day, you know. Had to adapt to his health. Have a seat."

"No, I think I'll powder my nose and then set the table. I'm up anyway," DeeDee said and walked away.

Antonio got to his feet. "I'll go downstairs and start preparing the food."

After he started walking down the stairs to the kitchen, Erin said to Chris and me, "Will you boys be okay while I go check on Dad?"

"Should be," I said.

"Thanks," she said and headed off in the opposite direction from DeeDee.

With the partial breakup of the dinner party already underway, Preacher excused himself. Said he was going to go downstairs to John Allen's garage. Chris asked if he could tag along, leaving me to fend for myself with Louise.

Here I was again in a place I've often been since Autumn's passing. Invisible in the middle of a crowd. Even before Autumn, I could be with a group of friends or at a party and somehow melt in where no one paid any attention to me. I wasn't one to seek attention or conversation. I let people come to me. Being passive in social skills had its benefits and detriments. The downside of it being that I had few friends. The upside being that when I connected with someone, it was because I had time to study them before shaking hands. They say you can't judge a book by its cover — like being wrong about Chris — but you can get hints at their personalities. I'm not like my brother who can make friends with anyone, anywhere.

I took this moment to walk over to the balcony and watch the crashing waves. Even at low tide, the gusts whipped the ocean into a frenzy. Was it my imagination, or did Karen look like she was coming closer?

CHAPTER
SEVEN

Then it happened. Clouds wrapped around each other a half-mile offshore and formed a blue cone. A waterspout. It coalesced in an ethereal manner. Waves pounded the beach with the wind, sending bursts of spray everywhere. Rain poured in a deluge. Then water and wind wrapped around each other, reaching to the sky in crooked fashion.

Only Louise remained with me in the great room.

The waterspout twisted and churned a couple hundred yards offshore. I watched its movement for two seconds before my fear turned to dread.

It was coming right for us.

Without wasting another second, I shouted, "Tornado!" at the top of my lungs. My yell startled poor Louise, whose eyes were closed and was leaning to the side on the couch.

"Louise," I said, running to her side, "let me help you up. We've got to get to an interior room. That twister is heading this way."

I risked a glance out the window. Her eyes opened. She turned and gasped. The bottom of the funnel had reached where waves were crashing onshore, throwing up plumes of sand and water. The house vibrated like a train was approaching.

I helped her up off the couch by grabbing one of her bony

arms by the elbow. She smelled of old perfume and ointment.

"Come on, Louise," I said. "Hang onto me."

She moaned with worry. Her words came in quick gasps. "Clark. Clark. Help."

"Are you okay?" I asked as I rushed us across the living room to the opposite side of the house from where we came up the stairs.

"I. Am. Just. Short. Of. Breath. Is. All," she gasped from my side.

"Almost there!" I shouted above the growing din of the cyclone racing toward us. It was slow going, but we reached one door lining the wall. I hoped to find a closet on an interior wall. The waterspout was now on land, meaning it had become a tornado.

And from the looks of it, it was mad.

It toppled the palm trees standing in its path like dominoes. Down one went after another. Wind tossed the chairs and tables around the pool in all directions. Some went flying into a neighbor's property. Some flew against the house, while others ended up submerged in the pool.

I slid open the barn door leading into what looked like a guest bedroom. The bed was made. Nightstands flanking it were tidy. An open door led to an attached bathroom. There was a set of louvered doors to our right. Jackpot.

"Quick, in here," I shouted to Louise, leading her to a large closet. She rushed as fast as she could inside.

I stole a glance back outside through the picture windows at the approaching tornado. The sound was deafening. The twister was about to graze by the opposite side of the house and pass between homes. Destruction lay in its path.

As I closed the barn door and went to huddle with Louise in the closet, I heard it. Even above the calamity.

A single gunshot.

* * *

Louise and I squeezed together as close to the floor as possible. Her limbs weren't flexible. I was too tall for the confined space. The house shook and thundered. Multiple objects shattered and crashed outside the room. A grating rip came from the roof as the tornado peeled the metal back like the top of a sardine can. Not even the hurricane-force rating of the roof could withstand the ferocity of a twister.

Then silence. Eerie, creepy silence magnified by the knowledge that somewhere in the house, someone might be dead. As fast as the tornado formed and hit, it was gone, off to wreak havoc on the homes inland. I hoped this house took the brunt of the force, weakening the tornado as it moved farther ashore.

Louise gulped shallow breaths. One hand rested on top of the cane.

"I think it's gone," I said.

"Do you think it's safe to go out?"

I pursed my lips. Whoever had the gun was still out there. For the life of me, I couldn't see this time and place as the setting for a potential mass shooting. I figured that whatever violence had been wrought was over. If I was wrong, that was another matter.

I cracked open one louvered door, allowing natural light to pour in. "Did you hear the shot?"

Her painted-on eyebrows came together as she placed a hand covered in liverworts on her ear and twisted her fingers. "No, I turned my hearing aids off after we got in here. I didn't want to hear what was happening. Did you hear a gun?"

For a moment, I was jealous of her hearing loss. I wished I hadn't heard what I heard.

"I did," I said. "Do you want me to help you to the bed in this room to lie down?"

Now she had a fresh fear to accept. First a tornado, now a possible killer was on the loose.

"No, help me up."

I did. She leaned on me and gripped my shoulder, stronger than I thought possible for her.

"I'm stronger than I look," she said. "I'll make it."

"If you're sure," I said.

"I'm as sure as ever."

I unfolded both doors of the closet, allowing her to exit first. She made a move toward the great room but stopped when she saw the bed. She put a hand to her head.

"On second thought," she said, "I think I will lie down for a moment and catch my breath."

"As you wish." I escorted her to the side of the bed and made sure she was comfortable. "I'm going to go see what's happening."

She grasped my hand. "Thank you, Clark, for helping this old woman. I'm forever in your debt."

I smiled and said, "I'm sure you would have done the same for me had the roles been reversed."

"I don't know 'bout that." She smiled. "I might have gone looking for your Irish friend."

I squeezed her hand before letting go. "Can't blame you there. Look, I'll leave the door open. If you need anything, shout."

"Thank you. I just want to rest a bit."

"I understand."

I let go of her hand and walked to the bedroom door, sliding it open. What I found looked like a scene from a catastrophe movie.

They had filled the house with vases and sculptures. It had been a miniature art gallery. Now, most of the artwork not hanging on walls had toppled over or shattered. Several paintings had fallen. Others hung at odd angles, while the rest looked untouched, including the magnificent painting above the fireplace.

That wasn't the most unsettling part.

When you are in a house, you're only supposed to see the sky through windows. Unless you have a skylight, which there weren't any in this house. That is, before the tornado.

Rain fell in the southeast corner of the home where the metal roof had been peeled back. That area was open to the bottom level where the living room was being flooded. I couldn't believe my eyes.

After being stunned by the condition of the house, I set off toward where I thought I heard the shot.

As I passed through the great room, Chris came running back up the stairs.

"You, okay?" I said as he joined me.

"Yeah, I'm fine. You?"

"Shaken, but otherwise fine. Where's Preacher?"

"Down in the garage. He was showing me John Allen's auto collection."

A blood-curdling scream arose, not from John Allen's bedroom, but from the room beside it.

Chris and I locked eyes. "Was that Erin?"

"Sounded like it," Chris said.

We ran across the great room to the two doors atop the stairs. Erin said one was John Allen's bedroom, the other was his office. Both were wide open. A section of his bedroom was visible through the doorway on the left. Like the room Louise and I entered before the tornado, everything looked neat and clean. Like entering a hotel room after check-in.

Erin was visible through the crack in the office door. She stood in the middle of the room with her back to us. Something was in her shaking hand. By this time, DeeDee had reappeared. Preacher, Antonio, and Cade rushed up to the top of the stairs.

We ran into the office. Erin looked at us, wide-eyed, unable to speak. It was easy to see why.

John Allen was slumped back in his office chair with a bullet wound to his chest.

Then I saw the object in her hand. It was a gun.

* * *

I've helped to investigate two murders. One involved the victim getting clubbed over the head with a trophy. The other died after being run through with a gladiator sword.

The only guns I've come across were in the holsters of the police officers I had been around.

To tell the truth, guns made me uneasy. We didn't have them in our house growing up. I've fired nothing more lethal than a BB gun when a friend and I drove around his neighborhood one night in high school shooting people's mailboxes. A few cheap beers played a role that evening. The only time I've touched a real gun was when my grandpa let me hold the service pistol he carried during the Korean War.

Until now. I pulled a tissue from my pocket.

"Erin," I said, grabbing her attention.

The whites of her eyes were visible as she pulled her gaze away from her father.

DeeDee rushed into the room followed by Cade. DeeDee screamed. Cade stood speechless. Rain poured through the gap in the roof around the corner from the office. Antonio and Preacher stood shoulder-to-shoulder at the door. Chris stood at my side, content to let me take the lead.

"Erin," I repeated, "Let me have the gun."

Her mouth opened, but no words came out.

With the tissue, I reached for the gun. Her thin hand opened to let me grab it. I wrapped the tissue around the grip and pulled the gun away. I set it down on the edge of the walnut desk and walked around to John Allen.

His eyes and mouth were open. He stared lifelessly at the ceiling. The bullet wound was to the left of center in his chest. The bullet passed clean through. It had buried itself in the wall behind him, leaving a neat hole.

When I placed a hand on his wrist to check on the off chance for a pulse, he blinked, and his mouth closed.

I jerked my hand away. My heart pounded in my chest. Everyone gasped or screamed behind me.

John Allen's eyes closed for a second and then burst open.

He croaked, "It's in the…"

The life faded from his eyes.

CHAPTER
EIGHT

I turned to the room and said in as calm a voice as I could muster, "Someone call 911."

Antonio was the first to reach for his phone. He dialed and held it to his ear.

No one else moved.

Erin stood alone. She hadn't moved from her spot. DeeDee cried with her face buried in her hands. Antonio pulled her into his embrace. She sobbed into his shoulder.

Cade's mouth was clinched in a tight line. Tears rimmed his red eyes. He shouted at his sister, "You killed him! You shot Dad!"

"I didn't do it!" Erin shouted. "The gun was laying on the floor when I got here. I picked it up because that's what I do."

DeeDee explained to Chris and me, "It's true. She does."

Cade didn't believe her. He rushed at Erin, but Chris restrained him with a beefy arm.

"Calm down, son," Chris said in Cade's ear. "Let the authorities render punishment."

Cade's face was red. Tears welled in his eyes. He struggled in vain to break free from Chris's grasp.

"There, there," Chris said to him. "Let's step out. Catch our breath."

What seemed like a suggestion from Chris was more of an order. He took Cade by the elbow and led him from the room.

Thankful that Chris had diffused the confrontation, I took a moment to assess the situation.

Antonio clicked off the phone in frustration and stared at the screen. "That's not good."

"What's not good?" Preacher asked.

"Phones are down," he said, holding his in the air.

As one, except for DeeDee, we checked our phones. There was a red X over the 5G network symbol at the top of the screen. A corded phone sat on the edge of John Allen's desk. I used the tissue to pick up the receiver and hoped I wasn't wiping away the killer's fingerprints.

Lightning flashed and thunder cracked outside the window behind John Allen's desk. The office would have a marvelous view of the ocean were it not for the driving rain from Karen. Why would the maestro have his desk facing away from the window?

I put the phone to my ear, then placed the handset back in the cradle and shook my head. "Landlines are dead too."

"What do we do now?" Preacher said.

"Can you go out to the road and see if there are any authorities about?" I asked.

"Ten-four. Be right back," he said and jogged from the room.

I tried to think like Detective Gomez. What would she do in this situation?

"Okay," I said, "here's what we're going to do. Let's leave this room and shut the door. This is a crime scene now, and we don't want to disturb anything."

No one disagreed.

"What about Erin?" Antonio said.

Erin's eyes searched mine. She tightened her jaw in a tight line and shook her head from side to side. A tear ran down her left cheek. She used two shaking hands to twirl her blonde hair in a spiral over one shoulder. An involuntary stress reliever.

I said, "I'm going to take her to a bedroom and lock her in until the police arrive."

I thought of Cade trying to attack her a moment ago. Keeping her away from the others might keep her safe as well. Besides, I had another reason to get her away from everyone.

"You heard him," Antonio said. "Let's all go downstairs."

I shepherded everyone from the room except for Erin. We hung back a moment. Chris and Cade came into view from somewhere right of the door and followed Antonio and the others to the elevator to the left.

I turned to Erin. She said through clenched teeth, biting out each word, "I. Didn't. Do. It."

* * *

After taking a moment to survey the contents on top of the desk, I ushered Erin from the room. As I closed the office door, I took one last look at John Allen, slouched back in his chair with a bullet wound to the chest. A sad end to a legendary Hollywood figure.

By the time I led Erin to the other side of the house, everyone poured out of the elevator down below and headed to the dining room on the ocean side of the house. This upper level afforded superb views of the lower level.

Outside, the sky darkened as the sun went down through the windows above the front door. It was an eerie scene. Sunset on one side of the house. The outer edges of a moody tropical storm on the other.

I started to guide Erin by the elbow to the room Louise and I had huddled in during the tornado. Erin's perfume was intoxicating. She hadn't said a word since her denial, perhaps waiting for more privacy, which was part of the reason I wanted to escort her to a room.

She stared at the wood plank flooring as we crossed through the great room. We paused as Preacher re-entered through the front door and stopped. His head and shoulders were wet from the rain. He noticed the others heading toward the living room.

"Preacher!" I called down, getting his attention. He looked up at me. "What's the situation?"

He shook his head. Water dripped from his brow. His shirt was soaked. "Good and bad," he called up to us. "It peeled a corner of the tin roof back like a sardine can. There must be water running down through the ceiling somewhere in that part of the house. Worse yet, the twister knocked over palm trees, blocking the gate. Rest of the house looks okay. Can't say the same for the neighbor's house on that side. Looks like it took the brunt of it."

Erin had mentioned the strength of the metal roof. Not even it was immune to the strength of a tornado.

The fence was too tall to climb without a ladder. Storm surge had pushed its way up to the dunes. There was no escape by going out to the beach. The whirlwind had trapped and cut us off from the outside world. Rain and wind wrapped us in our temporary prison.

"Did your dad have a ladder anywhere?" I asked Erin.

"Not anything tall enough to get over the fence."

I rubbed the back of my neck. To Preacher, I called down, "Did you see anyone about?"

"Not a soul."

"Thanks, Preacher," I shouted.

"Want me to see if there's a chainsaw in the garage so we can cut our way out?"

"Can you get to the trees to do that?"

He looked up at me with a blank expression. "No, I guess not. Never mind."

"Don't worry about it. Go dry yourself off. Thanks for going out."

He raised two fingers to his head in a mock salute and headed off, disappearing from view.

With the phone lines out, the only way we had to check for updates on the storm was to turn on the TV and hoped we could get a signal.

"How long will the generator last?" I asked Erin after she pulled the tissue from her face.

"For as long as it's needed, I guess. It runs off a propane tank we have buried beside the house. They topped off the gas in it last month."

"That's a positive, at least."

We reached the sliding barn door that led to the guest bedroom. I pushed it open and directed Erin inside, leading her to the bed. The mattress dipped under what little weight she carried. She sat on the edge and ran her hands over her eyes. I took a deep breath, trying to take stock of the situation. I pulled the phone from my pocket and checked the screen. Still no network.

After everything that's happened in the last twenty minutes, I needed to sit down. I did so in a comfortable chair in the room's corner, facing Erin.

She stopped crying. "I should have listened to him."

"What do you mean?"

"He told me someone was trying to kill him." My jaw hung open. She continued, "There had been some... oddities that occurred recently. We chalked it up to Alzheimer's. That he was slipping and imagining things. He'd claimed things had gone missing too, but we would find whatever it was he thought was stolen stuck someplace random. He just forgot where he'd stashed stuff."

"It's a shame what that disease does to people. I've had men in my family die from it."

"Such a nasty way for a person's life to end," she said.

I could think of worse ways to go. "It is."

"Now what?"

I shrugged my shoulders and ignored her question. "What happened?"

"I went to Dad's bedroom to check on him when the tornado hit but didn't quite make it and hid in a closet until it passed. I heard the shot while I was in there." She paused. Her bottom lip quivered as she twisted her hair into a ponytail. "Scariest experience I've ever experienced. I knew someone had finally gotten to him. When I figured it was safe to come out, I ran next door to his bedroom, but he wasn't in there. Next, I went into his office and found him dead."

"Where did the gun come from?"

She voluntarily opened and closed her right hand. The same hand I grabbed the gun from. Her body quaked as she twirled her blonde hair between two fingers. Her face was red as tears rimmed her eyes. "It was on the floor. Didn't think about it. Just picked it up. I'm OCD like that."

"Everything has a place, and every place has a thing?"

She nodded. "Cade is like me in that regard."

"Then what?"

"You and Chris came into the room."

"He was shot when you got there?"

"Yes."

"You say you didn't do this, even though you held the gun right after he was killed?"

"I swear to you I didn't do this." Her mouth compressed. "Dad wasn't in his bedroom when I went to check on him. I had visions of finding him in his closet lying on the floor again."

"Had you seen that gun before?"

"Yes. Dad kept it in a drawer in his desk. An old Hollywood carryover. In case an armed intruder came into the home."

I didn't live my life in fear like that. "So, the would-be murderer comes in and grabs the gun while John Allen is sitting at his desk and then shoots him with it?"

She raised her hands, palms up. "Your guess is as good as mine."

"Is it? You live here, after all. You were aware he had a gun. Where was it in his desk?"

She looked in the air for a moment and moved her right arm, mimicking the opening and closing of a drawer. "Let's see. If you're sitting at the desk, it was in a middle drawer on the right side."

"Who else knew about the gun?"

"I don't know."

"That's not helping your cause."

"Why would I kill my own dad?"

"I don't know you well enough to answer that question. You tell me why you didn't kill your dad."

A gust of wind thrashed against the side of the house, causing it to creak a little. Rain pelted against the window. Even though Karen had been downgraded to a tropical storm, she still carried a significant amount of water within her clouds. Her winds were calmer, but she could still soak the coast.

"Don't worry," she said. "The foundation under this house is built with rebar buried far into the bedrock. We aren't going anywhere."

I let out a puff of air. "That's good. So, why didn't you do it?"

"Dad was my everything. My entire world has revolved around him since I graduated from college. He offered me a grandiose sum of money to be his personal assistant. I said I'd pass and try my turn in the corporate world. When Mom died a year later, I reconsidered. Mom had handled most of his scheduling and needs."

"Was she sick for long?"

Her lips spasmed into a momentary frown before answering. "No, it was quick, thankfully."

It was bad enough that her dad had just been murdered, but here I was having her dredge up memories of her other departed parent.

"Did you have any fights with your dad?"

"No. He would only get mad when I tried to keep him from eating too much sugar."

"Ah, that's something you and I have in common. My dad has a never-ending sweet tooth."

She snorted and tried to smile.

"Let's say you didn't do this," I said.

"I'm telling you. I. Didn't. Do. This."

"Then who did?"

"That's what I think this dinner party was all about. Twice in the past month, Dad almost died. Once, his cane broke as he was walking down the front stairs of the house."

"What was the cane made of?"

"Wood. Ash, I think."

"A hardwood," I noted. "Did anyone examine the cane after the incident?"

"We did. Looked like a clean break," she said.

"Or someone cut it," I suggested. "I tinker with wood projects in my shed. Wood doesn't break cleanly to my knowledge. It splinters."

"Right," Erin said. "Dad didn't say anything, but I had my suspicions."

"Do you still have the cane?"

"No, we threw it out. He had spares."

"Great." My voice dripped with disappointment.

She leaned away from me. "Hey, how was I supposed to know it could have been evidence?"

"You're right."

Her body bent back in my direction but stopped. "He liked to see the best in people. I would have thought it was an anomaly had he not had to go to the emergency room a few days later."

"Why was that?"

"I'm still not clear about that. He takes many medications. I think someone slipped something into his pills and caused him to have a reaction and pass out."

"Who took him to the emergency room?" I asked.

She fingered the charm on the end of her necklace. "I did. Found him lying on the floor in his bedroom closet."

"Goodness," I said.

"He felt the after-effects for days." She patted her stomach.

"Gotcha," I said. "You think he planned this dinner party to bring all the suspects together?"

"That's my guess. And he wanted you to figure out who."

"No pressure there," I said in a half-hearted attempt at humor.

She got it. Smiled. "Yeah, no pressure. But that was Dad. He had grand expectations for everyone in his universe."

"Including you?"

"Yes, including me. He pushed me to be one step ahead of him all the time."

"Did he push you too far?"

"No, he didn't. I'm stronger than I look."

"That's the same thing Louise told me earlier."

She rolled her eyes. "Ah, Louise."

I wasn't sure whether to believe her innocence, but if she claimed she didn't kill John Allen, I had to listen. "I assume your dad thought everyone here tonight was a suspect, including Louise."

"Oh, yes. Including Louise."

I didn't voice the fact that Erin's inclusion in the meal put her in the same category. "What's her deal?"

"She's thrice widowed."

"How long ago did her last husband die?"

"I'm not sure. All I know is that she would have liked to have married Dad."

"Really? How did your dad feel about that?"

"He wasn't interested."

"Do you think she could have carried a grudge against him for his lack of interest?"

Her shoulders raised and dropped. "All I know is that she was relentless in her pursuit. Who knows? Maybe her pursuit of dad was her way of fighting boredom after living in her big house all alone."

I placed a finger on my bottom lip. "What about Preacher? He said he handled your dad's money."

"Right, he does. Dad used to have a guy in Los Angeles but had Preacher take the reins when we moved here."

"What's his background?"

She tried to laugh. "I thought it was a joke when I first met him. He was a financial analyst for a massage chair company before hanging out his own shingle."

"That's, uh, interesting. How did they meet? He doesn't seem very old. I'd figure they would run in different circles."

"Yeah, Preacher is closer to my age," Erin said without giving away a number. A lady never tells. "I'm not sure how they met, but he's good on the piano. He comes over and plays for Dad in the studio downstairs."

"Has your dad changed his will or anything lately?"

"Not that I'm aware of."

"What about Antonio and your sister, DeeDee?"

"Aye-yi-yi," she muttered. "They're a hot mess. Been dating since she moved here."

"When did she arrive?"

"Not long after Dad and I got here."

"What does she do?"

"Dad set up a charity foundation to teach music in schools. Where funding for those sorts of programs keeps getting stripped away, Dad wanted to help keep them going, so he established a fund. She is the head of it."

"Ah, that's nice. What about Antonio?"

"He sells insurance."

"Was your dad a buyer of it?"

"No, Dad was already insured. He updated all of that after Mom's passing."

"Doesn't mean Antonio couldn't have tried to sell him a new one."

"Could have. He and DeeDee come here for lunch often. I didn't always stay for those, so I don't know what they talked about when I was gone."

"Why didn't you stick around?"

She shifted on the bed, stretching her legs out. I draped an arm over the side table next to me. At some point, we went from me questioning her about possibly killing her dad to having a casual conversation about family and friends. I sat up straight in the chair.

"Her being here gave me a chance to get out and do things on my own. I tried to have a life too, you know."

"Of course."

"Besides, DeeDee and I don't always get along."

"I understand that. I have an older brother who I clash with. I'm an even-keeled guy, but sometimes he brings out the worst in me. Don't know why that is."

She pointed at her chest. "That's how it is with me and DeeDee. I try to be as nice as I can to everyone, but when she's around, it's like I can't wait to bring the claws out."

"Are you that way with Cade?"

"Him? No. He's the baby of the family and self-absorbed."

"I got that feeling."

"He's on his phone constantly. Every conversation revolves around him and what he's doing. He never asks about me or Dad or anything else."

"Makes sense. Because he was the last one born, your parents coddled him more."

"Coddling is an understatement. He always gets his way and isn't afraid to fail because Mom and Dad never let him. Went to college for art. He's a gifted painter himself, believe it or not, but could never make money selling his own. Instead, he finds museums with art and paintings in storage and brokers deals with private buyers."

"And he gets a cut?"

"Yup. Makes decent money doing it. He has an eye for it and a list full of buyers. He knows what they like, so when something becomes available, he knows who to call." She pointed at a painting of a beach scene on the wall. "Most of these come from Cade. Dad wanted to support him when he started the art brokerage business. You know that painting over the fireplace we have? Cost Dad a small fortune. Cade couldn't believe his luck in even finding one by Antoine Le Nain. Sold Dad on it."

I chewed on that for a moment. So, they say Cade wasn't talented enough of an artist to make a career out of it, but he had enough of an eye for what might capture his clients' tastes to stay in that arena. Wind blew against the house. The rain outside picked up with renewed ferocity.

"Let's get back to this dinner party. You think your dad brought these specific people here because he thought one of them was trying to kill him?"

"I do."

"If it wasn't you—"

"It wasn't."

"If not you, then tell me why?"

"Dad had the gate code changed last week after he came home from the hospital," Erin said. "It was frustrating because I was the one who had to inform everyone. Why would he change the code if he thought I wanted to kill him?"

"Good point. Do they have the new code?"

"Nope, besides me, you're the only person who knows it."

I couldn't think of anything else to ask her. The evening has been a whirlwind, pardon the pun, since my arrival, as I tried to recall what happened before the shooting and where everyone was supposed to be at the time of the murder.

"Look, I'm going downstairs and talk to the others. See if we can call the outside world." I held out my hand. "Let me have your phone."

"My phone? Why?"

"Because I don't want you communicating with anyone outside of this room." I pointed at the floor. "They all think you killed your dad and should be a prisoner. They looked at me like I was law enforcement, even though I'm not. The first thing the police would do is take away your phone."

Her eyes drilled into mine. "The phones and Wi-Fi are down right now. It's not like it has much use now. Do you think I did this?"

"All evidence points to you, and you know it."

"But?"

"But others might be worth looking into."

She stood, handed me her phone, and tried to hug me. I held her at arm's length and instructed, "Don't leave this room. It's as much for your protection as anything else."

The lines above her eyebrows wrinkled. "I guess that's the best answer I could have hoped for. I reiterate, I didn't do this."

"Then who did?"

When her mouth opened and closed without an answer, I left the room and blocked the sliding barn door, locking her in.

CHAPTER NINE

I placed my back against the nearest wall. Looked up and closed my eyes. The rain and gusts continued to pound outside.

If Erin denied being the killer, but didn't know who was, then where did that leave a potential investigation? The one man who could help was dead. He invited me here, allegedly, to help find a would-be killer. That killer struck before John Allen could relay his suspicions.

Or did they? Could more than one person have reason to kill the composer?

Despite the enormous, open space I stood in, I stared at the floor, trying to assess the situation. First, someone, likely Erin, shot John Allen. I needed to barricade the office as well to make sure no one snuck in and disturbed evidence. Which left the question: did I need to get back in there? If he threw this shindig together for me to figure out who might want him dead, could he have assembled the evidence against the suspects?

If the murderer wasn't Erin, learning the identity of the real one and having this case wrapped up with a nice bow when Detectives Gomez and Moody arrived could be an enormous relief to them. They will be busy enough in the aftermath of Karen.

The only person in the office when Chris and I entered was

Erin holding a gun. She vehemently denied doing the deed. Then who else could have? When the tornado hit, Cade was downstairs in the laundry room. DeeDee was powdering her nose. Antonio was in the kitchen preparing dinner. Louise was with me. Preacher and Chris were together downstairs.

The gunshot occurred during the cataclysm, after Louise and I hid in the guest bedroom closet. Time was a blur during that time. I couldn't remember how much time passed between when I heard the shot and then Erin's scream. That space could have given someone else time to leave where they were, commit the crime, and return.

The situation reminded me of Agatha Christie's Murder on the Orient Express, where it was discovered that many of the passengers aboard had motives to kill businessman Edward Ratchett. Solving that crime took all of Hercule Poirot's skill and expertise. I wasn't on that fictional character's level.

Many of the motives for Ratchett's slaying stemmed from an incident in his life. He fled from the United States to Europe to escape his past. Had John Allen done something similar in Hollywood which caused him to bolt in his cross-country move?

I crossed through the great room, glancing over the balcony. All the other attendees sat or stood around the dining room table against the seaward side of the house. DeeDee and Antonio huddled together. Louise slouched in a chair, half-asleep. Preacher and Chris stood together, conversing in hushed tones. Cade sat on one edge of the bench seat against the window, staring at his phone. If the internet was out, I wasn't sure what he'd be doing on it. Playing Candy Crush, I guess. When people get addicted to their phones, they'll find any reason to stare at the screen for hours, regardless of what's going on in the world around them. I lost count of the number of times I've been on the beach and walked past entire families sitting in their beach chairs, all staring at their phones. That's not how I liked to spend my vacation, but to each their own.

As I approached the steps to head down and join them, I changed direction for John Allen's office. The sun had gone down, and the sky was dark. With the power out, there were no path or lamp lights to give an indication of the current weather conditions.

I placed my hand on the barn door and stopped when I heard water flowing behind the wall in the room beside the office. I slid over and pushed that door aside to enter John Allen's bedroom. He had a four-post bed against the wall. I imagined him waking up to magnificent sunrises through the window across the room. Papers were arranged in neat rows atop the duvet. Twin nightstands sat on either side of the bed. A picture of John Allen and his late wife was atop the small table on the other side of the bed. A cello and bow stood on a stand in a corner. The room contained the most beautiful artwork I'd seen in the house yet. There were also photos of John Allen with various members of Hollywood royalty against one wall.

The rushing water sound grew louder, but it didn't come from this room. I crossed the space and slid open the closet door. This room was larger than my bedroom. Expensive suits hung on one rack. Various shirts and pants hung on another. A bench lay beside a display of Italian-made shoes. In the far corner, the back corner of the house, was a rectangular opening.

It was from this corner where the rushing sound came. Water dripped from the ceiling, down through the hole. I navigated through the closet to that corner, looking down through the opening. It was dark down the hole. I pulled out my phone, turned on the flashlight, and shined it through. Directly below, about fifteen feet down, was a hamper containing wet, rumpled clothes.

I stood straight and killed the light. "Ah, a laundry chute," I said aloud to no one. "That's handy."

Water cascaded through the ceiling above it, dripping down in the corner where the sheet metal and plywood underneath had been peeled back from the roof. There was nothing I could do to stop it. Managing the damage was the farthest thing from my mind, and I suspected anyone else's.

I returned to the bedroom and went to the bed, placing a hand on the comforter. For a person unimaginably wealthy, to the touch, the bedspread felt, well, normal. Like any other bedding you could purchase at Target. A reminder that John Allen used to put his pants on one leg at a time.

He arranged the papers on the bed in five columns along its length. I couldn't help myself. Without touching them, I bent forward to see what they were. John Allen had taken some care in laying them out.

The left column held three sheets. Letters from an insurance company. The first thanked John Allen for signing up. Another had information about his new policy. The third was a letter dated a month later, confirming cancellation of the account. It was from a company I didn't recognize. However, the name of the insurance broker was familiar. Antonio Bianchi. DeeDee's boyfriend.

The second column was a form containing a list of purchases with large and varied amounts at the end of each line. Atop the bill of sale was the company's name: Howard Art Brokerage.

The middle row contained a stack of papers. Receipt printouts of payments to a numbered account. I picked up the stack and leafed through them. They were of various amounts, each under a thousand dollars. A quick bit of mental math tallied it all to a shade over five-hundred thousand dollars.

Column number four held two handwritten letters done in flourishing script. The handwriting was feminine. The first letter's content was steamy enough to take the wrinkles out of a seersucker suit. My cheeks flushed just reading the first two lines. The other suggested a change of attitude. One begging its recipient to take her back. Both were signed by Louise Collins.

"Oh my," I whispered, moving on to the fifth and final column. It had a piece of paper on top of an opened envelope. The paper had a letterhead that made my skin crawl. I cringed every time I got an envelope from this agency. The IRS. It was addressed to The Cheerful Note Children's Music Organization, ATTN: DeeDee Howard. The envelope had markings on the front, showing that DeeDee received it through certified mail. Very official. I glanced at the first paragraph of the letter. It was asking for more information to clarify details on a recent tax return. An audit.

If John Allen invited me here this evening to figure out who might want him dead, then these papers must have been for my benefit. Once we could get word to the outside world of John Allen's death and unblocked the gate, the police would swoop in. This could be my last chance to be in this room. I whipped out my phone and snapped pictures of every sheet of paper in the layout.

What I saw on his bed wasn't a collection of random papers. What I saw on his bed was motive. Multiple motives.

CHAPTER
TEN

I stacked the papers in the order they'd been laid out and stuffed them into a drawer in John Allen's nightstand. If these were for me to see, I didn't want the others coming in to find out that the patriarch of the family suspected them. I could explain my fingerprints to the authorities later if the topic arose.

Instead of taking the stairs down to rejoin everyone, I used the luxury of the elevator. It was the first time I'd been in someone's private lift, and I wasn't sure what to expect. It seemed like a smaller version of a normal elevator like you would come across at any Myrtle Beach hotel.

A tone beeped, alerting me of the car's arrival on the first floor as the elevator doors whooshed open. I stepped out into a wide hallway. Elegant paintings depicting musical motifs lined both sides, lit by recessed lighting. The hall led to two doors on opposite sides and an elevator at the end. A pot containing a fiddle leaf fig lay beside the elevator.

The aroma of seafood directed me to the kitchen. I turned left and went that way, following my nose. Upon exiting the hallway, I came to the open space of the kitchen and dining room. Many of the open Styrofoam containers from the Sea Captain's House were picked through. To my right, the dinner party participants all sat at the table, eating a somber meal.

My stomach growled. I hadn't eaten since lunch. Antonio hopped up from the table and came over to where I stood by the kitchen island.

"We couldn't wait any longer," Antonio said. "We were ready to eat."

"I can't blame you," I said. "If nothing else, it's a distraction."

"You're right there." He hmphed and then showed me what was in the food containers and where to find plates, forks, knives, and cups. Most of the gang had wine glasses in front of them. I poured two sweet teas. He looked in the direction of the dining room table where the party gathered.

Although they had food on their plates, no one was cramming food into their hungry mouths, as Antonio said. DeeDee held a wine glass in one hand and held the other hand against the side of her head. Her mouth hung open, speechless as her head swung back and forth. Cade had a fork poised above his plate, but it didn't move. He had one arm folded against his torso, no doubt to ease the pain of an upset stomach. Preacher spread one hand over his chest and stared into the distance. Louise leaned sideways in her seat away from everyone. Her eyelids were heavy.

Chris ate with aplomb.

Antonio watched me gather food onto two plates. "Wow, you must be hungry."

"I am, but I thought I'd get Erin some food."

"Why would you get her anything?" he snarled.

I shrugged my shoulders. "Prisoners need to eat too."

"If you say so." He tapped his foot and stood at my side. His coiffed dark hair had a touch of gray around the edges. He wore a merino wool lightweight V-neck sweater, layered over a white shirt with a black windowpane pattern. A red paisley tie over a navy background completed the ensemble. I imagined him walking into one of the upscale men's clothing stores on King Street in Charleston, seeing a mannequin wearing that outfit, and telling the clerk to bag it up while pulling out a platinum credit card.

When he didn't appear to be in a big rush to get back to the dinner table, I asked him, "So, you sell insurance?"

"Yeah. I have an agency."

"How is that?"

"My firm? Busy," he said. "I sold State Farm for years and decided I might do pretty well by myself. So, I branched out, started an LLC, and fifteen years later, here we are."

"Is it going well?"

He stood straight and lifted his chin. "It is. It is."

"How long have you known DeeDee?"

He cast a glance in her direction. "A little under three years."

"How did you meet?"

He placed a hand on the counter and leaned on it. "She moved here after her dad and joined one of those Myrtle Beach Facebook Groups. The one called 'Local and Loving It.' Anyway, she was asking for someone to help her with renters insurance, and I replied. She contacted me, we sat down, discussed her move here and her needs." He spread his hands wide. "And here we are."

"Yes, here we are. Good story."

"Thanks."

Without looking up from where I spooned fluffy mashed potatoes onto a plate, I asked, "Did you ever try to sell her dad any insurance?"

He pressed a hand against his cheek and peered over my shoulder, lost in thought. "I tried to do his homeowners policy, but he already had a person for that."

"Win some, lose some," I said, using a set of tongs to place a steamed-to-perfection lobster tail on Erin's plate. "Why do you think she did it?"

He looked away. "I thought about that while you were upstairs with her."

"And?" I stacked a lobster tail on my plate. When in Rome.

"I figured she was sick of her old man." Antonio glanced back at DeeDee. She was dipping a chunk of lobster in butter at the table. "Not that he was abrasive or mean or anything. He was just, I don't know, difficult."

"Difficult? How?"

He looped a finger in the air around his ear as DeeDee had earlier. "The dementia. It was making him tough to deal with. Erin had to babysit her old man. That wasn't part of her job description, nor was she trained to do it. She tried her best, though."

"Why not hire a caretaker or something? Not like they don't have the money to do so."

"Pride and privacy. After his wife died, he retreated from the public eye. It was soon after that they'd diagnosed him with Stage One Alzheimer's. Then he left Hollywood. DeeDee told me he used to be someone sure of his talents. Not boastful, but he knew when he walked into a room of top movie composers, he stood above the rest."

"Literally," I said. "He was a tall man."

Antonio snorted and wiped his nose. "That he was."

I loaded my plate with a generous helping of mac and cheese. I've tried to get in better shape, but we all have an Achilles heel. Cheesy goodness was mine.

"I'm sure he had a will," I said. "Do you know anything

about it?"

He tapped a finger on the counter. "A chunk was supposed to go to his foundation that DeeDee oversees, and the rest was to be split equally among the kids."

"Who gets the house?"

"Erin, if she wanted it." He leaned in. "But this place is just a drop in the bucket, if you know what I mean."

I glanced at Chris, who was the first person to make me aware of John Allen Howard's net worth. "Yes, I know what you mean. Had there been any recent changes to the will?"

"Not that I'm aware of."

DeeDee hopped up from the table and walked to where Antonio and I were conversing in front of the smorgasbord. She pointed at one plate I was building. "That for Sis?"

"One of them is."

She reached for and handed me a small Styrofoam container that hadn't been opened yet. Someone had written a capital "P" in blue ink on the lid. "Give her that. It's her favorite."

* * *

Back upstairs, I crossed the house to Erin's cell, for lack of a better term. She huddled on the bed in an upright fetal position, crying into her knees. She unfurled as I entered and tried to compose herself.

Bad allergies are a curse I was born with, exacerbated by the southern coastal climate. They were bad as where I grew up in Ohio but got worse after I moved here. The "yellow fog" of pollen in the early spring as the plants and flowers awaken from the chilly winter was one of my least favorite times of the year.

Ragweed was my enemy during the early summer months. I always carried a few tissues in my pocket.

I offered one to Erin. She accepted with a soft "thank you" and filled it with snot.

She looked up with red-rimmed eyes. I held the plate I had put together for her in one hand. Steam rose from the mashed potatoes. Everything else was lukewarm. Rain spattered against the window. I set the plate on the bed beside her and walked across the room to sit in the comfy reading chair.

She sniffled and wiped her nose with the back of her left hand. She wore no ring. Blonde hair fell across her face. She pushed it back with the non-snotty hand.

"Thanks," she said, taking hold of the plate. "I can't believe they let you feed me."

"I didn't give them a choice. Everyone has to eat."

"Even the person they believe killed Dad?"

I tilted my head forward. "Yes, even that person."

She poked the fork into the mashed potatoes and savored a bite. For all she knew, this could be the last meal she would eat that didn't come from a prison cafeteria. I let her sample the other items on the plate before getting to the matter at hand. She ate like a person who skipped breakfast and lunch but passed on the peas. I dug into my food. The extra portion of mac and cheese was bland. Disappointing.

I wondered why DeeDee would suggest peas for her. Probably a sibling rivalry sort of thing. I'd do the same if Erin had been my brother instead.

"Tell me why you didn't kill your dad?"

Her jaw opened. She set the fork on the plate with a clink. "Why do you keep asking me that? You still think I killed him?"

"I don't think anything. Yet. You haven't convinced me that you didn't pull the trigger."

"There's Preacher for one thing."

I held out a hand with my palm outward. "I'm not asking who else might have done it. I want to know why you didn't. If there's even the slightest motive, they'll find it, and you'll spend the rest of your life in jail."

Her eyes hardened, and her jaw set. "I loved him. I adored him. Even though I spent most of my waking time with him, I always felt safe. Secure. He made me laugh. We had good times together. I wouldn't do this. I couldn't do this. I never even held a gun in my life before you found me in his office."

Even though I'd never fired a gun before, I wondered how difficult it would be to pick one up and fire it. It was less than six feet from where I found Erin in the center of the office to John Allen's desk chair. Could anyone miss from that range? I knew about recoil when firing a gun. Would that throw off her aim, or would it matter in the split second between squeezing the trigger and the bullet emerging from the barrel?

I asked, "Any bad times?"

"Not many."

"Recently?"

"More frequent, yes."

"Because you had to do more personal care than organizing his professional life?"

"How did you know that?"

"I spoke to Antonio while I was getting food."

She rolled her eyes. "That guy doesn't shut up."

"Not your favorite, I take it." I tore off a chunk of lobster, drowned it in a small plastic cup of melted butter, then stuffed it in my mouth. "That might be my favorite."

"It is good, isn't it?"

Speaking with her and watching her eat, she didn't seem like a woman who murdered her dad in cold blood. I wasn't a human lie detector, but the conviction she showed in denying her role in the shooting, speaking with her now, and watching her body language suggested truthfulness. Erin was absent in all the papers John Allen laid out for my benefit. I took that as he didn't consider her a potential murderer.

Although, as I've learned in the two other murder investigations that I'd been a part of, sometimes it's the person you least suspect, which led back to the beginning.

"When I first came in here," I said, causing her to look up from her plate, "you mentioned Preacher. Why?"

She looked at the ceiling, then down, poking the food on her plate. "When Dad was at the height of his career, many sycophants tried to be around him. Like little remoras feeding off the scraps of food left behind by the sharks they attach to. Many people offered to perform personal tasks, or offer their professional services, hoping to gain favor with Dad."

I held up a finger. "Let me guess, this is where you came in."

"Correct. DeeDee and I came to him after Mom died, and he was at his most vulnerable. Mom fulfilled the role I have now. After losing her, Dad didn't know what to do. He flailed about for months, saying yes to everyone who approached him. People took advantage."

"Snakes," I hissed.

"Right. There's all manner of lowlifes in Hollywood. They just wear Valentino suits. DeeDee would continue running his charity, and I left my marketing job to work for Dad."

"What about Cade?"

She batted a hand at an invisible fly. "Pfft. Cade always did his own thing. He was more artistic than me. DeeDee is good on different instruments. She and I are the organized ones, like Mom. Cade is like Dad in that regard. He was in art school around that time. Was a fantastic painter." She pointed at me. "Don't tell him I said that."

"My lips are sealed."

"Anyway, he graduates, tries to sell his artwork, fails at it, and asks Dad for a loan to start his art brokerage business."

"Nice."

"Yeah, he always got what he wanted. Here, it worked. He has a strong business going."

"Good for him. Back to Preacher."

"Right. So, after I took the job, I shooed all the leeches away. After Dad got sick and he scaled back on his work, fewer and fewer of that sort came around. Until we met Preacher. I'll tell you this," she said, tipping her fork up and down. "He's a sneaky one. I don't remember where or when Dad met him, but when I was introduced to him and he said he was a financial planner, I was like, 'here we go.' To Preacher's credit, he waited until he got into Dad's good graces before trying to sell him any type of service."

"And then he did, I take it."

"It was odd. Preacher came over every day for a week until Dad signed off on something. Then a month went by without Preacher before he reappeared."

"Any idea why?"

"Nope. They said nothing about it to me."

I hadn't had time to read the letters pertaining to Preacher and Antonio that John Allen left on his bed. If Erin was telling me all she knew about it, then I'd move on.

"When was the last time you saw your dad?"

She placed a palm on her forehead. "Uh, it would have been just before I went to get ready. Cade and Louise were the only ones here. No one else had arrived."

"What was the last thing you said to each other?"

She clasped her hands around her knees. A tear streamed down her face. "I think I just told him I was going to go get ready."

"No malice or venom?"

Her gaze went distant. "No, none of that. We'd had a good day."

"Did you see anyone entering or leaving the office around the time of the tornado?"

"No."

"Was the office door open or shut when you went into his bedroom?"

"Shut. I had to walk by it to get to his bedroom. If it had been open, I would have seen him in there."

"Right. How long after hearing the gun did you go to his office?"

"I don't know. It was such a bizarre moment that I lost track of time. Where were you when it happened?"

"Huddled in a closet across the house with Louise."

"Oh, I bet that was fun. Make sure you still have your wallet."

Without realizing it, I shifted in the seat to see if I could feel it in my back pants pocket. I could. She was joking, I think.

"What makes you say that?"

"If she was after my dad for his money, then she might not be above stealing to get more."

"I assure you that if Louise had sights set on your dad for that reason, then I have little to offer her in that department."

She regarded me. "You have other things to offer."

I didn't reply to that. "If you were in your dad's room when it happened, then I assume you saw what was on his bed."

"Yeah, just a bunch of papers from what I could gather."

"Did you look at any of them?"

"I didn't. I was more concerned with where he was. Besides, he does things like that. Usually with music sheets."

"They weren't music sheets."

She cocked an eyebrow. "What were they?"

"An assortment of statements and letters, both printed and handwritten."

"From whom?"

I pointed at the floor. "Everyone downstairs other than Chris."

"That's odd."

"I think he meant them for me to see."

"Why do you think that?"

"Each of them indicated a motive in killing him."

She put a hand over her mouth. "After the first two attempts on his life, he must have been assembling background, trying to come up with a reason someone was trying to kill him."

"Both times that happened, with the cutting of the cane and with the poisoning, did you try to figure out who did it?"

"We did but couldn't figure it out. By the time we figured his fall and poisoning weren't coincidences, it was too late to go back and try to figure out how both incidents occurred."

"Did you expect another try on his life?"

"You know the saying. If you don't succeed, try, try again."

CHAPTER
ELEVEN

I laughed. That was the second time she attempted to break the tension with a joke. Like something I would do. Erin and I had more than a few things in common.

"Yeah," I said. "That's true, I guess."

"Unfortunately."

The food on our plates was disappearing. The night outside the window grew darker. An eerie silence ran through the house, punctuated by the occasional gust of wind whistling through the ripped tin roof.

There was no telling when the phones would come back online, much less when help would arrive. The last time I checked, the tide was still up to the dunes. We couldn't walk out to the beach and get up on the roads via a beach access path.

If the National Weather Service considered coastal flooding a possibility with Karen's passing, I figured they would have ordered an evacuation of at least those living in Zone 1 along the beach. Then again, I didn't know the hard-and-fast rules about that sort of thing.

Karen threw us a last-second curveball and came closer to land than they'd predicted. Growing up in Ohio, the meteorologists there had it easy compared to those here. I watch the local FOX affiliate for my morning news, and I've heard meteorologist James Hopkins mention how the coast provides a greater challenge when predicting the weather. It's a well-known joke that if you don't like the weather in Myrtle Beach, wait five minutes.

It could be minutes or hours before the authorities could get here and take over this house. A crime scene now. If I was going to be stuck here, I might as well investigate a murder, even if it appeared to be an open-and-shut case.

"Are you trying to stare a hole in the floor?" Erin asked.

I snapped to attention. "Don't think so."

She laughed a snotty laugh. "You were concentrating on something so hard I could imagine lasers shooting out your eyes and gouging the floor."

"Sorry, just thinking." I smiled.

"About what?"

"A couple of things. Can I believe you? If you didn't do it, who did?"

"I can only answer that first question. Yes." Her voice and face displayed sincerity. Not that it meant she didn't do it. The best criminals could put on believable fronts. Was Erin one of those? I didn't know her well enough to draw that conclusion. Our conversation here and the papers on John Allen's bed led me to think she might be innocent. But how? We heard the shot and found her in the room a minute later.

Everyone was accounted for. Louise was with me. DeeDee was in a bathroom. Cade was down in the laundry room. Antonio was in the kitchen, readying the food. Chris and Preacher were on the bottom level. If Erin was telling the truth, then someone else was lying.

I thought about what my mom might tell me. Means, motive,

opportunity. The motive question was laid out, literally, by John Allen. Four potential motives existed to him. None of those involved Erin. Could he have turned a blind eye to her and didn't consider her a suspect? Could someone in her family provide a motive for her to have done it?

Means. Who had access to the gun? That left me with opportunity. Who could have done it? The only people upstairs at the time of the murder were DeeDee and Erin.

"What now?" she asked.

I rolled my shoulders and stood, reaching out for her empty plate. She handed it to me. I said, "I'm going to talk to them. Try to single them out, starting with your sister."

A smile flashed across her face before she could conceal it.

"Do you and DeeDee have issues?"

"Just normal things siblings argue about. Do you have a brother or sister?"

"An older brother," I said.

"Then you know what I'm talking about."

Did I? My brother and I didn't grow up in a wealthy environment like Erin and DeeDee. We likely had different issues. Of course, it has surprised me in the past when coming across wealthy and famous individuals. I learned they can have problems like what we common folk have.

"Yeah, we're grown men now, and still sometimes squabble like we're little kids when we get together. I love my brother, but he has a way of getting under my skin."

"Right," Erin said. "Same with my siblings. We can get along one moment, then at each other's throats the next. We can bring out the worst in each other."

Enough for one or both of them to frame their sister? I opened the door and leaned a shoulder against the opening. I stacked our empty dinner plates on top of each other in my right hand. My left held two empty plastic cups nesting with each other.

"Before I go," I said, "two questions. Do you want more drink?"

She sat up on the bed. Her hair hung over one shoulder. "Yes, please."

"I think I saw a bottle of wine floating around down there."

She held up a hand. "No thanks. I'm recovering."

It took me a moment to get what she was saying. "Oh, I'm sorry. I understand. I had a rough patch where I relied on the bottle more than I should have after my wife passed. Water then?"

"Don't worry about it. Yes, that's fine. What's your other question?"

"It's not really a question. You didn't answer mine."

"Which one?"

"What did you and DeeDee fight about?"

She did a slow eye roll, then told me. It made me happy to have a simpler life.

* * *

I exited the room and set the plates on a table near the stairs. Voices echoed up from the dining room. A woman laughed. I placed my hand on the door to the office containing the body of John Allen. A shiver ran up my spine.

I pushed the door aside. He was still in the same position. It was sad and a relief at the same time. Sad that he was dead. A relief that someone hadn't moved him. Or that he'd come back to life.

Closing the door behind me, I tiptoed into the room. Elegant shelving lined both walls. Books filled the shelves. Many were leather-bound with gold embossing on the spines, although more than a few popular modern hardcovers were mixed in. Daniel Silva, Brad Metzler, Brooke Vitale, Steve Berry, and David Baldacci were a few I found.

Careful not to touch anything, I shoved my hands in my pockets to resist temptation. I was here to observe, not muddle a crime scene. The woodgrain surface of his desk wasn't neat. Far from it. A stack of off-kilter, unopened mail lay in a corner. I wanted to stack them square to each other. The piece of mail at the top of the pile had a Bank of America return address.

Part of the business on the third envelope down was visible where the two above were off-center. Grou was all I could make out of it. It caught my eye because the rounded part of the G was shaped like a fish jumping out of water. A 1 and a 4 were visible at the start of the next line. The top envelope obscured the city.

In front of John Allen, in the middle of the desk, was a paper with five rows of five lines bunched together with musical notes written out by hand. Sheet music. A Mont Blanc fountain pen lay on top of the sheet. He must have been writing a musical piece when the murderer came into the room. I took a picture.

I knew the feeling with my writing. When I'm in the middle of planning or writing a book, sometimes I'll get a flash of inspiration and stop what I'm doing so I can write it down or get it onto a Word document. If it had inspired him, then I could understand why he would take the extra time to come in here and get it down on paper.

He and his chair were three feet from the desk. Had he pushed himself back when the assailant entered? Did the gun blast cause the chair to roll across the hardwood floor?

I knelt to examine the area behind John Allen. His desk sat in front of a wall with another elegant painting of a ship crashing through waves.

Getting back to my feet, I looked once more around the room to see if I'd missed anything. When nothing stood out, I exited, closing the door behind me.

Crossing to the balcony, I looked down at the party gathered around the table. DeeDee and Cade seemed to spat. Chris and Preacher stood chatting off to one side. Louise was using a knife to cut her green beans into smaller bites. Antonio sipped on a beer, taking it all in.

I called down, "DeeDee!"

Everyone except Louise turned their heads in my direction. DeeDee and Cade stopped the verbal jousting. "Yeah, what is it?"

"Can you come up here for a moment?" I said, crooking my finger.

She let out a breath and tried to stare me down, big hair and all. I stood my ground. She was a woman who likely wasn't ordered around much.

Grabbing her wine, she stood, pushing her chair away from the table. She took a sip, then said, "Be right there."

As she crossed the room, angling for the elevator and disappearing below, Cade rubbed a hand over his face and slouched back on the bench seat against the window. Some people light up a room when they entered it, others when they left it. The body language among those at the dinner table relaxed upon DeeDee's exit.

What was I getting myself into?

A moment later, the elevator dinged, and the light above it lit. The doors whooshed open and out walked DeeDee, wine glass in hand. With her head held high, she joined me in the great room. She plopped down on the other end of the plush couch from me.

She sipped from the glass and rubbed a hand over her forehead. An identical gesture to the one Cade made a moment ago. He seemed relieved when she departed. Could she feel the same now that she had a break from verbally jousting with him?

"What's this about?" she demanded. She seemed like a woman who liked to control every situation. A person who exuded confidence.

I considered how to ease my way into this conversation with her without tipping her off that I was raising a line of inquiry. Judging by her bossy demeanor, there would be no tiptoeing around the subject. I was a nobody to her. Why give me the time of day? I wasn't her guest at this party.

We were all waiting for the same thing. For the phones to come back up so we could call the authorities to come cut us out of here and make an arrest while they were at it. The mystery didn't seem as open-and-shut as that.

Could it have been Erin who pulled the trigger? It seemed likely considering where everyone else was in the house when the tornado struck and the shot was fired. Unless someone was lying. Her conviction in telling me she didn't do it was one thing. I'm not a human lie detector. She might be a talented actress.

I was convinced that John Allen invited me to help nab his would-be killer. If he laid out all the evidence he had gathered beforehand, why did none of it include Erin? Did he not think she'd tried to kill him? Did he have reason to believe she couldn't have been behind either attempt?

If not Erin, then who? The only other person who I'm sure

was close to John Allen at the penultimate moment sat across the sofa from me.

Her head bobbed and nodded with a will of its own. She had trouble focusing. I wondered how many glasses of wine she'd had this evening.

"DeeDee," I said, grabbing her attention. "Your sister says she didn't do it."

She poked a tongue into the inside of her cheek. "She says she didn't do it? Of course, she did. We all heard the shot. She was the one holding the gun when you found her. Besides you and Louise, she was the only one up here."

DeeDee left out herself from that equation. "She's still denying it," I said.

She took a long gulp of wine and then clinched her jaw. "How could she not be? We all knew she was tired of being Dad's caregiver."

"Would she kill him over it?"

She drained the last of her wine and looked around for another bottle. "She might. Just to put him out of his misery."

Callous. This was her dad we were talking about. "Was it that bad?"

"It was. His memory was gone. He'd forgotten how to use the bathroom. Could you imagine changing your parents' diapers?"

A little vomit surged to the back of my throat. "Nope."

"That's what Erin had to do. I mean, he'd still go by himself most times, but there were accidents."

"It's the circle of life, I guess. They change ours when we're little. We change theirs when they're old."

She stared at me for a moment, then laughed. "I hadn't thought about it like that. I bet my kids can't wait for that day to come."

"You have kids?"

"Yep. Both in college. Two years apart."

"Where do they go?"

"Zach is a senior at Berkeley. Heidi is in her second year at Stanford."

"Must be smart kids."

She put a hand on the side of her face. "You're telling me. Zach was reading on a high school level by the time he was six. Heidi is a prodigy on the violin."

"Must have some of her grandad's blood in her."

"She does. He was so proud of her. We're all creatives. Cade is a wonderful painter. Erin can tickle the ivory. I play a little violin myself, but not like Dad could or Heidi can."

"You must be proud."

DeeDee raised her chin and threw her shoulders back. "Very."

Now that the ice was broken, and DeeDee was disarmed and lubricated by the wine, I took this as my chance to poke around her story.

"Where were you when the tornado hit?"

She closed her eyes, perhaps reliving the moment, then reopened them. "In the bathroom powdering my nose."

"What did you do?"

"I heard what sounded like a freight train coming, heard someone shout about a tornado, and I got down and huddled in the shower until it passed."

"Did you hear the shot?"

"I did. Even with the ruckus, it was difficult to miss."

As was the shooter's aim from point-blank range. "When you heard it, who did you first think pulled the trigger?"

"Erin. She was the person in closest proximity to him."

"Gotcha. So, you head a charity your dad set up?"

She smiled, thankful for the change of topic. "I do. He called it The Cheerful Note."

"What's your role there?"

"I arrange for funding and introduce the program in schools."

"How were donations?"

"Good." She cocked an eyebrow. "Do you want to donate?"

"Let me think about it." If the papers from the IRS were any sign, the answer to her question would be a fat "no." I wanted to pick back up on something we lost track of. "A moment ago, when I asked if your dad's decline would cause Erin to put him out of his misery, you said, 'She might.' Do you have doubt about her reason for doing this?"

"No, no doubt. None of us knows each other's breaking point. I guess she'd reached hers."

"But to do it here, at a dinner party, doesn't that sound unlikely? If she lived here, she could have done it any time the house was empty and blamed it on a gardener or intruder and created an alibi for herself. Instead, she did it with all of us around and was found holding the smoking gun."

She waved her fingers and studied her empty wine glass. "That's what appears to have happened."

CHAPTER
TWELVE

DeeDee got up and left without another word. I stared at the end of the couch she'd vacated, thinking about our conversation. Something in it tickled the back of my brain, but I couldn't place a finger on what it was.

I pulled my phone out of my pocket and checked the screen. Still no signal. The storm pounded outside. A flash of lightning revealed palm trees ripped from their roots. The chairs and tables that had been around the pool were scattered about.

The realization struck that we might be here for hours, if not all night. If I was going to pull an all-nighter, I needed one thing. Coffee. And what does coffee do? It brings people together.

I eschewed the elevator and opted for the stairs. Everyone clustered around the dining room table as I reached the lower level. DeeDee had already refilled her wine glass. Cade sat in the same spot. His head was down on the table with his arms wrapped around it. Much the same way I used to take naps at my desk in elementary school. He had likely reached the same conclusion I had about how long we might be stuck here. Maybe his phone died.

Antonio rubbed DeeDee's back. Preacher and Chris were deep in conversation. Those two had huddled together ever since the tornado passed. Chris could sell saltine crackers to a camel in the desert, and I suspected Preacher could do the same. Louise's chin rested against her chest as she softly dozed sitting upright. At least she'd figured out a way to escape the evening.

I walked over to the table and got everyone's attention. "There is an Astra automatic espresso machine over there. I've wanted to get one for my store, but they're out of my price range. Since it looks like we're going to be here for a while, can I interest anyone in a cup?"

Half of them were, except for Cade, Louise, and Preacher. He said he preferred tea. I took orders, familiarized myself with the coffeemaker. The espresso machine I used at the bookstore was archaic by comparison. After I prepared DeeDee's caramel macchiato, I dug through the drawers on the coffee bar and found a box from the Charleston Tea Plantation. Someone here had good taste in tea.

A few minutes later, any verbal altercations between Cade and DeeDee had melted away, replaced with the calming effect coffee can provide. At least the most recent glass of wine DeeDee had poured sat half-full on the table in front of her. I had hoped a drink with espresso might sober her up. Whether it be from the actions of sipping something hot and that getting into your belly or the mild psychoactive effect, coffee had a way of easing the mind.

I took a sip of an excellent café au lait, a beverage I'd developed a taste for after Autumn and I took a trip to New Orleans one year just before Mardi Gras began. During that week, I frequented Café du Monde in the French Quarter for this specific beverage. I preferred to drink straight coffee with a little of crème, but when presented with the opportunity to use an Astra machine, I was going to go with one of my favorite beverages. I didn't regret it. This was up there with New Orleans's finest.

"How's Erin?" Cade asked.

DeeDee slapped him on the arm. "Who cares how she is. She killed Daddy!"

Cade rubbed his arm but didn't retaliate. "She's our sister, Dee."

Before this escalated further, I said, "She's shaken, that's for sure. Stunned."

"I'd be stunned too if I upped and blew my dad away during a hurricane," Antonio said.

"Why do it now?" I ventured.

"She'd had it, I guess," Cade said. "I know Dad was tough on her recently. She'd told me as much."

"Mmm hmm," DeeDee concurred.

"Did any of you ever give her a break?" I asked. "Step in and take care of John Allen so she could have time to herself?"

Cade and DeeDee glanced at each other. Like it was an alien thought. I didn't include Preacher or Antonio in the question because I didn't think it was their place.

Louise perked up. "I'd come over and spend some time with him so Erin could run errands, go do doctors' appointments and such." She pointed across to Cade and DeeDee. "They were always too busy."

Antonio held up a placating hand. "Hold on. DeeDee and I came over and had lunch with him two, three times a week so Erin could do her thing."

DeeDee crossed her arms so hard it caused her puffy hair to bounce. "Yeah. I may not have been here all the time to care for his needs, but I did care for him. I had his charity to run and relied on him to help steer the ship. Besides, Cade rarely showed his face."

The man in question's face turned beet red. "Look, I'm a busy man. I work hard to do what I do. You know I'm on a plane or in a hotel room most days."

"Yeah, I'll give you that," DeeDee said, wiping a tear away. "But you still don't come around. Even more so as of late."

Cade held his hands out, palms up. "What can I say? I have a life to lead."

I understood where Cade was coming from. Before my parents sold their home in Ohio and moved here a couple of years ago, I would see them once or twice a year. Autumn and I led busy lives that weren't conducive to paying regular family visits. My older brother saw my parents even less as he traveled the globe. In John Allen's defense, Cade lived nearby in Little River. It's not like it would be that difficult to visit.

I caught myself at a crossroads as I sipped my coffee. How could I steer this conversation in a way to ask questions about who might have killed John Allen other than Erin without letting them know that she might not have done it? Everyone here, except for Chris and Louise, was a suspect. Perhaps Preacher was innocent as well. He and Chris were in the basement together when the tornado struck.

That left Antonio, Cade, and DeeDee.

During our coffee chat, Chris had kept making eye contact with me but added nothing to the conversation. There was a lull after Cade's statement. I sensed Chris's eyes boring into the side of my head. I looked his way. He jerked his head up and to the side. A not-so-subtle hint.

I drained the last of my café au lait. "Hey, Chris. Want another cup?"

He looked down at his half-full cup. "Sure."

We headed to the coffee bar, away from the other dinner guests. I set about making myself a cup of regular coffee this time. Jamaican Blue Mountain pure blend. Nothing but the finest in this house.

"What's up?" I said to him when I was sure no one could hear us. The dinner table was around the corner, so a wall should muffle our speech.

"Hello Inspector," he said after we were away from the rest of the dinner party. "Why were you up there so long with her?"

I snorted, leaned in close, and whispered, "She swears she didn't do it."

He took a step back and didn't look surprised.

"I wondered. You wouldn't have spent that much time with her unless there was a story to it."

I shrugged. "I'm always looking for a good story."

"Yeah, I know. Can't blame you. I'd want to spend as much time with that beautiful creature as possible, too."

He spoke the truth, but that wasn't my reason for closing ourselves up in the guest bedroom upstairs.

"I don't know. She was holding the gun when we walked in. Whether she compulsively picked it up off the floor when she first saw it is the debate. All we have is her word." I glanced at my phone. Rain poured in a torrent outside. "Phones are still down."

"What are you going to do?"

"I guess we'll have to do this the old-fashioned way. Interviews, logic, and reasoning."

"Like Sherlock Holmes."

"Exactly."

"I'll be happy to help."

"Yes. That's elementary, Dr. Watson."

He rubbed his hands together. "The game is afoot."

"Hey, if I'm the Sherlock in this scenario, that's my line."

"I'm not apologizing," Chris said with a grin.

It was a pleasant break in the tragic consequences of the evening to inject a little humor. "You looked like you wanted to tell me something. How were the cars downstairs?"

He held up a hand, signaling that we had more important matters to discuss. "It's Preacher."

"What about him?"

"We got separated when the tornado roared through. He disappeared."

"How so?"

"We were down there and looking at this exquisite 1955 Mercedes SL300 Gullwing. You know, the ones where the doors raise up?"

"Like a seagull?"

"Yeah, like that. Anyway, I was sitting inside of it when we heard the twister. Preacher got on his tiptoes, looked out the window, and informed me a tornado was coming our way."

"What did you do?"

"I lowered the doors to the Mercedes and hunkered down. When I looked out, Preacher was gone."

"Was he in any of the other cars?"

"No, he wasn't. After the thing passed and the noise died down, he came back through a door connecting the garage to a recording studio. There's a narrow hallway that separates them from where you can hop on the elevator or climb the stairs."

I tapped the counter with a finger. "So, he could have gone anywhere during the thing."

"Yeah."

"Did you hear the gun go off?"

"I think I did. Heard a pop during it all. I figured it was a transformer or something that blew outside."

"It wasn't. How long was it until you saw him again?"

"I can't remember. A minute or two."

"What was Preacher like when you saw him again?"

"Shaking. Bad. He had to hold his hands together to keep them from quivering."

"He had just lived through a tornado. Could have been stress and shock manifesting itself."

"Or, if Erin said she didn't do it, maybe he'd just killed a person."

I tried to think back to if the house lost power during it all. I wasn't sure. Louise and I were in a dark closet in a dark room the entire time.

"Did the power ever go out in the home?" I asked.

"It flickered for a moment before the generator kicked in."

"I wonder how that would affect an elevator in transit between floors? Like, if Preacher took that as his opportunity to do it, and he was halfway up or down, would the elevator stall?"

"Depends on the elevator. The main elevators at OceanScapes can run on a limited basis under a generator."

"What about that one in your offices across the street? It doesn't travel much higher or lower than the one in this house."

My question brought back memories of sneaking around the resort one night while investigating the murder of Paige Whitaker and getting caught. If Natasha hadn't left me her keycard, I would have never done that and gotten in trouble. On the flip side, Paige's murderer may have never been caught had that not happened. That was also the night that I tried to pin the murder on Chris. But I digress.

Chris said, "It has an emergency battery that if the power goes out, it will take the passenger to the nearest floor and let them out before shutting down."

"So, if Preacher was on his way up to kill John Allen, he might have been let off on a different floor."

"Yeah," Chris said. "Or on his way down."

"In which case, Antonio might have seen him getting off the elevator and going down the stairs."

"Right."

I pressed my tongue to the inside of my cheek. So much for Preacher not being a suspect. "Need to talk to Preacher."

CHAPTER
THIRTEEN

I asked Preacher if he could show me the cars. He asked Cade to join us since a few of the cars were shared by him and his dad, but Cade declined and stayed in his spot. I figured getting away might help him take his mind off his dad's death, but I was grateful he didn't take Preacher up on the offer. Antonio didn't show any interest. DeeDee didn't care. Louise snored.

This was my preference, as I didn't want any of the others near us as I questioned Preacher. Chris volunteered to join us, saying he didn't get a full chance to look at the cars earlier thanks to the tornado.

Coffee cups in hand, the three of us descended the stairs. None of us wanted to chance getting stuck in the elevator. The stairs ended in a hallway that bisected the house from front to back. I couldn't judge if it was in the center of the home or not. Two doors faced each other on opposite sides midway down the hall. The one on the right-hand side was made of steel and had a glass inlay, head high. The other door was a typical wooden door.

A golden record of John Allen's most famous soundtrack, The Duelist, hung on the wall outside of a recording studio. I peeked in as Preacher led us to the other door but couldn't see anything. It was dark.

He opened the wooden door and flicked a light switch with his left hand and led us into the garage. Chris preceded me. The cavernous interior was lit by evenly spaced LED bay lights. They cast a clean glow over an impressive array of classic and modern cars. An ancient Harley-Davidson was among the collection, for which Chris made a beeline.

"I saw this in here earlier," he called over his shoulder. "Didn't get to look at it."

The reason Chris rode with me to the house was because a chromed-out Harley was his only mode of transportation. I still found it humorous when he rode past the bookstore on Ocean Boulevard while wearing a three-piece suit on his way to and from OceanScapes. Not a typical sight like you would see during Bike Week.

The garage reminded me of Dirk Pitt's hangar in the Clive Cussler adventure novels, except this room wasn't as cavernous as described in the books. Four rows of three vehicles, twelve total, filled the space. Everything from a 1911 Model T to a sleek newish Aston Martin graced the concrete. I spotted a red 1998 Porsche 911 among the crowd. That was my dream car in high school. A tool bench sat in a corner below a pegboard with various gadgets, tools, and equipment hanging from hooks.

"Not a bad bunch of vehicles, wouldn't you say?" Preacher asked me.

"Not at all," I said.

"I have a confession," he said.

My heart jumped. Chris was on the other side of the garage, out of earshot. As I wondered what juicy secret Preacher wanted to confide in me, he said, "After I met John Allen, he invited me to play piano with him."

"How did you meet?"

"Cade took him to the 88 Keys Piano Bar one night. It's near Antonio's business. I used to play there on Wednesday nights. He spoke to me after I finished and invited me to his house."

"Fascinating. You never know what talents a person possesses when you first meet them."

He batted a hand. "Anyway, when I got here and found these cars, I never wanted to leave."

"I don't know that I would either," I said. It was quite a collection. I didn't know what half of them were, but they were still beautiful to look at. "Where were you when the tornado went past?"

He turned to me, blinked, and said, "I ran across the hall to the studio. I knew it was well insulated and," he pointed at the ceiling and hanging lights, "you weren't likely to have things that could fall on you."

"Makes sense. Why didn't you take Chris? He probably didn't know that about the insulated room."

Preacher tilted his head in Chris's direction. "Look at him. His muscles are bulging through that shirt. I figured that the man could take care of himself."

"True," I laughed, then stopped. "Aren't we on the opposite side of the house from where the tornado hit? Wouldn't you have seen it through those windows up there?"

He turned to look up at the thin windows at the top of the wall facing the ocean. During the day, they provided natural sunlight. Now, it was black through the glass.

"We did. I saw it first. I yelled 'twister!' or something to your friend and high-tailed it out of here."

"Yeah, but you ran towards the tornado. Wouldn't that trump any perceived safety of the studio?"

He rubbed his chin. "What can I say? It was the heat of the moment. I panicked and got out." He looked like a man reliving a traumatizing experience. Which he was. This was a night none of us under this tin roof would soon forget.

"Where did you go?"

"Into the studio. With all the sound-dampening stuff on the walls and ceiling, I figured it was about as protective of a place as I could get. Where were you when it happened?"

I groaned. "Huddled in a closet in an upstairs bedroom closet with Louise."

He snickered. "That woman sure enjoys getting intimate with men."

"It wasn't an intimate encounter. Then you returned to the garage afterward?"

"Yeah, after the sound died down, and the ceiling didn't collapse on me. I remembered I left your pal in there and felt foolish for leaving him." The corner of his lips curled down. "I apologized to him."

"That's good, I guess."

He looked across at Chris, who was leaning down to look in a car window. The expression on Preacher's face didn't change. "I'm glad he was okay, at least."

"Chris said your hands were shaking when you reappeared."

He wrung his wrists and gave a sheepish smile. "Yeah, it terrified me, to be honest."

"It was scary. How well did you know John Allen?"

He rocked his head back and forth. "Okay, I guess. To be honest, it kinda surprised me to get the invitation."

"Yeah, why?"

"It's been a few months since I spoke to him."

"How did you get word of the invitation?"

"The man called me himself at the beginning of the week. Said he was having a shindig at his place tonight. I'd seen the weather reports about Karen, but the weatherman said it should pass by with little harm." He bounced his shoulders. "So, I came. Had nothing better to do this evening. It's always nice to be around John Allen."

"Why is that?"

Preacher turned and cast his eyes around the garage. "Because coming here has its perks."

"Do you know his kids well?"

He waggled his hand. "A little. John Allen would have me come over and play piano with him."

"What did he like to play?"

"Oh, piano, double bass, viola, clarinet. He could have been a world-class violinist in his own right. That's what he played the most, I think. DeeDee is superb." He closed his eyes for a second. "He'd work himself into a sweat performing Bartok's Violin Concerto No. 2. That's an intense piece right there. Then he could almost bring you to tears with a rendition of the second movement of Tchaikovsky's violin concerto."

"I bet. Did he ever play any of the music from his movies?"

"Not really. I'd ask him now and then, and he would tell me that he didn't like to play his old pieces. That he'd hear them and think about how they can be better. He didn't want to look back."

"I'm like that with my writing. Once I've written a story, beta readers read it and give their feedback, then my editor goes through it with a pair of scissors to make it readable. After that, I don't look at them again."

"You're a writer?"

"I am."

He leaned away and regarded me with a curious look. Then stuck out his fist. I bumped it. He waved a finger in the air. "My man. Something told me you were a creative sort. That must be why you're here. John Allen liked to surround himself with creatives. Like-minded people."

I didn't want to tell him the exact reason I thought I was here. "Maybe so."

"What sort of writing do you do?"

"I used to write action and adventures, but now I'm trying my hand at mystery novels."

"Like, murder mysteries?"

"Yup."

"Then tonight must be right up your alley. You could write a book about this; except you'd have to make the murderer more of a mystery."

"Yeah, I guess so. How was John Allen the last time you saw him? Health wise?"

"He was on the decline. They say he was nearing the end, sad to say. That poor Erin had her work cut out for her."

"Why didn't they have a caretaker stay here? It's not like they didn't have the money."

"Pride, I suppose. This family has that in spades."

"Both of the other kids seem like they're full of themselves. Erin seems, I don't know, more down-to-Earth."

His chin dipped. "I'll agree with you there. She was the one who, if you didn't know who she was, you'd never know she was the daughter of a famous movie composer. But DeeDee and Cade?" He let out a low, slow whistle. "Man, they're a couple pieces of work. Neither are ever wrong about anything. Everyone is below them. They acted like royalty without earning it, you know?"

I had the same impression from my limited interactions with both. I said, "Tell me about business."

"Not much to tell, I'm afraid. I used to be a financial advisor for an office chair company. Did that for twenty or so years. Got bored. I'd helped the company grow through various investments, and helped myself along the way, and had the idea to do the same for individuals."

"Like financial planning?"

"Exactly that."

"Ah, Chris does that for me."

Preacher looked over at Chris, who straddled the antique Harley. "I thought there was a reason I liked that guy."

"Did John Allen ever use your services?"

He scratched his arm. "Nah, never did. I mentioned it a couple times, but he said he had a person who managed his money out in Los Angeles."

From the glimpse of the papers arranged on John Allen's bed, that seemed like a lie. Here was a key moment. At first glance, the papers showed that John Allen had opened some kind of an account with Preacher. If I called Preacher out on his lie, then he would want to know how I knew that. I wasn't ready to reveal John Allen's incriminating document cache.

"Tell me," I said in a moment of inspiration, "when you heard the gun go off, who did you think fired it?"

"Honestly, I thought it was Antonio."

"Antonio? Why?"

"From what I could tell, John Allen didn't like Antonio very well, and the feeling was mutual."

"Any idea why?"

"I'm not sure. It seemed like maybe J.A. didn't think Antonio was good enough for his daughter or something. Maybe Antonio got tired of it and offed the old man to get him out of the way."

Chris moseyed over and led Preacher to an elegant green and white classic car and left me standing at the garage entrance. I made eye contact with Chris as Preacher walked away, letting him know I had gotten all that needed. For now.

A short while later, after I sat inside the Porsche and ran my hands over the dash, we exited the garage out into the hall. I drained the last of my coffee. Preacher led the way back up the stairs. I lagged behind. Chris and Preacher discussed something to do with cars and didn't notice when I put my hand on the knob of the studio door and tried to twist it.

The door didn't budge. It was locked.

CHAPTER
FOURTEEN

I stared at Preacher's back as he ascended the stairs in front of me, flanked by Chris. How did he hide in the studio if the door was locked? Did he lock it upon leaving and returning to the garage? If so, why? Was he hiding something in there?

How could he have run up the six flights of stairs, shot John Allen, and then returned to the garage? Antonio was, allegedly, in the kitchen. Would he have not seen Preacher hustling up and down the stairs? If he had, he surely would have mentioned it. Would Preacher have risked using the elevator with the tornado bearing down on us? It's possible.

I couldn't think of a way to broach the subject without revealing that I thought he could be a suspect. That meant I had to ask the others probing questions when he was out of earshot. With everyone gathered around the table, that might be difficult. Antonio seemed like the one who I might be able to pry away from there.

It was a precarious situation. Everyone, I assumed, thought Erin did it. Except for the actual killer.

We arrived back at the main level. Preacher moseyed over to the table and struck up a conversation with Antonio. Chris hung back with me as we looked out the front windows of the house.

The street was dark. Rain fell in solid sheets. Streetlights remained in silent darkness. Not a soul moved.

The clock on the wall approached eleven. What had seemed like an eternity since the tornado struck was, in fact, about three hours. From the way it looked outside, the night was just getting started.

"He lied to us," I said. "The studio room was locked. Unless he locked it on his way out, he couldn't have gotten in. That explains something else."

"What's that?"

"He told me he waited until he heard the storm die down to go out and check on you."

His eyes widened. "It's a soundproof room."

I pointed a finger at him like a gun. "Exactly."

"What do we do now with him?"

"Nothing for now. I don't know how he could have made it upstairs and back in the amount of time it would take to shoot him."

"But he was definitely up to something,"

"I concur."

We looked over to where Preacher stood with the others. He turned and made eye contact with us before quickly looking away.

"That's not suspicious at all," I said.

"Nope," Chris said, matching my sarcasm level. Which was high. "Should one of us go out there and try to flag someone down?"

I looked out the front windows. The night was black beyond the glow going out through the windows. "That's not a bad idea, but it doesn't look like anyone is about to flag down."

"You'd figure there would be at least one power truck out and about trying to restore power here. This is the Golden Mile. There's not a doubt in my mind that the people who live here take precedence over us common folk."

I laughed. Chris lived in a posh penthouse in Market Common. I wouldn't consider him a commoner. "True."

We approached the table. Cade looked up from his phone where there was a game being played on the screen. It might have been Candy Crush or another game like it. I wasn't too far off on my initial guess.

"What did you think of the cars?" he asked.

"It's a wonderful collection. That Porsche 911 is one that I've loved since high school."

"Did you look at it?"

"Yup. Climbed inside. Ran my hand across the dash. Asked it where it had been my entire life. It's beautiful."

He smirked. "I'll let you take it for a spin one of these days. That's one of my favorites as well."

The hair stood up on my arms. "That'd be awesome."

"Your sister tells me that, not only do you sell artwork, you're also a good painter," I said.

"A good painter?" DeeDee said. "He's a great painter. He'd just never admit it."

Cade's cheeks turned a light shade of rouge. "Thanks, Sis."

"Do you play music as well?"

"I don't," he said, then pointed at DeeDee. "That's her thing. As good as she says I am at painting, she's my equal on the violin. She could step in and handle the solo parts in Dad's pieces if she wanted to."

Now it was her turn to blush. "Dad trained me to play violin when I was a little kid. Later in life, when he developed arthritis in his fingers, he'd have me come in when he was composing for a film to play back the violin pieces he'd written to make sure they sounded correct. He was better on the violin than me, but I think he just liked to hear me play." She smiled sadly. "He still loved to play, though."

I thought of a heart-wrenching bit of music from the movie, The Duelist, which won an Academy Award when it came out. I asked her about it.

"That wasn't me on the recording," DeeDee said, "but I spent hours with Dad getting that one down pat. He knew it had to be perfect because the film was destined to be a hit, and the music is often what makes a film."

I scratched a fingernail on the counter. Upstairs, she told me she played a little violin. Either she was being modest about her abilities, or she was trying to downplay her skills for another reason. "I wouldn't mind hearing you play sometime."

A sad smile crossed her face. "In the future. Preacher and I used to play in the studio downstairs. Now there's a fine piano player."

"He'd mentioned that he played. Is your musical background the reason you run your dad's charity?"

"It is," DeeDee said. "Dad started it back home, but I needed to be near him to do it well. Daddy rarely did Zoom or Facetime or anything like that. He mostly met with people in person or talked to them on the phone. He'd make exceptions for friends in the industry."

"How was that going? The charity."

She glanced at Antonio before answering. "It's going well. We give the gift of music to kids in elementary schools. Exposing them to musical play at an early age keeps them interested as they get older. With more schools reducing or axing their arts budgets, music has taken a hit. We go into schools around Los Angeles and now here in Horry and Georgetown Counties and donate instruments. I play a little concert, explain who I am and who my daddy is, tell them the movies he's done, and then play a piece from a soundtrack. When I perform his more famous music, it's something they all recognize."

"It perks their ears up," Antonio said.

"Yes, it gets them interested. That's part of it. The other part is going into high schools and music academies and finding kids interested in going to college to study music. Daddy set up a scholarship fund for kids like that." She wiped a tear away from the corner of her eye. "I don't know what will happen now. Kids need music."

"Now, now," Antonio patted her arm, "your dad left something in his will to the charity to keep it going."

"I know, I know," she said. "It just won't be the same without him. Excuse me."

DeeDee wiped her nose, stood, and excused herself from the table, heading for the bathroom. Antonio followed her. If the IRS contacted her for an audit of the organization's funds, then it was possible The Cheerful Note was strapped for cash. If DeeDee needed the money enough, would she kill her own daddy to get the funds?

We watched DeeDee close the bathroom door behind her. Louise stayed awake. She placed her elbows on the table and folded one arm over the other. "DeeDee told us that Erin claims she didn't do it."

"Yeah, that's what she told me," I said.

"But she was holding the gun," Cade said. "She went looking for him when we all parted. What was her story?"

"She said she went into his bedroom and then closet, looking for him," I said. "She was afraid he'd passed out again. Then the tornado came, and she heard the shot. She waited until the twister passed and went into his office. She found him dead and the gun in the middle of the floor."

"Why did she pick it up?" Louise asked.

"Because she has a little OCD, according to DeeDee," I said.

"Yeah," Louise said. "Erin is the neatest and most organized person I've ever been around. That part makes sense."

I held a special place in my heart for organized people. Everything has a place. Every place has a thing.

Louise gasped and stood, backing away from the table. She crooked a finger at everyone sitting around the table. "If Erin didn't do it, that means one of you did!"

Preacher came around and placed a consoling arm around her waist. "Now, now, Ms. Louise. Look here. If you can believe them, how many innocent people do you think there are on death row?"

She took a moment to ponder his words. Her hands shook more violently than before. "True."

"There aren't many who confessed to the crimes they committed," Preacher said, as though he had every name on the ill-fated row memorized. "How many of them do you think tried to blame someone else for their crimes?"

"I see what you're saying," Louise said. "I think I need to lie down."

"Let me help you over to the couch," Preacher said and guided her away.

I had faced an obstacle in coming up here about trying to question Preacher and the others where they weren't within hearing distance of each other. It seemed as if that conundrum was taking care of itself. If I couldn't get to him yet, I had questions for the one who remained at the table. Cade.

He said, gesturing to a pair of empty chairs. "Go ahead, have a seat. Looks like it's going to be awhile."

Chris and I shared a look and then sat. A picture window was across from us, behind Cade. Our view was pitch black as the clouds covered the moon and the rain fell. I hated having my back to a room. It unnerved me not to see what was going on. A throwback to when I used to read Robert Ludlum's Jason Bourne novels.

"This is so nuts," Cade said, setting his phone aside. "Erin shot Dad. We're trapped here while this storm is going on. Cell phones are out. We're running on a generator. For all intents and purposes, we're cut off from the outside world. So, we sit here with Dad sitting dead up in his office." He waved a hand at me. "You have Sis locked up. Louise is a mess. Antonio and Preacher are like you guys. Stuck here until someone comes to arrest Erin and take Dad away."

"That about sums it up, laddie," Chris said. "What about the family? What's going to happen now?"

Cade twirled the phone in his hands. Worry lines creased his forehead.

"Come on," I said. "You all knew that your dad had little time left. Surely there were plans in place for his eventual passing."

"Yeah, there were," Cade said, passing a hand over his face, idly placing a hand on his phone.

"What sort?" I asked.

"Erin was going to sell this place," Cade said, "and split any profit between us kids."

"Why sell it?" Chris asked.

Cade bit his lip. "Because she had to spend all her time with Dad, the house would always hold terrible memories. Especially now with him being killed in the office."

"Good point," Chris said.

"What about the rest of his estate?" I asked.

Cade pursed his lips. "Dad has a substantial amount of assets, as you can imagine. The trick was dividing it up in a way that made us kids happy."

I crossed my arms. "Was he able to do that?"

"To a degree." Cade ran a hand across the table. "He split his estate four ways."

My brow crinkled. "Four? "There's three of you kids."

"Dad had another 'baby' as well."

I crossed my arms. "Did he have another wife or lover?"

"No, nothing like that," Cade said. "He and mom were childhood sweethearts, and as far as I know, never cheated on her. The fourth chunk of the estate was to go to The Cheerful Note organization DeeDee ran."

I swallowed hard. There was DeeDee's motive.

CHAPTER
FIFTEEN

Preacher rejoined us. "Louise needs to go to bed. She's tired."

"Looked that way," Chris said.

"The only bedroom on this level," Cade said, "is Erin's."

"I'm not sure we should allow anyone in there," I said. "If she killed John Allen, then I'm sure the police are going to want to search her room."

"She'll be fine on the sofa," Preacher said. "She was already asleep by the time I walked away."

Cade laughed. "She's been asleep half the evening."

Louise, it seemed, was a little older than my parents. I know from being at their house in the late evenings that Mom disappears into the bathroom at a prescribed time to dispense their nightly medications. I said, "I wonder if she missed taking her pills?"

"Ah," Preacher said. "That could be, but we don't have a way of getting over to her house to retrieve them. The wall on that side of the house is too high, and there isn't a gate connecting the two."

"If there were," Cade said, "we could have gotten out a long time ago."

Water dripped off the window frame outside. The dripping water reminded me of something I saw upstairs.

"Has anyone checked the laundry room lately?" I asked.

"No," Cade said. "I had no reason to go back in there after I folded my laundry. I was fortunate all my clothes got dry before the storm came."

"Well, they may not be dry now," I said.

"Why's that?" Cade asked.

"When I was in your dad's bedroom," I said, "I heard water leaking. I traced the sound to his closet where water was dripping down the laundry chute in the corner."

"Oh, no." Cade's eyes went wide as he half stood from his seat to look in the laundry's direction room. He ran both hands over his thighs. Then something seemed to calm him. "They'll be fine. My clothes are in a laundry basket on a table on the opposite side of the room."

I hooked a thumb in the laundry room's direction. "Mind if I go check it out, just in case?"

"Go for it," Cade said, sitting back down.

Chris joined me and we navigated our way from the dining room, through the kitchen, past the elevator, and down a short, dark hall. Elegant paintings of coastal settings in shadow adorned the walls.

"If I was one of these kids," Chris said. I found it funny that he referred to the Howards as "kids" even though he was about the same age as DeeDee, the oldest. "I'd be upset about DeeDee getting an extra portion of the estate."

"Yeah, me too."

I opened the door to the laundry room and hit the light switch. On a normal day, this laundry room would be a homemaker's dream. A set of stainless-steel top-of-the-line washer and dryer sat on opposite sides of a counter space with a farmhouse sink in the middle. Gray cabinetry was above the sink and counter. A laundry basket with folded clothes sat on an island with matching granite counters in the center of the room.

This, however, was not a normal day. Water dripped to the floor from a tall hamper in the corner from the laundry chute. We tiptoed across black and white tiles with an elegant design so as not to get wet to the corner. Water splashed with every step. Legs on the island kept it raised, allowing the water to flow to a drain in the middle of the room.

"That's a mess," Chris said.

I agreed, leaning over and looking into the hamper. A thick layer of soaked and folded clothes lay at the bottom of the basket. "There's about a foot of water in that basket."

Chris pointed to where the water disappeared under the island. "Thank goodness whoever designed this place installed that drain."

We both looked up to where the water fell in streams from the chute in the ceiling's corner.

"Looks like they'll have to add water damage to the chute when the insurance company comes out to inspect," I said.

"I'm sure they're covered," Chris said. We backed out of the room, turned off the lights, and closed the door. "What are you thinking?"

I put a hand on the door frame above my head and eased into it. "This is not what we signed up for."

Chris snickered. "True that, mate." He waited for me to speak next.

"First, Preacher disappeared before the gun went off. DeeDee was in a bathroom upstairs at the same time."

"That bathroom isn't too far away from John Allen's office."

"Right. She could have done the deed and snuck back into the bathroom with no one noticing. I think her charity was in trouble with the IRS. If she needed the chunk of money she was supposed to get in the will, then that could have been her motive for doing it."

"Maybe they were threatening jail time."

"I'm not sure." I pulled out my phone and pulled up the photo gallery. "Let's see what this letter says. Hmm. It says, "Dear Taxpayer, we're auditing your federal tax return and need a response from you."

"Oh, wow," Chris said.

"There's a checkbox beside a Form 990. I wonder what that is?"

"I think it's for nonprofit organizations."

"Makes sense if it's about The Cheerful Note."

"Does the letter say what it is they're looking for?"

I skimmed through the rest of it. "Not that I can see. There may have been a second page, but I was in hurry while taking the pictures. It did give a date for when they need a response and says if no response is given, more action will be taken."

"When's the date?"

"A month from last Friday."

"So, she has to get this figured out fast."

"If she was siphoning funds from the charity, then maybe she needed to figure out where to come up with the money."

"How do we check into that?"

"I'll think of something," I said. "Let's see. We have Preacher and DeeDee with murky alibis for the time of the shooting. Louise was with me. Antonio says he was hiding in a cabinet. Cade was folding his laundry here."

Chris's eyes roamed to the ceiling. "It's a short hike up those stairs to John Allen's office from the kitchen."

"I agree."

"Did he have anything laid out that might implicate Antonio?"

I scrolled through the pictures on the phone. "Looks like John Allen opened a supplemental life insurance policy and closed it a month later. Antonio's name is on the letters."

"Did he try to scam the man?"

"I don't think John Allen would have had these letters out in the open if there wasn't something fishy involved."

Chris ticked off three fingers. "DeeDee, Antonio, Preacher."

"Add Erin in there too."

"Despite what she says?"

"Yeah," I said. "Wouldn't you claim innocence if you know others have motives? All she needs is to cast enough doubt to walk away free if this ever goes to trial. I've read enough Grisham, Stuart Woods, and John Lescroart novels to know that."

"Have you asked her about the letters on the bed?"

"I have, but didn't go into detail because, until now, I haven't read what they're about."

"Maybe we should go ask her."

It was my turn to look up at the ceiling. "Yeah. Let's go."

We made our way through the kitchen and up the stairs. The others remained at the table in conversation. I don't think they noticed us leaving the floor. After climbing to the top of the stairs, we walked through the great room. Wind and rain swirled outside.

"It appears to be slacking off," Chris noted.

"Good. Then maybe we're close to being able to call the police and get out of here."

We reached the bedroom where I had blockaded Erin in with a chair propped against the door. I set it aside, knocked, and opened the door.

Erin was nowhere to be seen.

***

"Uh-oh," Chris said. "This isn't good."

I had no words. The windows in the room were both shut. I leaned over to look under the bed. She wasn't there either. Chris pulled open the closet door where Louise and I huddled together. No Erin.

There was only one solution, which became apparent at that moment. A toilet flushed behind the en suite bathroom door, then the sink started and ran for a few seconds before shutting off.

A moment later, the door opened.

"Oh!" Erin gasped and clutched a hand to her chest. "You scared me!"

"Sorry," I said, holding out a hand. "Didn't mean to startle you."

She took shallow, calming breaths. "No, it's okay. Did something happen?"

"No," I said. "Still waiting for the phones to come back up and the rain to die down."

This guest bedroom was on the north side of the house. The view out the window would have been of the Louise's estate had conditions provided. Still a solid rain. The fronds of the palm trees visible through the window were still. The wind had died. Progress.

Who in their right mind would hold a dinner party on the same evening as a tropical storm? Someone desperate to find out who was trying to kill them was the answer.

"How are you holding up?" Chris asked.

Erin crossed to the bed and sat down on the edge. "I guess I'm okay." She looked around the room and traced a finger over the bedspread. "Not much to do in here."

For a moment, I thought Chris was going to offer to keep her company. He was probably thinking that, judging from his expression.

"I have more questions for you," I said. "About the correspondence on your dad's bed."

"Shoot," she said, then put a hand over her mouth. "I'm sorry. Poor choice of words. I'll answer what I can."

I resisted a smile. "When the house received mail, did you go through all of it for your dad?"

"He still insisted on opening all his mail. He'd hand me the bills to take care of, but that's about it."

"You weren't aware of everything he received?"

"Only if he wanted me to be."

"You allowed a man with Alzheimer's to take care of his correspondence?"

"What can I say? Dad was a headstrong and proud man. That's part of the reason it became my job to care for him instead of hiring professionals. It's not like there's not enough room in this house to have a live-in caretaker."

I ignored the last part of her statement. "Let's start with DeeDee. Was The Cheerful Note having financial difficulties?"

"Not that I'm aware of."

"There was a letter from the IRS addressed to her requesting information about a recent return."

"A Form 990," Chris said. "I think that's how tax-exempt organizations file returns."

"I wouldn't know a thing about the taxes involved. We send

all of that to an accountant."

"Who is the accountant?"

"It's a firm back in LA. Do you need their number?"

"It wouldn't hurt."

Her mouth creased before opening a door on the nightstand and pulling out a pad of paper and a pen.

"Staying here must be like staying at a hotel," Chris said. "The room even comes with complementary stationery."

Erin smiled. "Dad liked to make sure we accommodated his guests. What few he had." She wrote a phone number and email address on the paper and handed it to me.

"Thanks," I said. "There was a note from Louise to your dad on the bed too."

Her eyebrow raised. "What sort of note?"

"Let's just say that its content would be racy even for a late-night movie on certain networks," I said.

"Why am I not surprised?" Erin rubbed her forehead. "That gold digger has been here almost every day, trying to put moves on Dad."

"The letter mentioned something about them spending an eternity together," I said. "Why do you think he left that note on the bed?"

"She got to a point where she wanted to marry him, but he rebuffed her."

"When was this?" I asked.

"A few weeks ago."

"Before or after the attempts on his life?"

"Before."

"Hmm." I pulled out my phone and brought up the pictures taken in John Allen's bedroom. "Another thing on the bed was a list of purchases made from the Howard Art Brokerage. Is that Cade's business?"

"It is."

"Any idea why it might be included with everything else?"

"Not that I know. Dad supported us and helped Cade stay in business."

"Was his business having problems?"

"I wouldn't call them problems, per se. He just sometimes struggled to make ends meet. Louise would pay him to come over and do some handyman tasks."

"What sort of tasks?"

"Putting together furniture. Hanging curtains. Changing light bulbs, air filters, and the like."

"Sounds like the type of things my parents would have me do," I said.

"Yeah. Then he'd go through spurts where he'd make a few big sales and fly off to who knows where to deliver art. Then he would live high on the hog, as you Southerners would say, for a while until his cash flow dwindled, and then he'd sell more. Rinse and repeat."

Chris and I looked at each other. We let the comment pass.

"Did Antonio ever sell your dad any insurance?"

"Yeah. Got Dad to buy supplemental life insurance a few months back."

"There was a letter of cancellation on the bed," I said. "Antonio didn't tell me about that. He said that he'd try to sell John Allen homeowners insurance."

"That's odd. I helped Dad get the information he and Antonio needed to create the life insurance policy but didn't know he'd canceled it, nor did I know anything about the homeowners. I know he's DeeDee's boyfriend and all, but I don't know how much I trust him."

"Hmm," I hummed. "The letter was dated a month after the policy's creation."

"I don't know what to say. You'd have to ask Antonio about it. Dad never told me he ended it. I think he took out the policy just to throw some business at Antonio. I think it was meant to help protect the charity."

"What is his and DeeDee's relationship like?"

She bobbed her head from side to side. "Seems like they're headed towards getting married. They've been looking at rings."

I crossed my arms. "What if John Allen didn't cancel the policy?"

"You mean, was Antonio behind it?" Chris said.

"Yeah," I answered. "Like, Antonio sold him on the policy, got everything done, but then he and DeeDee decided to get married. I'm no insurance expert, but could he have somehow written himself into the policy if he and DeeDee were married?"

Chris said, "That's beyond my knowledge, lad."

"Mine too," Erin said. "I don't know if supplemental life insurance policies pay out the same way as a will."

"I'll ask my insurance person," I said, then flipped over to another photo. "There was one more piece of paper on the bed. It was a stack of receipts with payments to a numbered account totaling five-hundred thousand dollars."

"What?" Erin shouted. Her face turned red.

"If we're going by process of elimination, that leaves Preacher."

"Preacher? Why would Dad give him half a million dollars?"

"I was hoping you could tell me that," I said.

"Of all the things you've asked me about, that's the one for which I have the least clue. I know Preacher tried to get Dad to move some of his money over to his firm."

"Maybe he was successful," Chris suggested.

"Goodness. Five hundred thousand dollars? That makes no sense. Can I see them?" I handed her my phone. She studied the screen.

"I don't know what these are for. It had gotten to where I handled all of Dad's money. I would have known if he was spending this type of cash."

"Could he have had money stashed somewhere you didn't know about?"

"It's possible, I guess."

"Looks like that was the case here," I said. "No clue what these are about?"

"Nope. You'd have to ask Preacher."

"Had your dad been in contact with anyone outside of the people in this house?"

"He's been video chatting with David Weller."

"David Weller? You mean the movie director, David Weller?"

"That's him. He and Dad worked on more than a dozen projects together and were close friends. Even after we moved here."

"Do you know what they talked about?"

"No clue."

"Can you get me in touch with him?"

She held out her hand. I passed the paper with the accountant's contact information back to her. After jotting down Weller's info, she passed the paper back to me. "This won't help right now, but if something happens and I end up in jail, there's David's contact information. Tell him I gave it to you. He was like an uncle to me."

I looked down at the paper. His name, number, and email address were written on it in neat penmanship. "Wow, can't believe you have his number memorized in this day and age."

"I'm organized like that," she said and tapped a finger on the side of her head. "I try to keep things like that up here. Phones can break or get stolen. I like to make sure I can get in touch with someone if need be."

"Like David Weller?"

"Yes, like him."

I stuck the paper in my back pocket. "Thanks."

"You might need it."

"When did everyone arrive?"

"Let's see. Antonio and DeeDee got here just before you. Preacher about an hour before that. Louise comes and goes as she pleases but was here first among those not in the family. Cade was here all afternoon working on his clothes."

"What were you doing?"

"Downstairs in my room, getting ready."

"You didn't know what the others were doing during that time?"

"I didn't."

I shot a look at Chris. He was staring at Erin's legs folded beneath her. Throughout this conversation, she would cast glances in his direction when I was speaking.

"Here's what I'm trying to work out," I said. That caught her full attention. "If your dad was as far along in Alzheimer's as you say, then how did he have the frame of mind to sort out the suspects, gather evidence, arrange this party, and get the crazy idea to invite me?"

"Don't forget that he had the frame of mind to change the gate code, according to you," Chris said. "And he was in his office writing music."

Erin's head turned from side to side in slow arcs. "I don't

know what to say."

"How about, he wasn't as bad off as you made him out to be?" I suggested.

Her face flushed. "You weren't here with him every day. His personality changed. He used to be this warm, loving father figure to us, and he became cranky and hateful and drove me to tears most days." She sat up straight on the bed. "Have you ever changed a baby's diaper before?"

"I haven't," I said.

"I've changed my niece's before," Chris said. "Once. Big blowout."

"Imagine doing that to a grown man," she said.

"Oh," Chris and I said in unison.

"We couldn't trust him in the kitchen anymore," she said. "He about caught the house on fire around the beginning of the year when he left the gas burner on after boiling water for tea."

"I get it," I said. "I feel for you, taking up this task of being his primary caretaker."

She wiped a tear away that was running down her cheek. She sobbed, "It wasn't easy."

"I'm sure it wasn't," Chris said. "I can't imagine having to do that for my parents, lass. You're a remarkable woman for doing it."

She looked up at him and blew a puff of air to get a strand of blonde hair out of her face. "Thanks."

After a moment, I said, "If something happens and you go to jail, is there a way for me to get back in if I need to?"

"There's a key under a planter of hibiscus by the back door. We have the gate up front to keep people from driving in, but there's nothing stopping people walking by on the beach. The boardwalk to the beach has a gate on the far end of it, but it's not locked."

I chewed on the inside of my lip. "In theory, I could park at one of the nearby public accesses and sneak in here from the beach?"

"You could if it came to it."

"Let's hope it doesn't."

CHAPTER
SIXTEEN

After Chris and I joined the rest of the dinner party on the main level, I sensed the mood had changed from somber to angry. That anger was directed toward me.

Antonio jumped up from his chair, bounded over, and stood inches from me. His face was red. He pointed a finger at my chin. "We've been talking."

"Yeah, about what?" I said in as cool a tone as I could manage while scratching my left forearm.

"You being here this evening."

"Yeah, John Allen invited me."

"No! Erin invited you."

"Yes, technically. She brought the invitation, but the invitation was handwritten by John Allen. What's your point?"

He dug his finger in my chest. I held off the temptation to bat it away. Escalating whatever was happening here was not the way to handle this.

"My point is, Clark, that none of us knows for sure that John Allen invited you. We're thinking you and your friend here are in on this."

Chris scratched his head. His slicked-back hair didn't move.

I laughed, then realized that's the reaction a psychopath

might have in a book to a claim such as Antonio's. "You think I killed him?"

"Maybe. You show up unexpectedly. None of us knew you were coming."

"Forgive me if John Allen didn't share the guest list."

He pulled his finger away from my chest and opened his hand like he wanted to slap me but put it down by his side, fist clenched.

"Listen," he bit off, "The tornado hits, John Allen gets shot, and you and Erin were there when the rest of us arrived. How do we know you aren't in on it? You've been up there for hours with her. We think you're trying to figure out how to pin this murder on one of us. We're aware of you solving a couple of murders. Then, I started thinking. If you know how a person goes about murdering someone else and how the police investigate, then you might know how to cover up a crime and pin it on someone else. That's why you've been asking us these questions."

I had three choices of how to manage this: laugh in his face, argue, or walk away.

I chose none of those. I had one question for him. "Did you discuss this with Louise?"

"Louise? What's she got to do with this?"

"We were huddled in a closet when we heard the gunshot. How could I have done it?"

He opened his mouth, but no words came out. Louise was still asleep on the couch in the next room. My guess was that they didn't consult her.

I pressed on. "Why in the world would I come into a man's home whom I had never met and kill him with his family and friends around?" I spread my arms out. "Come on. Do I look like a hitman to you?"

Antonio glanced at Chris, whose appearance could be that of a hitman. Everyone knew Chris was with Preacher when the gun was fired, so he was out of the equation.

I said, "You are looking for someone to blame besides Erin. Yes, I know my appearance here this evening seems like poor timing, considering what happened."

"You can say that again," DeeDee piped up from the table.

We were at a crossroads. No one at this table was likely to speak to me after this confrontation. They had no reason to. I had no authority. Telling them why John Allen brought me here would lead to the same result, so I was content to keep that to myself.

I unloaded my bullets. Emptied the chamber. Get it all out and see what happened. I was a stranger to these people as they were to me. John Allen wanted me to come here to figure out who wanted to kill him, not make friends. After spending a few hours with this lot, I wasn't sure if I'd want to make friends.

To DeeDee, I said, "Why was the IRS auditing The Cheerful Note?"

Everyone's heads whipped around to look at her. Her mouth opened but didn't respond.

Cade was ready to use all his bullets as well. Sibling resentment boiled over. "What is he talking about? Please tell me you weren't stealing money again?"

Antonio raised his voice. "Again?"

"Her first husband divorced her," Cade said. "He never prosecuted her for it, but she stole money from his catering company."

"Ah, ah," DeeDee stammered.

"Is this true?" Antonio asked, removing the arm he had

around her and leaning forward to get a better look at her face. His was beet red.

Her eyes fell. "Yes, it's true."

Cade set his phone on the table. A white charging cable ran from it under the table. He explained, "We'd get access to some of the sets for the movies Dad worked on. Somewhere along the way, DeeDee met Rich. He did the on-set catering for many of the movies Dad was involved in. She and Rich hit it off, got married, and had a couple of kids. Then, Rich's business kept losing money."

DeeDee's face was turning red. Had this been a Bugs Bunny cartoon, steam would escape her nostrils. She held up a finger to her brother. "Not another word."

With a straight face, Cade said, "It's not my fault you needed the money for all of that plastic work you wanted done on your face."

DeeDee lunged across the table at Cade and tried to grab his shirt before Antonio grabbed her around the hips and pulled her back.

"You miserable loser!" she shouted at Cade when Antonio shoved her back in her chair.

"Hey, I can't help it if you were Dad's least favorite," Cade shouted back.

She lunged again with renewed vigor. This time, Antonio was prepared and held her down.

Antonio's face turned red again. "This is not the place for this, DeeDee. Save it for after everyone goes home."

She pulled on the hem of her blouse to put it back in place and composed herself. Grabbing her wine glass that had somehow not spilled during the altercation, she said, "Well, at least I never had to ask Daddy for a loan."

From behind us, Louise yelled, "Children! Children! Antonio

is right. Save these juvenile squabbles for another time."

She walked to the table, fresh from her nap. A quasi-parental figure to fill the void left by John Allen's death. She covered her mouth and yawned. "Your dad wouldn't tolerate this nonsense for one minute. Don't behave like kids. You're grown adults. I have four children and six grandchildren. I hate to treat you like my children, but use your words, not your fists."

The redness on DeeDee's face ebbed. Cade stared at her with a confident smile.

I wiped it off his face. "Cade, Erin told me that sometimes you go through stretches of financial difficulties. DeeDee said something about you asking your dad for a loan. Are you one of these kids who tries to live off their parents their entire lives? What are you going to do now?"

It was his turn for his face to flush. "I haven't thought about it."

"Sounds about right," DeeDee said. "You don't plan anything. Just let Daddy take care of it."

"Probably live off the inheritance," Preacher noted.

"DeeDee," Louise said, resting a hand on the back of the oldest daughter's chair, "be nice."

It was admirable how Louise drifted over to take charge. Someone had to rein in the group.

"Yeah, let's not let this night descend into an airing of grievances," Antonio added, taking a sip of wine. "This should be about remembering a great man. We should thank Clark for catching Erin dead to rights."

I held up a hand. "No need to thank me. Whoever was first into the office was going to be the one to see her there."

"Unless she ran somewhere else before we found her," Preacher said.

"Good point," I said.

Despite everything Erin told me and her swearing she didn't do it, I had to admit to myself that she could be lying. As many times as I ran through the events of the shooting and aftermath in my mind, she or DeeDee still seemed like the persons who most likely could have pulled the trigger. They were the closest people to John Allen's office. I wouldn't be able to get any further in questioning DeeDee about The Cheerful Note and IRS letter here.

It was only a matter of time before the phones came back on and we could call someone to get us out of here, and report the murder, of course. Then, they would question everyone again, and haul Erin off to jail. After that, I didn't know if I'd have access to any of the people in this room, besides Chris.

Conversations around the dinner table resumed. Everyone spoke to each other, except for Cade and DeeDee. I made another round of coffee for everyone. Louise was especially grateful. She took a double espresso.

When Preacher came to pick up his coffee, black, he took the cup from me and sniffed it. "Mmm, that's going to be good."

"I'm telling you," I said, "I need to get one of these machines for my bookstore. Makes fantastic coffee."

"Well, get you one," he said, taking a tentative drink after blowing on the coffee's surface.

"These things are expensive," I said. "Money doesn't grow on trees for me."

He smiled. "The world would be a better place if it did."

I thought about that for a moment. "Would it? If everyone had easy access to money, then no one would need anything. People would stay home, get fat, and not work."

"But they'd be happy."

"Would they? Money can't buy happiness."

"Yeah, but it can buy a jet ski. Have you ever seen anyone not happy on a jet ski?"

I had to give him that and tapped his mug with mine. "Good point. The point I'm trying to make is if people somehow got free money, then many wouldn't want to work. Industries would break down. Many businesses wouldn't be able to find enough workers. Things just wouldn't get done."

"Yeah. Saw that during Covid," Preacher said, tipping his head.

Now that the ice was broken, it was time to spill the beans. "When I went into John Allen's bedroom to check on the leaking water sound, I noticed a bunch of papers laid out in rows on his bed."

"Really? What sort of papers?"

I described what I saw. "It looked like there was something on the bed about everyone except for you and Erin. There was a paper in one row that listed a slew of transactions, totaling half a million dollars. There was no name attached. It was easy to see who the other four rows were about because there were names on each document."

His eyes narrowed. "Go on."

I pointed toward the dining room. "Everyone in that room is accounted for by those papers John Allen laid out, except for you. Each row of papers had one of their names. Except for yours. When Erin denied killing her dad, you were the first person she mentioned. There's this one receipt with that whopping total on there and no name attached. It's about you, isn't it?"

He didn't lie or hem and haw. He came right out with it. "Half a million? Sounds like the arrangement I had with him."

"What sort of arrangement?"

He expelled a breath. "I have a client with a big offshore

hedge fund who promised enormous returns for investors. I mentioned it to John Allen and Louise one day here over lunch, when no one else was around. The fund only allows initial investments of a quarter million dollars. He and Louise are the only ones in this house who could afford that."

"And they bought in?"

"He did. She didn't."

"Louise didn't?"

"Yeah, she was interested, but didn't have cash available. The fund would have closed off investments this week."

"But John Allen did?"

"Yes, sir. He gave it to me in small batches, then I wired it to an island in the Caribbean in even smaller deposits to escape notice by the IRS."

"This isn't a legal fund, I take it?"

"Not here, it isn't."

"Gotcha."

"Will you keep this between me and you? I don't want the rest of the family to find out."

"I won't tell any of them," I said. I might tell Gomez, though.

CHAPTER
SEVENTEEN

I didn't feel like joining the conversation at the dinner table. With socializing, I've always been the type of person who would rather be approached than do the approaching. Mom called it my "shy streak." I called it my "I-don't-want-to-put-up-with-these-people streak." That is, until I got to know people better like I had Detectives Gomez and Moody. I was more comfortable with them now, so it was easy to meet them for lunch. Part of me would have preferred if Moody hadn't been at Toffino's yesterday and just been me and detective Gomez.

But I digress, after Antonio called me out over being here under these unfortunate circumstances, I sensed a wall being put up. They believed Erin did it. Case closed. She may have, but if she didn't, that meant the killer was at that table, carrying on like they didn't kill a person in cold blood several hours before.

I climbed the stairs. Instead of going into John Allen's office or bedroom or to where Erin was held captive, I stood on the balcony overlooking the bottom floor and the magnificent view of the ocean. My phone informed me it was after midnight. Still no cell phone signal.

The rain outside appeared to be slacking off. That was a relief. It meant we were closer to getting out of here.

I leaned against the balcony railing, cradling the warm mug in my hands, admiring what little I could see of the outside world.

Preacher had gotten John Allen involved with high-stakes offshore investing. The money man made it sound like a straightforward business deal, albeit on the shady side. If it was on the up and up, why did John Allen leave me the sheet with the transactions listed?

The IRS letter to The Cheerful Note could stem from DeeDee stealing money. Cade said she had done it before. It made me think of DeeDee like a cheating spouse. Once they are caught cheating, you might forgive them, but since they have broken that trust, you're afraid of them doing it again. Did she? Had she asked her dad for money to get the charity out of trouble, and he turned her down? If she faced jail time for tax evasion, then that might give her reason to kill him. The charity was due to get a quarter of John Allen's estate. Surely that would cover any back taxes due. Were her siblings fine with her, in essence, getting half of the inheritance?

Who had the most to gain? The better question, as far as driving motive, might be who had the most to lose?

If Erin was innocent, how was the murder performed? To this point, everyone's location during the time of the shooting was accounted for. Erin was the closest. DeeDee was the next closest. Could she have run from the bathroom where she holed herself up to the office, shot John Allen, and raced back? Besides Louise and I, they were the only people on the upstairs level. When Preacher disappeared from Chris, he could have taken the elevator up, done the deed, and gone back down. Cade could have used the elevator or the stairs. Same for Antonio.

I bit a nail. Closed my eyes, then opened them wide. What if none of this was as it seemed?

My musings put me so deep in thought that I didn't notice a person approaching me from behind. A hand touched my back. I jolted.

"Sorry," Antonio said, taking a tissue from his pocket and sopping up the spillage from the floor. "Didn't mean to startle you."

"No worries," I said. "Just came up here to clear my head."

"It must not be clear yet if you didn't notice my approach," he laughed. "I'm not a light foot."

"No, it's not," I admitted.

"Look, I just wanted to apologize for assaulting you like that earlier." His green eyes glowed with authenticity. "It was DeeDee who put that bug in my ear, not understanding why you were here."

"And you were speaking for her."

"A man has to protect his woman."

How far would a man go to do that? "I get it, and I agree with you. My being here, with what happened, seems curious. All I know is that Erin came to my store the other morning with a handwritten invitation from John Allen, inviting me to dinner this evening."

"He did that. Invite people he read about or saw on TV that he found interesting to dinner." He nodded his head absently. "Makes sense. So, you're a crime solver?"

"I don't know about that. I got wrapped up in one murder inquiry after I found a body by the backdoor of my business and was asked to poke around another one."

"I'd like to point out that you solved them both."

"I guess I did."

"Don't be so modest," he said, clamping a hand on my upper arm. "You helped put the bad guy away and brought solace to those families."

"Thanks. It's what anyone would have done."

"In a dream world, yes. In the real world? Not me. I would have let the authorities handle it. You've got gumption. I'll give you that."

"What can I say? I'm a curious person who likes puzzles."

"And that's what these murders are to you? Puzzles?"

"They are."

"That was like J.A. He loved puzzles, codes, and cryptography."

"Erin mentioned that."

"Yeah, he weaved messages to his kids in his movie scores."

"Really?"

"Yeah."

"What sort of messages?"

"His kids' names, pets' names, and so forth. Just little signatures hidden in plain sight."

"That's sweet." Both of us rested our hands on the railing and gazed out the windows. Voices echoed up from the open space below, accentuated by the now still night outside. Her exit happened in as swift a manner as she came. Karen was gone. Good riddance.

I turned and faced him. "You say you were hiding in the cabinets downstairs when the shot was fired?"

"Yeah." He massaged his hamstring. "It was cramped in there, that's for sure."

"What did it sound like?"

He ran one palm over the back of the other on the rail. "It was an extremely loud POP. Even above the twister, it stood out."

"Did you know what it was when you heard it?"

"I figured it was a gun or something electrical."

"In that moment where you thought it was a gun, who was the person who flashed in your mind?"

"Erin."

"Why?"

"She fought with her father."

"That's the only reason?"

He turned away and leaned his elbows on the rail. "Yeah."

"You know, I asked that question to several people here."

"They all agreed with me, didn't they?"

"A few. One person said they thought it was you."

"Yeah, who was that? No, let me guess. Preacher?"

I didn't need to answer. The look on my face gave Antonio all he needed. He snorted. "Preacher? Why would he say my name? I barely know him."

"Said John Allen didn't think you were good enough for his daughter."

His tan complexion reddened. "He's just mad that I got to her first."

"Oh? Was he interested in DeeDee?"

"I think so. I mean, who wouldn't be?" He pointed down at the table where we could see the tops of everyone's head, including the big-haired DeeDee.

If I wanted to get tossed over the balcony, I would have said, "Not me," but didn't.

"Besides, how could I have done it? Run up the stairs where you could hear my footsteps echoing through the house. Shoot him, run back down, and get back in the cabinet. I can move well for a man my age, but not that well."

I admitted, "Seems like a stretch."

He held out a hand. "No hard feelings then for calling you out?"

"I have thick skin," I said, clasping his hand. "Don't worry about it."

With that, he walked off, going down the stairs.

I made a mental note to ask Chris when he first saw Antonio after the tornado, as the two of them were the first to arrive at the office door after me.

Antonio was replaced a few moments later by Louise. She arrived at the top of the stairs, shaking her head in disgust and staring at the floor. She didn't seem to notice me as she crossed into the great room from the landing and veered toward a short walnut cabinet near the seating group. Opening the door, she kneeled, rummaged around, pulled out a glass, set it on top, stood, then closed the door, holding a bottle of brandy.

She pulled the cap off and poured two fingers into the glass. She gulped it down in one swig and refilled her glass. I stood still. She moseyed in my direction, not stopping until she was within five feet from where I stood.

"Oh, Clark. Didn't see you there."

"No worries. I like to remain invisible as much as I can. You're just lending credit to my image."

She laughed and sipped the brandy. "Thank you for being here. Your sense of humor is welcome on a night like this."

"Can't say I'm glad to be here, considering the circumstances. Still, I like to make the most of any situation."

"That's admirable." She fake spit in the direction of the dinner table down below. They carried on in conversation, voices muffled by the distance. "So much better than that lot below. Except for your friend, Chris. Can I keep him?"

"I don't think he's up for adoption."

"That's a shame," she scoffed and then did one of the most surprising things I had seen all evening. She pulled off her hair.

I almost spilled my coffee. She wore a tan wig cap underneath, tight to her narrow skull. She held the wig to her side and cradled the brandy in the other.

"Now that John's gone, I guess there's no need to put on appearances."

"What was your relationship like with him?"

She tilted her head from side to side. "Good. Friendly."

"Did you come over often?"

"I'd lunch here a couple times a week. He never came to my place."

"You live next door?"

She pointed to our left. "Yup. Over there. Thankfully, on the opposite side of where the tornado went through."

"That's nice. Both that your house might have been spared from the twister and that you're so close. How did you first meet John Allen?"

"I have a smaller fence around my property. I was out back gardening one day before they put his up. Struck up a conversation, welcoming him to the neighborhood."

"Ah," I said.

"Yeah, it went from there. I take back what I said a moment ago. I invited him and Erin to my place for lunch not long after they moved in. They came, and I thought they enjoyed it, but they never seemed inclined to return."

"How did you end up over here that often?"

"It just came about. We exchanged phone numbers early on, and he would text me, asking me if I had lunch plans."

"Like a friendly neighbor would do."

"Yes, something I'm afraid people don't do as much of anymore."

"The people in my neighborhood get together for cookouts a couple times a year. We get along and look out for each other."

"Must be nice. Not much of that here on the Golden Mile. We keep to ourselves."

I pointed to our right, toward where the tornado spun through. "What about that house over there?"

"Don't see them much. It's used as a rental."

"A common theme among these beachfront homes."

"After being landlocked in the middle of the country most of my life, I don't know why I'd ever leave."

"I was the same way growing up in Ohio."

"I was from Indiana. We were practically neighbors."

"Almost. I lived on the southeastern border across the river from Huntington, West Virginia."

"Then maybe not as close as I thought." Louise sipped her brandy in silent contemplation. "Thank you again for doing what you did for me earlier. I could have died. I'm in your debt."

"Don't mention it."

"Clark, you're too modest." She wheezed, "You know, when we were in that closet and heard the gun go off, I didn't think we'd find Erin in there."

"Who did you think we'd see?"

"DeeDee."

CHAPTER
EIGHTEEN

Her comment didn't surprise me. Not at this point. "Why do you think it was her?"

"Her dad confided in me that his charity organization was being audited. He let her run it because he couldn't do much with it."

"Why was it being audited?"

"He told me over lunch that they questioned the amounts in the contributions being reported."

"How would the IRS figure that out?"

"I'm not sure. Could be they were looking at the taxpayers' reported contributions and the numbers didn't add up."

"That's what my accountant is for."

"Mine too."

"Do you know if John Allen had talked to his accountant about it?"

"He had."

"What did he say?"

"That he only knew to report what DeeDee told him to report."

"Could she have been siphoning off donations?"

"Looks that way. She asked for the money to pay the IRS, and he refused to give it to her. He told me she had to learn to dig herself out of her holes."

"And to dig herself out of this hole, you think she wanted a hole dug for him?"

She drained the last of the brandy in one gulp. "That might have been her only recourse. She stood to gain a lot of money from his death."

I emptied my mug. The coffee had gone cold during our conversation. The only word I had for her was, "Thanks."

Louise set her glass on the banister. I had visions of it falling off and shattering into a million pieces below. I grabbed it while she put her wig back on.

She straightened the fake hair and composed herself, grabbing the cup from my hand. "Thank you, I needed that. Back to the funny farm down there. You should join us."

I glanced down at the empty coffee mug in my hand. "I think I'll do that."

Once we returned to the dining room, Chris looked up from his conversation with Preacher. "There he is."

"Yeah, here I am," I said.

DeeDee and Cade shot evil looks at me. The rest seemed uncaring. I could deal with two of the six not liking me. Besides Chris, I didn't figure that I would see any of them after tonight.

DeeDee had another glass of wine in front of her. Cade's cup of water was untouched. The ice had melted long ago. Chris, Preacher, and Antonio held bottles of Stella Artois in their hands. I was inclined to go back to the coffee bar but didn't want to seem like I was ditching the crew too much. I believed that my comings and goings throughout the evening led to Antonio's accusation earlier. From their perspective, my avoidance of them could be a sign of guilt.

The night outside was still. Hurricane Karen's stay in Myrtle

Beach didn't last long, but she didn't go out without at least a parting shot. Good riddance, Karen.

At that moment, Cade's phone chirped. Then Preacher's. Then Chris's. Then mine.

Chris held up his phone. "Phones are back online."

I pulled mine out. Sure enough, I had bars and several new emails where the phone had been offline for several hours.

Everyone looked at me.

"What now?" Antonio said.

Our collective gaze moved up to the balcony, thinking about what and who was up there.

I said, "I'll call the police."

* * *

I went upstairs to make the call. Chris joined me. We stood outside John Allen's office door. The walls of John Allen's bedroom muffled the sounds of trickling water from the closet.

Erin's sobs echoed across the great room. Outside, darkness reigned, but the first twinkle of stars became visible in the southern sky. Karen had reached out to Myrtle Beach for one last reminder of the power of nature before moving north. I hoped my friends to the north in Wilmington and Morehead City stayed safe.

"Here goes," I said.

"Do it, laddie," he said. "Make the call. This is your territory."

I called Gomez. She picked up after half a ring.

"Must have had the phone in your hand," I said.

"Yeah, trying to get updates on the storm."

"Did you make it out okay where you are?"

"Yeah, I'm fine here. Just rain and a few gusts. A tornado

spun up in Garden City and headed in this direction but dissipated. How are things in Surfside Beach?"

"I'm not sure." I scratched my head and for the first time considered potential damage to my house. It's close to Garden City where the first tornado rolled through. "I'm not home."

"Where are you?"

"Up on the Golden Mile. We had a tornado brush by the house we're in."

"Goodness," Gomez said. "Are you okay?"

"I'm fine. But look, the reason I'm calling you—"

"I take it that this isn't a social call. I'd hoped you were calling only to check on my well-being." The disappointment in her voice was clear.

Over the past year, I had sensed a connection between the two of us. Now was not the time to explore that. Unfortunately.

"There's been a murder."

* * *

An hour later, with spotlights illuminating the area in front of the gate, a member of the MBFD took a chainsaw to the trees blocking the way. Gomez and Moody stood side-by-side with their arms crossed, flanked by crime scene technicians, waiting to get in.

Chris, Antonio, and I watched from inside the gate. The grinding of the chainsaw ripped through the trees and the night air. The lights illuminated the immediate vicinity. A swath of destruction lay in the tornado's wake. The house across the street was vacant. One of the many rental properties in the area. The tornado had torn away its roof, with a section of the house attached to it. Windows shattered where a tree had fallen against the house. I was sure this was a microcosm of the damage.

Forms in the dark night emerged from their homes after hearing the chainsaw. Perhaps, like us, they had also been waiting for help to arrive. Up here in this section of the Golden Mile were homeowners unaccustomed to hardship. They paid someone to do the menial household tasks such as grass cutting, landscaping, and tree removal. Well, that latter project is better served by professionals, such as the firefighter cutting through the trees on the other side of the gate.

While we waited, I asked Antonio with a raised voice to carry over the grinding of the chainsaw, "I forgot to ask. Who did you first see after the gunshot?"

He leaned away and cocked an eyebrow. "Now is a weird time to ask that question."

"I know," I shouted. "Just passing the time."

His mouth puckered in concentration. "Cade, I think. He eased out of the laundry room."

"What about Preacher?"

"It wasn't long after seeing Cade that I saw him and your buddy there come up the stairs."

"Ah, okay."

With a flurry, the first tree fell in two. The crown of the palm fell to the side. Its landing was softened by the halo of palm fronds. The trunk thunked to the ground. Antonio clapped. Two burly members of the MBFD hefted the tree sections away from the gate. Four minutes later, the second tree suffered the same fate.

Antonio went to the control box on our side of the gate, pushed a button, and the gate opened.

Gomez and Moody came straight to Chris and me, while Antonio met with the firefighters.

Gomez was dressed in her typical navy pantsuit. The specific style changed each time I saw her at work, but they all looked the same to me. A police badge hung at the end of a long chain, dangling from her neck.

Moody wore a gray sport coat over khaki pants with a navy button-up shirt. No tie. Skechers shoes rounded out the ensemble.

I would give him the benefit of the doubt in thinking that the grizzled detective's clashing look could stem from having to get dressed in the dark, but this was normal. He wore a nice golf polo the evening we wrapped up Connor West's murder. That was the only time I've seen him not look like he shopped at thrift stores.

"Moody," I said, shaking his hand. He had the grip of a dead fish.

"Clark," he returned. He shook Chris's hand and grunted. His normal rejoinder.

Gomez and I didn't engage in the same formalities. We were familiar enough with each other.

Antonio joined our group, and I introduced him.

He clasped his hands together and said, "I wish we could have met under better circumstances."

"Me too," Gomez said, looking up at the front of the house. The lights used to shine on the fallen trees emanated enough light to make this side visible. "Didn't you say there was damage?"

"Yes," I said, pointing toward the right back corner of the stately home. "It's on that side of the home. The tornado passed right between here and their neighbor's place."

Moody whistled. "You're fortunate."

"Trust me," Chris said, "we know."

"Run through it," Gomez said to Antonio, Chris, and me. "What happened?"

As I had already given her my version of events, I stayed quiet and let Antonio take over. Knowing Chris and his somewhat shady past, he'd likely only speak if a judge compelled him to. After hearing Erin describe Antonio as a yapper, it wasn't a surprise to hear him start.

"John Allen invited us here for dinner this evening," he said. "We were waiting for him to come out of his bedroom and join us. He'd been in there a while, so I volunteered to go down to the kitchen and get everything ready to eat."

"How do you know him?" Gomez asked.

"I'm his daughter's boyfriend."

"What's the name of the daughter?"

"DeeDee."

She made a note on her phone. "Okay."

Antonio continued, "I was sorting out the plates and plasticware when I heard what sounded like a freight train outside. I turned and saw the tornado bearing down on us and hid in the first spot I could think of. In a cabinet. A moment later, I heard a loud pop. At first, I thought it was a circuit breaker or a transformer outside blowing. Then, after it passed and the sound died away, I heard Erin scream upstairs."

"Then what did you do?" Gomez said.

"I rushed up the stairs behind Preacher and Chris and found Clark with Erin in the office where John Allen had been shot. She was holding the gun. Clark," he nodded at me, "took charge and talked her into handing over the gun."

"Erin's his daughter?" Gomez asked.

"Yes," Antonio replied. "She was his personal assistant, and as he got sicker, his caretaker too."

"He was sick?"

"Yes. Alzheimer's disease."

"That's sad," Moody said. "My pops had it until the end."

"Yeah," Antonio agreed. "John Allen was getting on toward the later stages of it from what they told me. Poor Erin had to deal with most of it herself."

Gomez waved a hand at the grand estate. "He had money. Why not hire someone to look after him?"

"Pride," Antonio said. "Pure pride. He told them when he learned he was sick that he wasn't going into a nursing home, nor were they to hire anyone to care for him. He didn't want people to see him vulnerable."

The thought processes of the rich and famous baffled me sometimes. I've learned in life, especially after Autumn's passing, that it's okay to be vulnerable. No one is going to think less of you for showing that you're hurt. It's just that many people were too stubborn to see it that way. John Allen included.

"What do you think was Erin's motive for doing it?" Gomez said.

Antonio rubbed his arm. "I think she got fed up. The disease changed him, you know. Made him difficult to deal with. DeeDee told me that John Allen used to be the kindest man but started to get nasty with people. Especially with Erin. I've been over here for lunch and seen him get hateful with her."

"What would he do?"

"He'd lash out at her if she did something he perceived as being wrong."

"Such as?"

"It could be little things. Like, the other day, for instance, she handed him his pills to take with his lunch. He looked at them, said they were the wrong ones, threw them at her, and berated her for five minutes. DeeDee and I just sat there and watched in horror."

"What did Erin do?"

"Bless her heart. She took it. Took a pounding. Didn't argue or fight back."

"Then what happened?"

"When he finished his tirade, she went to the kitchen and got the schedule of his medications and showed it to him. She had the right pills."

"What did John Allen do then?"

"He apologized. Said he thought it was bedtime."

"What time was it?"

"Noon."

"Oh," Gomez said. Her shoulders slumped. "You think she snapped?"

"I guess so," Antonio said.

Chris added, "She went to check on him just before the tornado hit."

"It's possible that he said something to her then that caused her to snap," Antonio said.

"We'll figure that out," Gomez said. "Where is she now?"

"I have her locked in an upstairs bedroom," I said.

"Good," Gomez said. "Thanks for taking care of the situation."

"I'm good for something now and then," I said.

She flashed a quick, coquettish smile. "You're good for more than that." To Antonio, she asked, "Where is everyone else?"

"Sitting around the dinner table."

"Okay. Go join them. Chris, you too. Detective Moody and I need to talk to Clark for a few minutes."

They excused themselves and climbed the stairs back to the front door, where they disappeared into the house. After they were out of earshot, Gomez said to me, "Is that what happened?"

"More or less. I wasn't around him when the gun went off."

"Where were you?"

"As far as I know, he's telling the truth. I was in an upstairs closet with one of John Allen's neighbors."

"Ooo, you go Clark," Moody said, punching me in the shoulder. "You sly dog."

"She's old enough to be my grandma," I said. "She and I were the only ones left in the great room upstairs when I saw the tornado form and come toward us. I got her up off the couch and rushed her over to one of the guest bedrooms as fast as her feet could shuffle. Then we got in the closet. I heard the shot. Waited for the twister to pass. Heard the scream and found Erin."

"Were you the first to find her?"

"I was."

"What did you think when you did?"

"That, oh my goodness, she shot her dad."

"Had she given any indication of enmity towards him?"

"I'd only met her on Monday. She came to the store and delivered an invitation. The next time I saw her was when she answered the door here earlier this evening. To answer your question, no, she hadn't. She seemed sadder than anything else about his progressing condition."

"Did you talk to her afterward? Get her version of events?"

"I did. She said she went looking for her dad in his bedroom closet when it happened. His bedroom is next to the office where he was found. She heard the shot and rushed in and found the gun. At least that's what she said."

Moody snorted. "That's what they all say."

Gomez gave her partner a cross look. To me, she said, "Do you think she did it?"

I thought about all Erin said to me, what the others said about Erin's relationship with her dad, and what I knew about the shooting. I was honest when I replied, "It's possible."

She studied me for a beat. "But you have doubts."

"Yes."

"Why?"

"She swears she didn't do it."

Gomez eyed me and looked off into the distance, crossing her arms and tapping a foot.

"What?" I asked.

Moody stood silent.

She blew out a breath. "Is this another Connor West situation?"

"You mean, do I have an intuition that she didn't do it like I did with Edward Moore? No, I don't. She said she didn't do it."

"What did she say happened?"

"She said she was in his bedroom looking for him when the tornado occurred."

"Where is that in relation to where he was shot?"

"Right beside it. She said she heard the shot while she hid in a closet. One thing that I thought was interesting was that she couldn't recall how long it was between the end of the tornado and coming out of his bedroom and going next door to his office and finding him."

She bit her lower lip. "There's an unknown period where she has no alibi."

"Yes."

Gomez nodded. "Thanks, Clark. I'm going to go examine the

body, then to have the crime scene techs go up and do their thing. Moody is going to take statements from everyone. I've already called the medical examiner. She'll be here as soon as she can."

"Then what?"

"We'll have to send everyone away from the house while we carry on the investigation."

My stomach fluttered. "Do you want me to stay for it?"

"No, I don't."

My voice went an octave higher than usual. "You called me in when Connor West was found on the beach."

Moody said, "I did that. Remember?"

"Yeah, I do." He woke me up early on a Monday morning with four terse text messages requesting my presence between the State Park and Springmaid Pier. That led to two of the craziest days of my life, which included a sword fight in the middle of a fake Roman Colosseum and figuring out who killed the locally famous star.

"We appreciated your help on that," Gomez said.

"And Paige Whitaker," Moody added.

"Let us handle this," Gomez said. "It's not your job. Go join the others, and we'll be with you shortly."

"Sure thing." I stared at the ground and found a small rock to kick.

Moody gave me a sad smile beneath his beard. Gomez touched my wrist, sending a pulse up my arm. "Thanks, Clark. I hope you understand."

"I do." I climbed the stairs, rubbing my arm, thinking about Gomez's soft touch and being told to sit on the sideline. Again.

***

Moody pulled everyone into a bedroom, one by one, to take their statements. Gomez joined him a short while later after investigating the body. When they called me into the room, I sat on the bed and recounted the events of the evening, almost verbatim from what I'd told them earlier. I mentioned John Allen's last words too because I'd forgotten earlier. There was likely more that I'd left out, but only because so much happened in a short span, it was difficult to keep up with.

After more questions and a gunpowder residue test, we were released. Louise, Chris, Cade, and Antonio all said they had fired guns recently, so the test might not mean much in the end. Preacher hadn't fired a weapon, but he had tinkered with cars. The forensics technician explained that even if they found the fused particles of barium, lead, and antimony, they could have come from brake pads.

The bottom strip of the sky on the ocean horizon had a faint glow. Otherwise, it was still dark. Chris and I climbed into the Jeep. I wasn't in a hurry. Antonio guided DeeDee to a Tesla. Cade stood beside a sporty Lexus. Preacher hopped up into a GMC Denali truck. Louise shuffled out the gate to the sidewalk and turned right before passing out of view beyond the fence and ambling away.

The streetlights shined to life as other house lights came on.

"Power is back on," Chris said, stating the obvious.

"Yup," I said, tapping a thumb on the steering wheel, staring at the entrance.

The front door opened and out walked Officer Nichols, guiding Erin by the elbow down the stairs to a patrol car. Her shoulders sagged. Tears rimmed her eyes. She shook her head, repeating the words, "It wasn't me. It wasn't me. It wasn't me."

Antonio had his arm around DeeDee's waist as they leaned against their car. Cade rested his hands on the open door of the red car. Preacher watched out the open window of his truck. Everyone watched as Nichols placed a hand on Erin's head so she wouldn't bang it against the top of the door opening as she settled into the back seat of the patrol car.

Nichols shut Erin's door, then got into the driver's seat. As they pulled away, Erin stared at me through the car window. She mouthed, "Help me."

CHAPTER
NINETEEN

We were first in the door at Mammy's Kitchen. The aroma of hash browns, coffee, pancakes, bacon, and sausage greeted us. The collective official smell of Myrtle Beach.

"What now?" Chris said as the server placed two steaming mugs of coffee in front of us.

I took a sip, savored, let the warmth pass through me, and said, "Go home and get some sleep, I guess."

"Yeah, that seems prudent. I already sent Tanzee a text letting her know I wouldn't be in today." Tanzee was one of the executives of OceanScapes I had met when looking into the murder of Paige Whitaker.

"I'll do the same with the store today. Winona and I were supposed to open this morning."

"That's not happening."

"Nope." The sky outside the window brightened with the first rays of the morning sun. Cars with their headlights on passed by. People were on their way to work or coming home from a long night out, as was typical in this part of Myrtle. Two joggers in spandex passed by. From the looks of things, you would never know Karen came through here less than twelve hours ago.

Chris's face blanched after taking his first sip of coffee. He set the mug down on the table, and said, "Needs some Bailey's."

"Might help after last night."

"What now with Erin?"

"I guess they'll hold her until she gets arraigned. I'm not sure what'll happen after that."

His head moved from side to side. "You're still not getting it. I think you think she's innocent. What are you going to do about it?"

I rubbed my chin. "I don't know. I'm tired. Just want to fill my belly and sleep."

"I hear ya."

"I might check on some things, though."

He sat up straight, raised his coffee mug, and pointed a finger that had been curled around the handle. "That's what I'm talking about. I knew you couldn't resist."

The server came and took our orders. After she departed, I said, "Here's the thing. Someone had made at least two attempts to kill John Allen before last night. At least that's what Erin said."

"Oh?"

"Yeah. That's what the papers on his bed were for. To establish motive." I took another sip of coffee. "If Erin didn't do it, then he believed the reason someone wanted to kill him was in those papers."

"And he left them for you."

"Yes, although he probably wanted to go through them with me and explain what they were."

"That would help. Too bad they're locked up in the house."

"That's not a problem."

"Why not?"

"I took pictures."

He tapped a finger on the side of his head. "Right. You did. Smart, laddie, but don't you think the police will find them and investigate?"

"Beats me. Gomez told me to stay out of it."

"You've heard that before. Didn't stop you."

"I can't help it." I took a meditative sip of the fresh coffee and let it warm my belly. "Here's the thing. I tried to ask everyone who they thought did it when they first heard the gunshot."

"That's a good question. Get that gut reaction. What did they say?"

I ran a hand over my face and looked out the window, trying to recall everyone's story. I should have kept notes on my phone. It wasn't too late to do that. I pulled it out and started the Google Keep app and started a fresh note.

"Let's see," I said. "Louise said DeeDee. Erin indicated Preacher who then said Antonio. DeeDee, Cade, and Antonio all pointed at Erin."

"That's a mess," Chris said.

"It's all a mess. That entire family is a mess."

"The other thing to consider is who could have done it. Only Erin and DeeDee were upstairs with him. Could someone have used the elevator?"

"I think you'd have to be suicidal to hop in an elevator with a tornado bearing down on you."

"Right, but Preacher disappeared when it happened."

I held up the index finger on the hand holding the coffee mug. "That was curious. Preacher told us he went to hide in the soundproof studio, but here's the thing, it was locked."

Chris's eyebrows jumped on his forehead. "Ah, if he was in there, he couldn't have heard or seen when it ended. He lied.

Where did he go?"

"Exactly. I'm sure Gomez caught that. Even if Antonio was hiding in a kitchen cabinet near where the stairs come up, he would have heard someone booking it up and down the stairs. Cade wasn't too far off in the laundry room."

"He would have had to use the elevator."

"Yup. After we found John Allen, I never thought to keep track of who went up and down the elevator."

"Not too many people did," Chris said. "With the house being under auxiliary power and all. Who would want to risk getting stuck in an elevator?"

"DeeDee did it when she came up to meet me for the first time after I got Erin's side of the story. I wonder if the elevator opened right up when she hit the call button, or did she have to wait for it to arrive from another floor?"

"You'd have to ask her."

"Yeah, but what are the odds that she'll speak to me again?"

"She didn't take too kindly to you. I overheard things she said about you."

"Like what?"

"Like, why were you meddling in their business? Just who did you think you were? That sort of thing."

How people regarded me was far down on the list of things I cared about. In this instance, though, it meant something. If DeeDee did it and was trying to cover her tracks, then she would throw up roadblock after roadblock to get me to stop. Would she behave that way to the police?

Opening my hands around the mug, I said to Chris, "Because that's why I was invited. I think she has a guilty conscience over something. Whether it's from killing her dad or this business with the IRS."

"Or both."

"There's that too."

Our server delivered a thick omelet to Chris and set a stack of fluffy pancakes, sausage, and scrambled eggs before me. Comfort food after a trying night. We dug in and ate in silence for a moment.

I speared a sausage link and held it up in the air. "There's something that keeps bothering me…"

"What's that?" Chris said between chews.

"After Erin denied doing it and I asked her who else could have done it, the only person she mentioned was Preacher. Not her sister, who was the only other person in the vicinity."

"He and I didn't go to the garage until after she left to check on her dad, so she wouldn't have known where Preacher was."

"Nobody used the elevator either," I mused, biting off a chunk of the sausage. Tasted like Neese's. Good stuff. "There's a time gap too. Erin left first, then DeeDee. Antonio went to get the food ready to serve. Then you and Preacher did your thing, leaving me with Louise."

"Where's the gap?"

"Erin. She first said she was going to go to his office to check on him, then went to the bedroom first."

"Why?"

"She found him passed out in his closet before. That's when they had to take him to the emergency room to get his stomach pumped. He'd taken the wrong pills."

"Didn't Antonio say her dad flew off the handle at her because he thought she screwed up his pills?"

"That's right."

"Was this before or after the ER?"

"I'm not sure. Seems like it was after."

Chris raised his hand on the tabletop, setting down his fork. "Let me play devil's advocate. If Erin was the one responsible for doling out his medicine, maybe she's the one who tried to kill him."

I sat up in my seat. "That hadn't occurred to me. It's possible, I guess. I wish I would have asked more questions about that incident. With as many motives floating around, it's possible she tried to give him an overdose, but wasn't the person who fired the gun."

"Now that's a frightening thought. Is there any way you can learn more?"

"I'm not sure how it works with a prisoner charged with murder. They might not let me see Erin, and I doubt DeeDee or Cade would talk to me."

"What about Louise?"

I flashed back to when she and I huddled in the closet. We shared a scary moment together. Even as strangers, we shared a bond.

"Good idea." I took a bite of pancake. Syrup dribbled off the chunk at the end of the fork and landed in the eggs. "I'll try that."

Chris said in a gruff voice, mimicking a certain long-eared green alien. "Do or do not, there is no try."

I smirked. "Ha. Here's the thing, Erin said she went to John Allen's bedroom first. Did anyone see her do that?"

Chris stared up at the ceiling. "His bedroom door was around the corner from the great room and out of sight from where we were. Besides, I didn't pay attention after watching her walk away."

"I bet you enjoyed that part."

He composed himself and said deadpan, "I hated to see her go, but I loved to watch her walk away."

"I thought so."

"I wish she wasn't accused of killing someone. Might've asked her out."

"Prisoners' need lovin' too," I said. "That's what conjugal visits are for."

He laughed, but I could tell he was thinking about it. "Sure, mate."

I stared out the window. If Erin was the first to leave us in the great room, how much time elapsed between then and when the gun went off?

Then, from out of the blue, it hit me. Was DeeDee's letter from the IRS and Antonio's life insurance policy for John Allen related? If so, the implications were enormous and chilling.

CHAPTER
TWENTY

The sun was rising over the ocean across the street as I popped into the bookstore and put a sign on the window informing patrons that we would open at noon today rather than nine. Chris hopped on his Harley and bid adieu. I sent a text message to Winona informing her of the delayed start time. There didn't seem to be any visible damage to the store or any buildings in the surrounding area. Only a couple of puddles along the edges of Ocean Boulevard were all that remained of Karen.

I went home, slept for two hours on the couch, hopped up, changed my clothes, and drove back to the bookstore. We opened at noon after I brewed a pot of coffee made from a bag of the Palmetto Blend from Grand Strand Coffee in Market Common. No customers were about, so I set Winona on a cleaning task and went back to my office.

Word got out about John Allen's death at the top of the noon news. My friend, Erica Sullivan, now anchored the midday news on WMHF and relayed the sad news as the lead story. Her pale skin, black hair, beauty mark, and dark eyes looked out at me from the computer screen atop my desk. She gave scant details. Perhaps that was all the police provided them with. They did not mention my name. Thank goodness.

Mom called five minutes after the news broke. I had told them about dinner at the Howard estate beforehand.

"Clark, you did it again," she said.

"Did what?"

"Get involved in a murder and didn't call me with the details."

I sighed and closed my eyes. "Look, it was a long night. I'm operating on two hours' sleep. Don't worry, I'm fine."

"If you say so," she said. "Come have dinner tonight. Tell me all about it."

Mom was a lifelong avid reader and watcher of murder mysteries with a keen eye for detail. She gave solid advice to me the first two times I investigated murders. We made plans for dinner at six. Dad would have a baseball game on the big screen.

I fell asleep at my desk. The next thing I knew, Karen was shaking my shoulder. I blinked open my eyes and wiped away a stream of drool from the side of my mouth. A puddle of the stuff pooled on my desk. I grabbed a tissue and wiped it up.

"Ah, hey Karen," I said.

"Gracious, Clark," Karen said with her southern drawl. "I thought you were dead."

I sat up and rubbed my eyes. "Sorry, long night."

"It's okay. You're the boss."

"What time is it?"

"A little after two. I just started my shift."

"Well, thanks for telling me. You didn't need to do that."

"I know that. I didn't come into your office to tell you I'm here. Figured you were back here working on your book. You're almost finished with it, right?"

"Yeah, I'm close. Two chapters left to go. What's up?"

"You have a visitor."

"Who is it?"

"That pretty detective."

I smiled. "Tell Detective Gomez I'll be right there."

"Will do, boss."

"What did I tell you about calling me that?"

She twisted a smile as she showed herself out. "I know. I just like ribbing ya."

"Thanks, Karen," I said to the closing door. I stood, stretched, and composed myself. Grabbing the empty mug on the desk, I left the office.

Gomez stood at the front of the store, looking out the front windows at the ocean across the street.

"Had lunch yet?" she asked as I approached.

I patted my stomach and thought about the pancakes I put down at Mammy's Kitchen this morning. Seemed like yesterday. That was the last time I'd eaten. "Nope. My stomach is going to start eating me if I don't feed it soon."

She snickered, then scanned the store. One customer browsed through the self-help section. Winona and Karen huddled behind the counter, going over books being held for loyal customers.

"Let me take you out," she said. "It's the least I can do for you containing the situation last night."

A private lunch out with Gomez without her partner piqued my groggy interest. "Where did you have in mind?"

* * *

A short while later, Gomez and I sat across from each other under an awning at Sharkey's Oceanfront Restaurant in comfortable rattan chairs. A wood table with a white top sat between us. The waves rolled in from the ocean fifty feet away.

"Love this place," I said as I got comfortable.

"Me too," she said, settling in.

A server took our drink orders and told us about the specials for the day. Sweet tea for me. Water with extra lemons for Gomez. Little evidence of the storm remained beyond extra debris on the beach and water pooling in the potted greenery dotting the periphery of the restaurant patio.

"Thank you again for taking care of the situation last night," Gomez said. Her ponytail shifted in the breeze. I couldn't recall ever seeing her hair down. She always tied it back. She wore her traditional pantsuit. I wore flip-flops and a purple Polo shirt over khaki shorts. My traditional uniform.

"No problem," I said. "When it happened, they all kinda looked toward me about what to do. I put myself in your shoes and imagined what you'd do in the same position."

"It seems like you made the right decisions."

"Thanks. What happened after you took Erin to the police station?"

The server brought us our drinks, and we placed our food orders.

After she departed, Gomez said, "She was stoic about it all. Almost seemed resigned."

"Did she confess?"

"No, that was all she would get worked up over. That she didn't do it."

"What did she say when you asked her who did?"

"She couldn't provide any information to clear herself. She admitted to being in the room next to John Allen's when the tornado came through. There was something else too which she might not have told you."

"What's that?"

"She and her dad got into an argument before most of the guests arrived."

"What kind of argument?"

"They didn't know the details, just that Erin and John Allen got into a heated dispute before most of the dinner party arrived. They heard them yelling from downstairs. Erin and her dad were upstairs."

"Who is 'they'?"

She dipped her chin, perhaps considering how much she could tell me. "His son, Cade, and the neighbor, Louise. They were the ones who told us. I asked Erin about it. She said it was nothing. That Louise and Cade were making more out of the altercation that what it was."

I tried to recollect the order in which Erin said the guests arrived. "No one mentioned that to me. They were the first two there. Cade was there all afternoon doing his laundry."

"Yeah, he was pretty upset when we wouldn't let him remove it from the home. Said he didn't have any clean clothes at home."

"He can afford new ones."

"Probably," Gomez laughed. "Anyway, he and Louise were downstairs talking about something or other in the kitchen when they heard the shouts echoing down."

"Did they do anything about it?"

"Nope. They said it had been happening more. So much so that it became commonplace."

"A shame."

"It is. It really is," she said. "I've been around families where something like this happens. Two people argue all the time until one day it comes to a head. It usually ends with a wife beating her husband over the head with something and him getting sent to the hospital. Not with outright murder."

"I don't want to know everything you've seen."

"Believe me, you don't. It's a tragedy how some people go through life and what happens in the end."

We sat for a minute and watched the waves break. A large family from one of the nearby hotels had several beach chairs set in a row. Wind rustled the edges of a multi-colored beach umbrella. A little boy and girl dug a large hole in the sand. The mom lay back in her chair with a paperback propped open on her chest, asleep. The dad drank a beer and watched it all like a Roman emperor regarding his court. The white-haired grandma people-watched, as I often do.

Three tiny sandpipers darted away from incoming waves, pecking in the sand for lunch after the waves receded. A majestic white egret stood on the beach, doing what Gomez was doing, watching the waves. The sea was flat all the way to the horizon. Thin white clouds wove an intricate pattern in the sky. Not too bad of a day after a tropical storm.

I tried to place what Gomez told me about Erin and John Allen's spat prior to the party into perspective. That would give her motive. Especially if she was still hot under the collar as the evening progressed. She didn't seem flustered when she greeted Chris and me and gave us a tour of the house. Perhaps she had learned to hide it.

"What are you thinking?" Gomez asked.

"Whether Erin did it."

"Do you not think she did it?"

"I had questions until now. Did you find the papers in John Allen's nightstand?"

"No." Her forehead creased. "What papers?"

I explained how I found them and my reasons for hiding the

incriminating documents from the other members of the dinner party. "I'm sorry. I was so exhausted that I forgot to tell you about them."

"You think he invited you to figure out who was trying to kill him?"

"I don't think it was for my glowing personality," I joked. "Did you learn about the other tries on his life?"

"We did. Moody is looking into them as we speak."

"From what Erin told me, there might not be much to look into. If they threw away the cut cane, then it's at the landfill in Conway by now. You might get more headway in figuring out who might have given him the wrong pills."

"That's our thinking. However, something had to have been used to cut the cane. If it's in that house, we'll find it. His family said that cane never left his side. Once we find whatever damaged the cane, we're hoping we can trace it back to the perpetrator. If it was a saw from his garage, then we'll take prints. It shouldn't be difficult to figure out who all had access to it."

"Which would leave Erin as the most likely culprit since she lived with him."

"It could. Everyone else there last night had access to the home."

A server delivered our food and departed. Gomez and I both ordered the grouper tacos.

"I get this every time I come here," I said.

Gomez picked up a taco, using her fingers to keep all the cheese, grouper, lettuce, and pico de gallo inside before taking a bite.

After I chewed and swallowed my first delicious bite, I said, "Look into Preacher Mobley's business."

"Why is that?"

"He roped John Allen into some sort of offshore fund where they were wiring small amounts of money to accounts in the

Caribbean to escape IRS notice."

"Sounds fishy."

"It does. I cornered him and asked him about it, and he told me what they were up to. Admitted that it wasn't on the up and up and not to tell the other family members about it. I didn't, but now I'm telling you."

"Hmm. How did you figure this out?"

"There was a form listing various transactions totaling half a million dollars in that stack of papers. It didn't have anyone's name on it, but of all the people there and all the papers on the bed, his was the only one without a name attached to it."

"Process of elimination then."

"Yup."

"Thanks, Clark. I'll get someone to check into it."

"What's going to happen to Erin next?"

"She's supposed to appear in court for a bond hearing this afternoon. I'll be present. The judge will introduce herself and make sure Erin has legal representation before determining if they will release her on bond. Then they will hold a preliminary hearing with ten days to set a trial date. Normal stuff. I'm sure the court will be packed."

I had no comment on that. We ate and chatted about more pleasant topics not concerning death. It was a pleasant change.

After the tacos disappeared and Gomez paid the bill, we walked out of the restaurant. We stood on the sidewalk, unsure of what to do next. The bookstore lay in one direction. She indicated her car was parked in the other.

"Thanks for lunch," I said.

"It was the least I could do." She smiled and touched the back of my hand. "Thanks again for what you did."

With that, she turned and walked away, leaving me with stirring emotions and questions. Namely, who at that party didn't want to kill John Allen?

CHAPTER
TWENTY-ONE

I went back to the bookstore and closed myself in the office after grabbing a cup of coffee. The store wasn't busy, and Karen didn't need any of my help. I realized that by leaving her alone in a quiet store I'd risked her watching Turkish soap operas on her phone. It was a problem we had when she had any downtime while on duty. I didn't care so much today.

My head felt like a bowl of pudding. Shoulders ached. Legs were tired. Sitting upright in my office chair didn't appeal to me. I unplugged the laptop and sat in a comfortable gray chair with an ottoman in the corner. Light streamed through a pair of windows set high on the outside wall. My office wasn't large but big enough to hold three bookshelves filled with writer's guides and collectible editions of books. My prized possession among them was a leather-bound edition of the Charles Dickens novel, Great Expectations with a handwritten inscription on the inside cover dating back to Christmas of 1903. It was in mint condition and still had gold gilding on the outside pages.

I collapsed in the chair, got comfortable, and fired up the computer, then brought up the web browser. After slipping the cell phone from my pocket, I pulled up the photo gallery. This was the first chance I'd had, since last night, to delve into the papers I'd found lying on John Allen's bed.

The first item I searched for was Grouper Insurance. Antonio Bianchi's firm. There were paid ads for Progressive and Allstate Insurances atop the search results, but Grouper was number three on the list, accompanied by an information block showing the outside of the building with links to his website, reviews, and driving directions.

The reviews were the first thing that caught my eye. It showed over twenty reviews with a 2-star rating out of 5. I knew enough about Google Reviews to realize that people who reviewed companies like insurance firms, government agencies, and utility companies weren't likely happy customers, dragging the ratings down. The number of stars wasn't as important as the content of the written reviews.

I clicked on that section and the first three reviews where someone took the time to write their opinion appeared. All were 1-star. Two parroted the same thought, in that they wouldn't do business with Grouper again. The third said the strong-arm tactics of the owner, Antonio, put them off, and they felt he forced them to sign up for a life insurance policy.

I went to the website. It was modern, clean, and displayed the many services offered. Realizing I wouldn't find any incriminating information there, I backed out and hit the News tab. Nothing was there except for a ribbon cutting at his business over five years ago.

Next, I looked up Cade's business, the Howard Art Brokerage. His website displayed at the top of the results. No Google info box here. I clicked. It took me to a simple page with a few art renderings. The business description underneath the business name reported that the brokerage gave art lovers a chance to own museum-quality paintings. It gave a phone number and email address. That was it.

Moving on, I looked up The Cheerful Note. The website displayed pictures of joyous children from poor schools playing shiny musical instruments. One picture showed John Allen in a full tuxedo with tails conducting an orchestra composed of young children. I smiled. That was cute. The About page gave the background of the business and what the organization had accomplished. It mentioned that they appreciated all donations, either monetary or of musical instruments, and gave a link to a page where interested parties could contribute.

I backed out of that page and searched the Google News section for The Cheerful Note. The list displayed articles from local news groups around the Carolinas, showing DeeDee presenting large checks to elementary school principals. John Allen appeared in a few, hunched over a cane. The time stamps were varied and dated back as far as three years. I sorted the results to display the most recent articles first.

My breathing faltered when I read the first two.

> *John Allen Howard's Cheerful Note Charity Under Investigation*
> *Did a Charity Under a Famous Movie Composer Steal Money from Donors?*

Those were instant clicks. I went with the top result first. The article read that the IRS was looking into claims that The Cheerful Note accepted donations of musical instruments, and instead of providing them to schools, sold them. Then they failed to report that income.

"Uh oh," I said to myself. "Looks like someone might go to jail."

The second article reported more of the same.

On a whim, I searched for all instances of "Louise Collins." Google found over 160,000 results. The first four results showed an author whose books were too spicy for my store. There were no pictures of the author, but after reading some of the book descriptions, I decided this Louise Collins was almost certainly a pen name.

The next page down was a Wikipedia page showing an actress of that name from Indiana, born in 1932. The Louise that I had met mentioned that she was from that state. She was old, but I didn't think she was that old. I went to the Wiki page, and it showed a handsome woman who was not the Louise Collins I'd met last night.

I went back and added the word "Indiana" to my search query. Again, the actress appeared at the top of the results, but there was less to sift through. This time, I found several articles about the death of an Arnie Collins, who owned several Cadillac dealerships in the Indianapolis region. He dealt with many ailments and passed away in his sleep one night.

If he was Louise's third husband, then this was where my search ended. I didn't know her maiden name or married names from her first two spouses. I wasn't advanced enough as a genealogical researcher to dig deeper than that.

I punched in Preacher Mobley next. A website appeared, advertising a full-service wealth management company named Premier Wealth, designed to help those on the Grand Strand grow their money while in retirement or accumulate the funds to live comfortably once their work was finished. Unlike Antonio Bianchi's Grouper Insurance, the reviews on Preacher's business glowed.

There was nothing in Google News about him or Premier Wealth.

I closed the laptop and watched the dust motes dancing in the sunlight streaming through the office windows. If the charges about The Cheerful Note proved true, then DeeDee would spend time in prison. Had the IRS offered her a chance to pay her way out of whatever hole she'd dug herself into and John Allen let her hang? Did Antonio try to sell the composer a shady life insurance policy?

How did Preacher factor into all of this? He said he had sheltered in the music studio during the tornado, but that door had been locked. He couldn't have gone in unless he had a key, or it was unlocked when he'd entered, but locked once he exited. That seemed far-fetched. The odds were that he was lying about what he'd done when he left Chris to fend for himself in the garage. What had he been up to? The power had blinked out during the event. He might have gotten stuck had he been in the elevator. So, where did he go?

***

A dejected Erin appeared briefly in municipal court that afternoon at the courthouse on Oak Street. I didn't attend, but it was the lead story on the evening news. They dressed her in an orange jumper. Her blonde hair was brushed long and straight. No ponytail. I wondered if she was on a suicide watch, and that's why they wouldn't allow her to have an elastic ponytail holder in case she could somehow strangle herself with it.

Two attorneys stood next to her. A man and woman. The tall older gentleman named Eric Paulicap flew into Myrtle Beach overnight on a private jet. He had a full shock of white hair dressed in a designer navy suit. He looked every bit like a Hollywood lawyer. The other attorney, Claudia DeMille, was local. Paulicap needed her presence to appear before the court as he was unlicensed in South Carolina. She did all the talking.

The camera showed a brief glimpse of Detectives Gomez and Moody sitting in the front row on the plaintiff's side. Our charismatic and steel-eyed mayor, Sid Rosen, sat nearby, as were other movers and shakers I recognized from the Myrtle Beach political and news scene. Everyone wanted to glimpse the late composer's daughter.

They went through the motions of making sure Erin understood the charges against her and that she had adequate representation. The body language from her attorney assured me that this appearance in court wasn't anywhere near his first. His elocution before the judge was perfect and practiced. Was Eric Paulicap also John Allen's attorney? If so, wouldn't he have a conflict of interest?

The judge set a date for a second hearing for the following week, at which they would finalize a trial date. A bailiff led Erin away. She hung her head as he guided her out the door by the elbow.

CHAPTER
TWENTY-TWO

One of Mom's specialties, and one of my favorites growing up, was chicken and dumplings. Not the rolled type. Her dumplings were fat and light as air, drowning in a chicken soup tasty enough to be on the menu at Paula Deen's restaurant at Broadway at the Beach. When Mom told me that was on the menu, I canceled my other dinner plan: frozen pizza.

The divine aromas of chicken and soup greeted me as she opened the door. The kitchen lay past a small hall separating the interior of the house from the garage. Beyond that was a large open area containing a sophisticated kitchen and living room. Dad had an Atlanta Braves game playing in the corner on a massive, curved television. Not a football game like I had figured would be on the screen. The Braves were in a chase for the playoffs, and my sports-loving dad would not miss a minute.

"Hi, Clark," she said.

"Hi, Mom," I returned, giving her a peck on the cheek.

"Got yourself into another sticky situation, did you?"

I took off my jacket and hung it on a hook by the door and sat on a cushioned bench to remove my shoes. Looking up at her, I said, "It's not like I meant to this time. It just turned out that way."

She placed a hand on her wrist. "Well, you need to stop doing that. You had us worried."

"When are you not worried about me?" I asked, with the corner of my mouth rising to a grin.

Mom looked up at the ceiling. "When you're here."

"I know. I know."

That's the thing about parents. As long as their kids are alive, they are never too old to stop worrying about them. I'm in my early forties and can't go anywhere without the cautious advice to "be careful."

"Come on into the kitchen. Dinner's ready. We were waiting for you before we ate."

"Thanks. You didn't need to do that."

"No, it's fine. The timer went off as you were pulling into the driveway."

"Great." My stomach growled. I hadn't eaten since Gomez treated me to lunch. "Any damage to the house?"

"No, we were fine. Got windy and dark with heavy rain, but otherwise no different from an afternoon storm in June. Any damage to your house?"

"A few branches fell off the loblolly pine in the backyard," I said, "but that's about it."

"Hey, Pipsqueak," my dad said in his deep voice as I entered the living room. He still called me that, even though I was taller. Not by much, though.

"Hey, Dad. Braves winning?"

"No score yet," he said, nodding at the screen where it showed the bases were loaded with Braves players in white with no outs. He sat in a light gray pleather recliner with his feet up.

"Looks like that's about to change."

"Yep," he said and took a swig from a bottle of beer. I cringed inside and hoped he wouldn't offer me one. Autumn used to call his light beers "corn water" which wasn't far from the truth.

As it would take a crowbar to pry Dad from his chair, we ate our dinner in the living room. He turned the volume on the TV down so as not to drown out our conversation, which he partook little anyway. His focus was on the game.

Mom sat on the other end of the matching pleather sofa from me. She placed a dishcloth over her chest to function as a bib for the chicken and dumplings. Her feet were up as well. Dad protected himself in the same manner. Except for my brother Bo missing, this could have been a throwback dinner to my teenage years.

It was Mom who got me into reading mysteries as a teen. She introduced me to the world of Sherlock Holmes in book form and Murder, She Wrote on the television screen. I've been reading mysteries most of my life but will never come close to reading the number she has. She was a stay-at-home mom to my brother and me. When she wasn't cooking or cleaning or keeping us from fighting, she was reading books from Agatha Christie, Dorothy Sayers, Sue Grafton, and the like. When she wasn't reading mysteries, she was watching them. She was a veritable encyclopedia for murder mysteries.

I cradled a warm bowl in my hands and leaned forward. If I spilled any of the broth, I preferred it landed on their dark hardwood floor rather than my clothes.

"Tell me what happened," Mom said after I'd taken my first bite into a fluffy dumpling.

"Chris and I got there and met everyone invited." I savored the bite, then described the house, the guests, and where everyone was when the tornado struck.

"What was John Allen Howard like?"

Dipping my spoon into the soup, I answered, "Never got to meet him. He got killed before I had the chance."

"That's a shame. I'm sorry. Bet you were excited."

"I was. Woulda been nice."

"How come you didn't meet him?"

"Erin said he was up in his room getting ready." I related the events of the evening, in detail to Mom. Her keen intellect in mysteries might help sift through something I may have missed.

I had finished my recounting at the same time Dad whooped when a Braves player hit a double, knocking in a go-ahead run.

"Here's the thing, Clark," Mom said after Dad calmed down. "You were there. You spoke to everyone. You know the layout of the house. You know the motives. If it wasn't Erin, you know who did it. You just have to figure out who and how."

"Yeah. Sounds simple. I'm not sure she didn't do it. Not like I had the strong hunch that Edward Moore didn't kill Connor West. I mean, it's possible Erin didn't do it, but not sure how anyone else besides DeeDee could have done it."

"What was her motive?"

I told Mom about DeeDee, the IRS, and The Cheerful Note. "Of everyone else there, her motive might be the strongest."

"She had opportunity as well."

"She did. Almost as good as Erin's."

"Where did the gun come from?"

"Erin said John Allen kept one in his desk."

"How could the killer have gotten the gun, come around the front of the desk, and shoot him?"

"Beats me. I'm not sure how these people lived. Maybe playing with guns was part of their lifestyle behind closed doors."

"Could it have been an accident?"

"I guess so. If it was accidental, Erin would have said so."

She said, "If you're in any way interested in figuring out who the real killer was, I'd look into the sister."

CHAPTER
TWENTY-THREE

The adage goes, loose lips sink ships. Of everyone I met at the dinner party, Antonio was the chattiest. Even Erin commented about his talking. If I were to learn more about DeeDee, the path of least resistance led me to his Grouper Insurance firm.

The following morning, a quick Google search led me to The Shoppes at Magnolia Row. The row housed specialty shopping and dining establishments, housed in architecture reminiscent of Charleston's downtown to the south. The Grouper Insurance office was between The Little White Dress and Barre Co. in a section with a pale blue facade. I planned my visit to arrive five minutes after their posted opening time, hoping he wouldn't be busy.

I pulled open the glass door. A bell chimed. The cozy lobby smelled of caramel. Aerial photos of various locales in Myrtle Beach adorned the walls. Comfortable seating sat opposite of a tall, dark greeting desk. A young, red-headed woman with her hair done up sat behind the desk, punching at a keyboard when I walked in.

She looked up and said in a sing-song voice, "Good morning. Welcome to Grouper Insurance. Do you have an appointment?"

I crossed the lobby in two steps and placed the fingers of my right hand on the edge of the glass-topped desk. It was cool to the touch. Various brochures, business cards, and flyers adorned the desk surface, split like the Red Sea to give a view of the attractive receptionist. A cup of untouched coffee sat in front of her.

I had thought about coming here under false pretenses and pretending that I was looking for a life insurance policy. Had I not been through the ordeal of the other night with Antonio, I might have. I figured that after what happened, he would know that I wouldn't be interested in anything he had to sell.

"I don't. I was hoping to grab a few minutes with Antonio."

She tapped a finger on the desk and her green eyes studied mine. I didn't blink.

Pushing her chair back and standing, she held up a finger. "I'll go see if he's busy. Have a seat if you'd like."

"Thank you," I said as she disappeared down a hall.

The aroma of her coffee rose from the desk. French roast. I thought about sneaking a sip but decided against it and sat in one of the comfortable seats. She returned as I crossed my legs.

"If you give him a few minutes, he'll see you. He's on a call right now."

Karen and Winona were handling things at the store, so they did not need my presence this morning. I had several hours to kill.

"Thank you," I said.

"Sure. Would you like a cup of coffee while you wait?"

I smiled.

* * *

Thirty-three minutes later, the coffee was long gone, and I had gotten the life story of the receptionist, Lisa. Antonio appeared dressed in a gray three-piece suit, with a scowl on his face.

"Clark, to what do I owe this honor?" he said, coming around the desk and shaking my hand.

I stood to get on even ground. In a low voice, I said, "I was hoping you could clear something up for me from the other night."

He glanced back at Lisa, whose head jerked down at that moment and stared at her computer screen.

"Yeah, let's step back into my office," Antonio said. "Cuppa?"

"No, I'm good. Lisa already took care of me."

"I'm sure she did," he said with a wink and led the way down a hall containing more photos of Myrtle Beach. The hall contained four doors. Door number one on the left was open, revealing a conference room with a long gray table and chairs. The first on the right was closed, as was the last one on the left. The door at the end was open, and that's where Antonio led me.

He closed the door behind me as we entered his cozy office. A brag wall behind his desk contained a marketing degree from the University of South Carolina and certifications from various insurance schools. More aerial photography pictures hung on the walls. A simple white wood desk took up most of the space. He went around his desk and sat while I took a sturdy chair that matched the desk. The room smelled faintly of cigarette smoke.

He unbuttoned his suit coat and shrugged it off, laying the expensive jacket across a printer stand next to him. Leaning forward, he laced his hands together on the desk. Jeweled cufflinks glittered in the light.

"That was quite a night we had, wasn't it?" he asked. There was hesitation in his voice.

"Oh, yes. Not one that we'll ever forget," I answered.

"I assume you're not here to discuss insurance."

My head bobbed. "In a manner of speaking, maybe."

He removed his hands from his desk and sat back. "How can I help you?"

"I'm a curious person by nature," I said.

"I gathered that. You'd have to be to get into murder investigations."

"Right. The other night after John Allen was shot, I couldn't help myself."

"Even though you were the one who found Erin holding the gun?"

I hadn't forgotten about him accusing me of the crime at one point that evening, but I didn't feel the need to bring that back up again. "Yeah, even so. I might not have if Erin didn't proclaim her innocence so fervently. I haven't been around too many murderers, but the two that I had, when it became clear that everyone knew they were guilty, took on this air of defeat. You know? Like there was no fighting it."

"But Erin didn't play it that way."

"She didn't."

"Who did she say did it?"

I bit the inside of my lip, deciding how much to reveal. Antonio was my best bet to get more information about the family. If I wanted him to talk, I had to give and take. "Preacher."

"Ah, that makes sense."

"Why?"

"From the minute Preacher first started coming around and everyone learned what he did for a living, we knew it was a matter of time before he tried to get at John Allen's money." He leaned forward again. "We all knew he was shady."

"Did you know that John Allen did, in fact, invest in one of Preacher's products?"

His eyebrows jumped. "No, I didn't. What kind?"

"Something offshore to the tune of half a million."

Antonio let out a long, low whistle. "Wow. That's a lot of dough. I mean, that's chump change to someone like John Allen Howard, but to the rest of us, that's a life's savings."

"Yeah, well, something happened there that caused Erin to believe Preacher was behind the slaying."

"Did you talk to him about it?"

"I did. He denied it. Had a story to cover his tracks. He said something interesting, though."

"What's that?"

"When I asked him who he thought did it before we discovered Erin with the gun, he said he thought it was you."

His neck flushed purple, as did his face as he sat erect in his chair. He bit his bottom lip so hard I thought he would draw blood. "Me? Why me? What did that snake think I had to do with this?"

Now the claws were coming out. Just what I'd wanted. "He believed John Allen thought you weren't good enough for his daughter, and you got fed up with it."

To my surprise, he hooted a laugh. "What? No, no, no. It was the other way around. JA respected me. His daughter, not so much."

"Because of how her first marriage ended?"

"That I don't know. Could be. Remember, me and you found out about that at the same time."

"Right," I said. "Good old Cade."

He rubbed a finger at a spot on his desk. "Yeah, DeeDee and I had a long discussion about that yesterday."

"Was it bad?"

He didn't answer for a moment, then pulled open the top desk drawer to his left and withdrew a small box. He set it on top of the desk. It was a black box with "Vicki Lyn Michaels Jewelers" silk-screened on the top.

"Got that last week," he said. "Was going to propose to DeeDee this weekend."

"Ah." This was no time to give my opinion, but to relax and let him speak. The tap was open now. Let it pour.

"I might take it back. She gave me this song and dance routine about how she needed the money and how she'd never do such a thing to me."

Those Botox injections needed doing from time to time to keep up DeeDee's appearance. Who knows what else wasn't part of her original equipment? I said, "As the saying goes, 'Once a cheater, always a cheater.'"

"Yup. Similar mindset. Don't know if I can trust her."

"Did you learn any more about the trouble she's having with The Cheerful Note and the IRS?"

"Nope. She wasn't going to talk to me about it." His face reddened. "Honestly, I'm not sure I want to know."

"How did the charity work?"

"They would get donations from wealthy donors to go out and purchase instruments for kids in schools. They could go online and purchase second-hand instruments with the donated money. Other times, people donated instruments by dropping them off at their office or by mail. She had many musical contacts dating back from when her dad was in the biz that helped. It's a good charity. I went to a few schools with her to bring instruments. She was never happier than to see a poor ten-year-old wrap their hands around a flute or other instrument for the first time."

"Sounds rewarding."

"It is." He scratched his chin and glanced out the window. "Say, there wasn't anything about me lying on his bed, was there?"

That he was ready to move past the subject of IRS malfeasance by his girlfriend to learn if I had any dirt on him told me that Antonio was also guilty of something.

"There were letters about some sort of life insurance policy."

He crossed one leg over the other and laced his fingers over his knee. "How many were there?"

"Two. One about opening a policy. The other was about closing it."

"Oh, yes. DeeDee and I were over at his house a couple of months ago for lunch. Erin went out to run errands. He brought up that he was worried about what might happen to his charity upon his death. I suggested he change his will to leave money in a trust and to open a life insurance policy that would pay in the event of his death."

"Why did he cancel the policy?"

"Because I promised him one rate, and it ended up being a higher one after going through underwriting. He told me he could do better if he used his people out in LA to do it, so he canceled."

"I bet that chapped your pants. Must have been a big commission to lose out on."

"It was, I'll admit."

"Did that make you angry?"

I'm not sure John Allen canceling the account made him as angry as me asking that question. His face flushed red again. "Are you suggesting that I'd kill him over a canceled insurance policy? That's ridiculous. I'm doing well for myself, thank you. I should throw you out for even thinking that."

I held up my hands in a defensive move. "Look, I don't know

your situation. We just met. For all I know, you could go out of business tomorrow. I'm sorry if I offended you."

He bit the inside of his cheek and raised his left eyebrow. His shoulders deflated. "I see where you're coming from. Look, I've made enough bank that I could retire tomorrow if I wanted to and live out my days in comfort."

"See, I didn't know that." That didn't mean he wouldn't try to squeeze money out of his clients to get there.

"Besides," he said, "I was down in the kitchen hiding in a cabinet when the gun went off. Remember?"

"Yeah, I do." Something about what he said tugged at the back of my mind, but I couldn't grasp the thought right then.

"I had no reason to kill John. I swear. Why kill the source of DeeDee's money if I was going to marry her?" He laughed a bit. "I said I could retire tomorrow if it came to it, but if I had to support DeeDee too? Hoo boy. I'd need a second job."

I laughed as well, if for no other reason than to show camaraderie. "I hear that."

"Speaking of needing more than one job to support someone, did you know Louise has gone through three husbands?"

"I was aware of that."

"She'd join us for lunch. Her mouth would start opening after the second glass of wine. Often, it wouldn't stop. Told us all about them."

"Didn't one of them own a few car dealerships?" At this point, I didn't want to reveal to Antonio that I had done my background research on all of them. Better to play ignorant than informed.

"Her most recent husband owned three. All luxury car brands."

"He wasn't hurting for money, then."

"Nope. He left most of it to Louise. They bought their house here not long before he passed away."

"How did he die?"

"Natural causes. She woke up one morning. He didn't."

"That's scary."

"I don't know what I would have done had I been in her slippers."

"That's one husband. What about the other two?"

He stroked a hand over the lower part of his smooth jaw. "Let's see. The first was a carpenter. Back in the sixties. Both got caught up in the times. She claimed to be a hippy. He overdosed on heroin. Scared her straight."

"It would me. What about her second husband?"

"He was the one she was married to the longest. A career car salesman."

"I sense a theme here."

"Yeah. After a while, he died, and she upgraded her model, so to speak."

"How did he die?"

"Liver disease. Louise said he was a big drinker. Drunk or buzzed all the time. He claimed that's what made him such a good car sales agent. A few drinks would loosen his tongue and cause him to be honest with prospective buyers. She said he could cover it up when engaging customers through chewing gum or smoking cigarettes, depending on the customer."

"Could you imagine going to a car dealership around here nowadays and having your sales rep lighting up in the backseat while you're testing a car down the 17 Bypass?"

He smiled. "Nope. Things were different back in the 70s and 80s. I used to smoke too."

Judging by the odor when I entered his office, it smelled like he still did. "Do you know what her married names were?"

"Ah, let's see. Gillespie and Andrews, I think. Not sure which belonged to whom."

I made a mental note of them to punch the names into my phone when I got back in the Jeep.

He glanced at his watch. "Look, Clark. Can't say this has been fun, but I have a meeting in ten minutes I need to get ready for."

"I understand. Sorry about insinuating your involvement in his death."

"No, I see where you're coming from. I do. Not sure why you want to get involved in it. Erin shot him. She's going to trial. Leave it be."

CHAPTER
TWENTY-FOUR

I drove past the Howard estate after leaving Antonio's Grouper Insurance office. It wasn't my intended destination. As the conversation I just had with Antonio spiraled through my mind, my Jeep drifted in that direction after turning down the street beside Fiesta Mexicana and driving toward the Atlantic.

That had been an interesting chat. Antonio claimed John Allen had canceled the policy over a change in premium rates, but would it make enough of a difference for a man who could afford anything? Was there more to it?

The last conversation I had with DeeDee made it apparent that she wanted no part of me. Getting a one-on-one with her like I did with Antonio just now seemed far-fetched. Antonio threatened to throw me out at one point. She would unleash the hounds if she saw me walking to the door. Still might be worth a shot.

I waited for a golf cart carrying two passengers more intent on their phones than the ocean to their left before turning right onto Ocean Boulevard. The two-lane road meandered in a semi-straight line as it separated a long activity trail, sand dunes, and the beach from the first row of immaculate houses facing the waves.

The distracted tourists in the golf cart ended up in front of me. With a long stream of traffic coming in my direction, I could only pray that the driver of the cart moving five miles per hour would take pity on me and pull to the side of the road to let me pass. No such luck. Not that I was in a hurry.

Tall sand dunes obscured any sight of the beach along this stretch of road. The masts of two catamarans poked above the sand and sea oats swayed in the gentle morning breeze. Several adorable, colorful beach shacks on stilts that would qualify for tiny-house status dotted this section by the ocean. A playground with a large wooden pirate ship lay at the end of this stretch before Ocean Boulevard made a sharp curve to get around the resort hotels and the Myrtle Beach Boardwalk. The cart veered into a beach access parking lot as the road curved, leaving me to wonder if the driver and his passenger knew that the road turned.

I rolled by them, then checked the side-view mirror in time to see them bump into a concrete barrier in the lot. The male driver seemed surprised and looked up from his phone. His wife never took her eyes off the screen in her chubby hand. People never ceased to amaze me.

I rolled the window down and rested my arm on the opening. The temperature was pleasant, not sticky. Dry air must have pushed Karen away.

After passing by a cluster of hotels ending with the Dunes Village Resort, I came to 52nd Avenue N. The northern boundary of the Golden Mile. Here, the sidewalks widened. The foliage was greener and lusher. Perhaps to help obscure the views of homes from us common folk.

Two trucks with cherry pickers from Santee Cooper straddled the road and sidewalk in different spots. Both trucks towed woodchippers. Workers used chainsaws to clear away shattered trees left in the tornado's wake that touched down the night of Karen. I dodged past them, raising two fingers off the steering wheel in a wave. They stared at me with disinterest.

As the Jeep approached the Howard Estate, I passed Louise's house. She didn't have a security gate out front. Among all the homes here on the Mile, hers was one of the plainest. Gray siding, brown shutters, and a roof with missing shingles. The only thing that stood out about her home was the landscaping. She had placed tropical flowers and shrubs in a manner pleasing to the eye.

Her back was to me as she stooped over a flower bed. She wore a long, thin shirt and a pair of light blue slacks that didn't make it down to her ankles. She was barefoot. I glimpsed her before she fell from view, and the Howards' home came into view. The gate was closed. A ribbon of yellow police tape was tied across it. The windows were dark. The driveway empty.

I pulled into the next beach access and turned the vehicle around and headed back. After passing the Howards' place, I pulled into Louise's driveway. She stood and turned, squinting to see who the driver was. I stopped the car. She walked over to the driver's side.

With the window down, it was easy for her to see inside. She held a hand over her eyes to keep the sun out. "Clark, is that you?"

"It is. How are you doing?"

She glanced around the interior of the Jeep, then responded, "I'm alright. Just tending to my flowers."

"Looks beautiful."

"Thank you." She smiled. Then more cautiously asked, "What are you doing up this way?"

I crooked a thumb inland. "Just came from a meeting with someone and was kinda driving aimlessly. I passed by here, saw you out, and thought I'd circle back and say hi."

"Well, hello."

"Are you okay from the other night?"

She pulled off a pair of rubber gardening gloves and held them together by her side. "Yeah. It was a frightful night, that's for sure. Poor John. Poor family."

"It's a tragedy."

She placed a hand on the window opening. "Thank you for protecting me. I might have had a heart attack had you not been there and pulled me into that room."

I put my hand on hers. "You're welcome. I'm sure it's what anyone else would have done had they been capable."

"Still, thank you. If there's ever anything I can do for you, let me know." She gave my hand a squeeze, then withdrew it.

"Maybe you could answer a few questions for me."

"I'll try."

"Did you know about the attempts on John Allen's life before the other night?"

"Yes, he'd told me. I was so worried about him. The one where Erin found him passed out in his closet was just scary. They say he'd taken the wrong pills."

"Erin mentioned she managed her dad's medication schedule to keep him on track. Do you know if anyone else did?"

She held a finger under her chin and thought. "Sometimes, when Erin would go out and about, and DeeDee and that boyfriend of hers would come over for lunch, I'd join them. DeeDee would give him a pill or two after he filled his belly."

"So, DeeDee was aware of what medications John Allen took and when?"

"She'd have to be, wouldn't she?"

"Anyone else? What about Cade?"

"Don't think so. He didn't come around as often."

That meant the two daughters were the ones most likely to have given him the wrong pills. They were also closest to him at the time of the shooting. "Were you around when his cane broke, and he fell?"

She pointed at the ground. "I was outside tending to the flowers when I heard the calamity. I rushed over to see what happened. Erin and Preacher were there helping him up. He drove John to the ER. I came back here, changed my dirt-stained pants, and rushed down to check on him. You know that poor man wasn't in the best of health."

"That's what they say," I said. "Erin said the cane broke clean. Like it had been cut."

"Oh, my goodness." She held a hand over her mouth. "No way. Who would do that?"

"Whoever had it out for him."

"True. Let's see. Preacher would come over and do handyman things for John."

"To keep in his good graces?"

"Probably so," she agreed. "Cade was handy with tools as well. He comes over here when I need something fixed."

"Interesting."

A big pickup truck roared by, going way too fast for this section of road. Louise watched it pass from view. She clicked her tongue and said, "Darn kids. Always in a hurry."

"We all were that age at one time. In a hurry to get everywhere."

"And then to nothing."

"That's about it." I laughed.

"Look," she said, "it was nice talking to you, but I have to finish this, so I can clean up and meet some ladies for a game of mahjong."

I played the game on my phone, but never in physical form. "Sounds fun. Thanks Louise. Nice talking to you as well."

I backed out of the driveway and drove toward the Boardwalk, thinking. Could Cade or Preacher have cut the cane?

CHAPTER
TWENTY-FIVE

Back at Myrtle Beach Reads, ensconced in my office, coffee cup in one hand, computer mouse in the other, I pulled the handwritten note from Erin with the contact information for John Allen's accountant and the director, David Weller. My stomach growled as I realized I skipped lunch. Maybe later. The coffee would help blanket my appetite.

The first task was to reach out to Weller. Erin only gave me his email address. I crafted a message letting him know who I was and how I was there the evening his close friend was shot. In the letter, I explained the attempts on John Allen's life before his murder and that Erin had mentioned the composer had video chats with Weller around that time. I inquired what those chats were about and if John Allen had mentioned his recent hospital visits. Then, I fired off the email, figuring that it would land in Weller's spam folder and never be seen again.

Next up was to contact the accountant. The firm was called Hinkle Accountancy. I did a quick internet search. Their office was in a modern styled building on a street off Santa Monica Boulevard. They appeared to cater to Hollywood's finest. From the pictures of the exterior and interior of the building, I judged you would have to be in the upper part of the entertainment industry income bracket to afford their services.

I pulled out my phone and dialed the number Erin wrote, not the one listed at the bottom of the website. They differed. As I wondered why the numbers were different, someone answered on the other end, grunted, and said in a cumbersome voice in need of sleep or coffee, "Peter Hinkle."

It took me a moment to remember they were three hours behind us here on the East Coast. We were past midday while they were getting started.

"Good morning," I said. "My name is Clark Thomas. John Allen Howard's daughter, Erin, gave me your number."

"Ah, yes. Erin. How is that girl?"

"Well, sir. You see, she's in jail."

"Jail?" he roared. "Whatever for?"

"They arrested her for shooting her dad."

His voice remained a high yell. "What? What are you talking about?"

"Did you not hear about his death?"

A moment passed. "No, I didn't. I've been in bed sick for a week. This is my first morning back. I've been in a haze."

I explained to him what happened that night and how they arrested Erin for the crime.

"Goodness. I can't imagine that sweet, sweet girl doing anything like that."

"To be honest, I only met her this past Monday. Don't know her too well. I must apologize for being the bearer of bad news."

"No, it's okay," Peter said. On this end, he sounded like he was crying. "John Allen was one of the kindest, most giving people I've ever met. He wasn't the client with the most money, but he was my favorite."

"He seemed that way," I said, having never met the late composer. His comment made me wonder who else was in his client portfolio.

"When my daughter Bess turned sixteen, she and Erin were best friends. John Allen composed a piece on the violin, especially for Bess. It was something simple. Not much. But it was special coming from him."

"I can imagine."

"Right. He said he had hidden Bess' name in the composition. I know nothing about music, but I took his word for it. No matter what, it was sweet and special."

"What does Bess do now?"

"She works for me, of course."

"That must be nice. Keep the business in the family."

"It is."

Offhand, I wondered about the future of my business years down the road. There were no children to pass it along to. Getting back on track, and off that depressing note, I said, "The reason for my call is that Erin said I should contact you."

"Why me?"

"Erin claims she didn't do it, even though she was caught holding the gun moments after we heard it fired."

"Do you believe her?"

"It's crazy, but I think I do," I admitted. "I'm not a private investigator or anything. Just a curious person who owns a bookstore here in Myrtle Beach." I related how I had been involved in solving two murders. "After the attempts on his life, John Allen invited me to his house for dinner. He had laid out a bunch of papers on his bed, which I believe he meant for me. I think he wanted me to help him figure out who was behind it all."

"But the tornado hit, and he didn't have time to explain what they were about?" Hinkle said.

Astute observation on his part. "Right, I had a question about one part of it, which is why Erin told me to call you."

He let out an audible breath into the receiver. "Look, there's an entire client confidentiality thing here that keeps me from giving information from parties not named on the accounts." Just as I figured that I'd hit a dead end, Hinkle continued, "In this case, I might dance my way around whatever questions you have, if it'll help. You just can't say you heard it from me."

"My lips are sealed."

"Fire away."

"You did the books for their Cheerful Note charity, right?"

"I did them personally." I heard the clacking of a keyboard on the other end. "Let me pull up their file. What is it you want to know?"

"There's a letter from the IRS regarding a Form 990. Know anything about that?"

"Umm. Here's where we get into a gray area. I can't comment specifically on it, but I will say that the money coming into their account wasn't matching up with what DeeDee was reporting."

"Was she embezzling money?"

"No comment."

I took the no comment as an affirmation.

"What I can say is that not all the donations they received were of the monetary variety. They would get hand-me-down instruments from parents whose kids were no longer in bands. They'd sanitize them and donate the used ones to schools."

"That's nice."

"I must say, I never cared for DeeDee. She was a few years

older than Erin and Bess but put on like she ruled the roost. Very bossy. Obtuse. Did her first husband wrong."

"Yes, I'm aware of what happened between them, and I had a similar impression of DeeDee."

He cleared his throat. My ears perked up. He said, "Now, John Allen had a lot of friends and performers in the music industry. Sometimes, they would be the ones to donate instruments, intending to put them up for auction."

"Noble."

"It should be that way, yes."

"Ah. I take it that it wasn't."

"Let's just say that many of those instruments never saw the light of day at auction."

"Wait, are you saying DeeDee was selling these collectors' pieces and keeping the money for herself?"

"I didn't say that, nor did I not say that, if you catch my drift."

After a few more minutes of small talk, I thanked him for his time and hung up the phone. There it was. Motive for DeeDee. If her dad caught wind of this, there's no telling how far DeeDee would go to cover it up.

An email notification appeared on the computer screen. I had a sharp intake of air when I saw who it was from: David Weller.

* * *

An hour later, after grabbing a to-go sandwich down the street from Surf's Pizza on the corner of 8th Avenue N and Ocean Boulevard, I was back in front of the computer and logged onto Zoom. Humphrey and Margaret were out front, stocking books and servicing customers. Traffic had picked up now that we were past lunchtime.

Weller's email included a link to a Zoom meeting at 1:30. Said he would be interested in chatting. Anything to help his dear old friend, John Allen Howard.

When the program started, I had to wait for the host to start the meeting. Five minutes after the appointed time, Weller appeared on the screen. He had a thin beard and gray hair had receded from his forehead. I could only see him from the torso up. He wore a plain black polo shirt. First, it was a legendary Hollywood composer who wanted to chat with me. Now, it was another member of Hollywood royalty. I had lost track of how many Academy Awards David Weller had won over the years, but there were three statues of Oscar behind him on a shelf below a painting depicting a man standing above two others in a darkened room. An Emmy was jumbled in there as well.

"Hello," he said with a sheepish wave. "You must be Clark."

I tilted my head forward. "I am. Pleased to meet you."

"Yes, I wish it were under better circumstances. Forgive me for insisting on doing a video call, but I abhor phones. They're too impersonal."

"No worries at all." This is something that I would be sure to tell my mom and brother about later. My friend Marilyn from the We Got Issues comic bookstore up the street would be jealous. She was a movie buff in addition to her love of comics. Weller had directed several of her favorite movies.

"John Allen was a dear friend of mine. We go way back. How can I help you? I must apologize. I'm pressed for time."

I held up a hand. "No apologies necessary. It's an honor that you would give me even sixty seconds."

He chuckled. "Please. I'm just a regular man in his sixties

who does something that entertains people. When I say I'm short on time, it's not because I need to be on set or in post-production on a movie. It's because I need to get my husky to the vet and then pick up my granddaughter from preschool at 3:30."

"That is normal." I smiled and then laid out the scenario involving Erin, the gun, and her professed innocence. "She mentioned that her dad and you had been in contact over the past few weeks. I just wanted to know if he had said anything about the cane or pill incidents."

He knitted his eyebrows together. "What cane and pill incident?"

I relayed what happened.

"Hmm. No, he didn't. It's strange. Usually, we're an open book to each other."

That wasn't the answer I was looking for. I had hoped John Allen would have told Weller everything, including dirt on the suspects. "What did you talk about, if you don't mind my asking?"

He looked at the ceiling and then back at the screen. "Let's see. It was mostly reminiscing about our times doing movies together. You knew about his Alzheimer's, right?"

"I did."

"Yeah, his mind was slipping, and I think he was trying to hold on to the memories that he had while he still could. We'd be talking about an experience that was vivid in my mind, but he had no memory of it. It happened several times. It was sad to see a man who was so intelligent and such a good person fall victim to this debilitating disease."

"Runs in my family. My grandfather and two of his three brothers died of the same condition."

"Then you know first-hand what it does to a person."

"I do."

We chatted about this and that, nothing related to the reason for my call. I had an out-of-body experience while we talked, seeing myself talking with the David Weller from a cluttered office thousands of miles away. Strange days.

He checked his watch. "Look, it was nice chatting with you, but I gotta run."

"One more question, if you don't mind," I said, holding up a finger.

"Yes, go ahead."

"That painting behind you. Where did you get it?"

He turned to see what I was talking about and spun back to face forward. "Oh, that came from John Allen's son, Cade. He'd brokered a deal between me and an art gallery from Georgia. Savannah, maybe. It's beautiful, isn't it?"

"It is. Who painted it?"

"I'm not too sure. It was either Benjamin West or Antoine Le Nain."

"Very nice. He told me he did business with galleries scattered around the country. Georgia is a simple drive from here once you make it out to the interstate."

We ended the virtual meeting a moment later. I folded the computer and wondered if anything useful came from that entire conversation.

CHAPTER
TWENTY-SIX

The time was just past two. I stretched my arms above my head and stared at the ceiling. Light streamed through the windows. There wasn't much to glean from the conversation with David Weller, at least not on the surface. The painting bothered me, but I wasn't sure why.

After exiting the office, I told Winona I was heading out. Karen had left for the day, replaced by Humphrey.

"Sure thing, boss," Winona said. She was behind the counter, sorting through special order books.

Before getting to the door, I turned on my heel and walked back to Winona. She had short, brown hair, was of average height and build, and had a red splotchy birthmark on the left side of her forehead. Her chestnut brown eyes and sideways smile gave away her wry sense of humor.

"Can't you see I'm busy here," she said, not looking up from a printed list of names and books.

"Real quick," I said. Humphrey lumbered near the back of the store out of earshot helping a customer.

She set the list down on top of an open box of books. In a more serious manner, she said, "Yeah, what is it?"

"You remember me talking about opening another store in

Garden City?"

"Uh-huh."

"The other day, I signed off on getting it off the ground."

"Wow. That's awesome. Congratulations."

"Thank you. The thing is," I said, running my hand along the edge of the counter, "this store is my baby."

She nodded. "It was yours and your wife's labor of love."

"Exactly. I don't want to leave it but want to grow the business. Hence, the second location."

"Sounds like you're in a pickle."

"Maybe. Maybe not. What if you ran the Garden City location?"

Her mouth opened, then closed. "Get out. You want me to run it?"

"Only if you want to."

Winona was two years removed from college. She was young and inexperienced. What she lacked in practice, she made up for in maturity and business management knowledge. The only way to gain experience is to do something, and everyone had to start somewhere. I worked with Winona for several months, gauging her, before giving her more responsibilities. We were at the point where I considered her my second-in-command. Her work ethic was on par with Karen and Margaret. Neither of them were possible choices. Margaret informed me she was ready for permanent retirement, and Karen was content to work here a few hours a week while her husband fished. I didn't want to hire someone new to run the Garden City location. I would rather promote from within. Winona knew my vision for how I ran my business, and I felt she could bring that mentality elsewhere.

She ran around the counter and wrapped her bony arms around my neck. "Thank you! Thank you! You won't regret this.

I've been hoping you would ask me. My parents will be so proud."

"I'm sure they will. I'm proud of you, too. You're a remarkable young woman, and I think you'll do well. You're a keeper."

She let go of me and stood back, wiping a tear from her eye. Made me misty-eyed too, but I tried to hide it.

"Thank you," she said again.

"You're welcome. I don't have a timeframe yet, but I'll start training you for the gig on the next schedule I write."

"Sounds perfect."

I glanced back to where Humphrey was attending to the customers, then said to Winona, "You took music courses at Coastal, didn't you?"

"Got a bachelor's degree in Music General Studies. I was so jealous of you getting to meet John Allen Howard. He, John Williams, Howard Shore, Michael Giacchino, and Hans Zimmer play on a constant loop when I'm at home."

"Yes, it's a shame that I never got to meet him," I said.

Her lips compressed. She looked down at the counter. "It is. A tragedy."

"I have a question for you about music."

She wiped away the tears that were already flowing from the news of her impending promotion. "Sure. What is it?"

I pulled out my phone and scrolled through the photo gallery before arriving at one specific picture. Holding out the phone where she could see the screen, I asked, "Does that mean anything?"

She grabbed the phone from my hand, placed two fingers on the screen, and slid them apart to enlarge the image. Her eyebrows met in the middle. "That's odd."

"What is?"

Before she could answer, Humphrey approached the counter, leading two shoppers with a stack of books. He saw her tears and gave me a perplexed look. I shook my head at him as a hint not to ask about it in front of customers. He nodded in understanding and set the books on the counter before Winona, where she had resumed her position. Her face held both a big smile and a perplexed look at the same time.

After the delighted customers departed and Humphrey plodded off to help someone else, Winona and I drew close. She whispered one word, and everything changed.

The Cheerful Note office sat in between the offices for a security company and bike shop in a strip of businesses sandwiched between car dealerships on Jason Boulevard. A frontage road to the 17 Bypass near the 501 interchanges. The building shouted "boring!" It was rectangular and boxy with silver and dingy brown accents. An establishment one ignores when seeing all the shiny new vehicles surrounding it. I crawled past a row of Jeep Gladiators at Myrtle Beach Chrysler Jeep, remembering how I found Connor's West's abandoned in the 2nd Avenue Pier parking lot a few months ago.

DeeDee's blue Tesla was parked in front of The Cheerful Note door. The charity's name was painted onto the picture window beside the entrance. The doorknob was shaped like a saxophone.

I pulled open the door, and a bell rang above my head. Bright lights lit a reception area which had a long desk. An open box labeled "Donations" was in front of it. A few random instruments lay inside it. Behind the desk sat a youngish man with a shock of brown hair that didn't look like he had combed it in years. I measured the same timeframe as to when he last shaved. Bright green eyes emanated from the mask of hair.

His voice was melodious. "Can I help you?"

"Hi. Maybe. Is DeeDee here?"

"She's in the back, taking inventory. Can I help you with anything?"

If this guy knew anything about the IRS being on DeeDee's back, I would be beyond surprised. "Not likely. I just want to ask her about something. She and I met the other night."

"Oh, you were at her dad's house."

"She told you about it?"

He waggled a hand with long fingers like those of a piano player. "Some. She said they were all over there for dinner when a tornado hit the house and almost killed everyone. Said she was nearby when she heard the gun go off."

"Did she seem surprised at who was holding the gun?"

His eyes lit. "You must be that Clark guy. That's the G-rated version of the way she referred to you. Asking a lot of questions."

"I guess so." She must have told this guy more than he was letting on. "What's your name?"

"Ken. Ken Baker."

"Nice to meet you, Ken."

"Same. To answer your question, no, it did not surprise her to find Erin holding the gun. It surprised her it happened, but not by who did it."

This wasn't the time to mention that the "who did it" part was still up for debate. If he and DeeDee had a close relationship, he might clam up if I informed him about why I was here.

"Why is that?"

His head cocked to the side. "Things had been rocky between Erin and her dad. DeeDee had been going over there more often to give her sister a break. That's all I know."

"Roger."

He uncurled his legs and stood, towering over my head. "Come this way."

I wanted to ask him what the weather was like up there, but said, "How tall are you?"

"An inch below seven feet."

"Did you play basketball?"

"No. Had no interest. I play piano and percussion."

"Ah," I grunted, as though he explained everything.

"This way," he said and guided me through a door leading to a long hallway. He had to duck to get through. With all his hair, I imagined I was being led by one of Chewbacca's relatives. The hall was dim. Framed photographs of DeeDee and Ken presenting groups of happy, smiling children with instruments lined the walls. John Allen appeared in a few.

He led me through an open door at the end of the hall and into a warehouse lined with row upon row of musical instruments. Trumpets, saxophones, tubas, clarinets, you name it. A section reserved for pianos lay at one end. There had to be a thousand instruments here. Easy.

DeeDee held a sheaf of papers in one hand while rummaging through a large box of brassy instruments. A pencil perched behind one ear. Her once coiffed hair was now disheveled. Red rings rimmed her eyes. Weariness had replaced the aura of confidence. She had lost her dad and her long-time boyfriend in a matter of hours. After watching her put away glass after glass of wine the other night, it surprised me she was sober at present.

"DeeDee," Ken announced.

She looked up at him and down at me. The disappointment was clear on her face, which turned a shade redder.

"Why did you let him back here?" she snarled.

Ken didn't seem to take offense. He brushed her off like a gnat. "Because he seemed like a nice enough guy and said he'd met you the other night."

Her mouth drooped. She reached out and rubbed his arm. "Okay. Thanks, Ken. I know we don't get many people who come here to see me, but next time come ask me before bringing them past the desk."

"Sure thing, DeeDee."

He nodded at me and ducked through the door on his way back up front.

After he departed, DeeDee's features softened. "You'll have to forgive Ken."

"I do?" I had no reason to do that. He made a face-to-face meeting with DeeDee easy to get.

"He's autistic. Doesn't always say the right thing in social situations, but a near virtuoso on a piano, xylophone, and marimba."

"Interesting."

She set the papers on a shelf, then squared her shoulders back to me. "We might as well get to it. What do you want?"

I had rehearsed how I could ease into this conversation with the combative DeeDee, but maybe now her guard was down. "Tell me about the IRS."

One eyebrow pressed down and the other one jerked up. "The only reason you're asking is because you think I might have shot Dad instead of Erin."

"I'm only trying to sort out what happened."

Her shoulders sagged as she leaned against a shelf. "Okay. A while back, one of Dad's orchestra members caught wind of what we were doing and donated a violin she'd used in recording the soundtrack to a movie. Said she had two more like it. Thought

I might get something out of it."

"Did it go to auction?"

"Most of the collectible ones we receive do, but I knew there was an underground market where certain types of instruments could fetch exorbitant amounts of money in Asia. Someone I know from back in Hollywood put word out that this instrument was available. Next thing I knew, the instrument was packed in a crate bound for Hong Kong. We pocketed a million dollars, minus my friend's fee, of course."

My eyes bulged. "A million dollars?"

"Oh yes. It's amazing what people from overseas will pay."

"Did you do this more than once?"

"I did. It was so easy. Dad kept having friends donate old instruments. I'd turn around and auction most of them, but the ones that were true collector's items, I turned around and sold in the underground economy."

That was an interesting way to put it. "I did not know there was a black market for musical instruments."

She raised an eyebrow. "After being around some people I have, you learn that there's an underground market for about anything."

"Can't say I'm surprised. What did you do with the money?"

"I had to pay my guy a small commission, then put most of the rest back into The Cheerful Note."

"But not all of it?"

"No, I kept some for myself."

"Do you take a salary from the charity?"

"I do, albeit a small one."

"And you did the backroom sales of certain instruments off the books. If you kept some money for yourself, no one would be none the wiser, right?"

"Something like that."

"Where does the IRS come into the picture?"

"I'm not sure. All I know is that one day, a certified letter showed up that I had to sign for. I thought it was a prank, but after showing it to our accountant and lawyer, they assured me it was quite real."

"What did your dad say about it?"

"It devastated him," DeeDee said. "He couldn't hide his disappointment in me, nor should he have."

"What are you going to do about it? The IRS, that is."

"Pay back what I owe. I have the money for it."

"Let me ask you, point-blank. Was the money going to come from your dad's estate? I understand you were to receive one chunk and The Cheerful Note was to receive another. That would go a long way to making amends with the government."

She bit a nail and muttered, "Antonio." She balled her fists, and, for a moment, I thought she was going to take a swing at me. To my surprise, she didn't. "Look, if you think that was a motive for me to kill Dad, then you're wrong. If I don't pay the IRS pronto, they're going to cuff me and put me in jail. Dad's estate is going to be tied up in probate court for a year due to its size and all the pieces in it."

I relaxed my arms at my sides. "Okay then."

She crossed her arms. "What's your theory? Let's hear it. If not Erin, then who?"

"I'm not too sure now. Chris and Preacher were down in the garage when it all happened. Cade was in the laundry room. Chris told me Preacher disappeared during it all. I asked him about it, and he said he hid in the studio across the hall."

"That would have been a great place to hide," she said.

"I agree. Here's the thing, after we all went downstairs and Chris and Preacher led me through what happened, I tried the studio door, and it was locked."

"Makes sense. Even with all the security in the place, Dad kept that door locked. There was so much money in that room with Dad's music collection and studio equipment that he couldn't risk someone getting inside and stealing anything. It was double protection from thieves. He had a break-in one night when we lived in Los Angeles. The thieves grabbed instruments and equipment worth millions. We were all in Bali at the time."

Must be nice. "So, when he had his new house built, he wanted to make sure it was better protected."

"Yes, something like that."

Getting back on track, I said, "Besides Erin, you were the closest person to your dad when the gun went off."

Her stance shifted. "Yes, around the corner. I'd finished in the bathroom and was coming out when I heard the noise. I saw the tornado coming and ducked back in and closed the door. That bathroom is in the middle of the house, and I've seen the movie Twister enough times to know to put as many walls between you and a tornado as you can. I ducked down in the shower and covered my ears, but I still heard the gun. It's funny though."

"What's funny?"

"That isn't the right word. Strange might be more appropriate. The shot was distinct, even above the commotion. When I heard the gun, it didn't sound like it was coming from the level we were on. It sounded like it was below us."

"Below?"

"Uh-huh. It was weird. I didn't think about the sound coming from Dad's office until I saw everyone rushing to it."

CHAPTER
TWENTY-EIGHT

The conversation with Winona turned everything upside down. My chat with DeeDee did it again. Foremost being her intuition that the gunshot was beneath her. How? I couldn't ask Erin about it. I could pass the information along to Gomez, but she would tell me to keep my nose out of it. Which I didn't want to at this point. Besides, I was sure they would learn the same thing, wouldn't they?

Here was the other thing. Just because DeeDee had the money to sweep her fraud under the rug, it didn't mean the IRS was going to let her get away with it. Yeah, she could pay back what she owed but still face prison time.

Over a week passed while Erin awaited her next court appearance. I worked shifts at the store covering for Humphrey when he came down with the flu and missed two days. I was near the end of completing my first solo novel and was working on a deadline with it. The publisher wanted to release it in the Spring, and it needed to get done so they could offer it for early reviews.

With all of that happening, I didn't have time to dig any more into what happened the night of John Allen's death. I wasn't too sure what else I could learn without a warrant, since I'm an average Joe, and Gomez told me to lay off. She has that habit.

I was surprised on the next Thursday morning. While consuming a bowl of old-fashioned brown sugar and cinnamon oatmeal on the back deck of my house overlooking Lake Vivian, my phone rang. It was Gomez.

"Clark," she breathed into the receiver. "This is awkward, but I didn't have anyone else to call."

I set the bowl down on a metal side table and sat up in my Adirondack chair. Her tone sounded urgent. "What is it?"

"I need a date."

That was the last thing I expected her to say. "A date? A date for what?"

"There's a fashion show happening at the Chapin Museum tonight, and it would look bad if I showed up by myself. Stupid social pressures being what they are and all. Chief Kluttz tabbed me to represent the police department this year. They do it every fall for charity."

"Ah, fun. I thought you had a boyfriend?"

"Him? He's not, er wasn't my boyfriend. We were . . . friendly is all, but we aren't on speaking terms now." She paused. "As of today. Look, I know why you haven't asked me out."

My jaw dropped. I never articulated that thought aloud, much less in my brain. That didn't mean what she said wasn't true. Also, I was aware she was seeing someone but didn't know much about him or their relationship. Until now. "Why is that?"

"Autumn. If I hadn't told you my thoughts on the circumstances surrounding her death, who knows where we'd be right now."

"Wouldn't that be awkward? You being a lead detective and me occasionally helping to solve crimes."

"Let me worry about that. I'm not looking for a romantic

entanglement with you. Tonight would be platonic."

Deep in my gut, parts of her statement comforted and disappointed me at the same time.

When I said nothing, she continued, "Look, I'd owe you one. You'd be doing me a huge favor."

"Now, Gomez—"

"Please, we've known each other long enough. Let's drop the formality. Call me Gina."

"Gina," I said, trying it on for size. My agenda for the day consisted of working during the midday and coming home. My social life was nonexistent. I'd been hesitant to get back out and spend time with friends. Most of them were originally Autumn's anyway, and there was always an awkwardness when I was around them. The close friends I had when I went to Coastal Carolina all drifted in different directions in the years since graduation. An evening with Gina Gomez. Why not? What did I have to lose? "Okay. I'm in. Tell me more about this fashion show."

* * *

She picked me up at my place at ten till seven that evening. I wore a navy blazer over a Ralph Lauren button-up shirt that I kept buried in my closet for special occasions and a pair of Kenneth Cole khakis. Name brands are something my brother, Bo, told me were important. I've never cared. Tonight was different. This was Gina Gomez off the clock. I wanted her to see that I tried to look presentable. A final pose in the bathroom mirror as Gomez arrived informed me that I had accomplished that mission.

The sun was on its descent to the bottom of the horizon for the day. Orange and purple clouds traced designs in the sky to the west. The Evening Star, Venus, glimmered in the southern sky. A soft cool breeze fluttered across my exposed skin, a hint of the evolving seasons. Changing leaves rustled. One of my neighbors was grilling hamburgers. I couldn't tell which one, but the unmistakable aroma floated in the air.

For once, she wasn't driving her police-issue sedan. A shiny blue newish Toyota Camry sat in the driveway, still dripping with water from a nearby car wash. Tinted windows obscured Gomez, but I could see her form applying lipstick in the rearview mirror.

I went around to the passenger side and opened the door. A Tahitian vanilla fragrance from an air freshener dangling from the rearview mirror whacked me in the face as I sat down in the comfortable leather seat. She was placing the tube of lipstick back in her slim pocketbook when I said, "Hello, Detective Gina."

The contrast of lipstick to shiny, white teeth revealed a rarity. She smiled and looked radiant even in the dim car interior. I couldn't see exactly what she was wearing, but it fit her well. She laughed. "Clark, when I told you to stop calling me Gomez and call me Gina, it also meant that you could drop the formality of Detective."

I smiled back. How couldn't I? "I know. Thanks for picking me up."

"It's no problem. I figured it would be easy since you were on the way from my place to the Chapin Museum. Then, I tried to navigate this maze in Deerfield and had to turn around to find your place."

A grin spread across my face. "That's one thing I love about this place and being on a dead-end street. The only traffic is from the people who live here. No one passes through my section of the neighborhood at random."

"It has its benefits. You look handsome."

My cheeks warmed. "Thank you. You had the benefit of seeing me outside your car. I can't see you too well, but I'm sure you look lovely."

She tugged at the hem of her dress. "This old thing? I keep it in the back of my closet for these rare occasions. Don't know the last time I wore it. I was thrilled that I still fit into it. Too many heavy lunches with Moody doesn't do the body good."

"I can imagine. Welcome to Myrtle Beach."

"Not a dieter's paradise." A smile crossed her face.

"That it is not."

In a more serious tone, she said, "Listen, no shoptalk this evening. No murders, no nothing."

That was all I ever spoke to Gomez, er Gina, about. What would we discuss? I was never one for small talk. "Sure thing."

She put the car in gear and wound our way back out of the neighborhood and turned left onto Business 17, heading toward Myrtle Beach. We cruised by the Ocean Lakes, Lakewood Resort, and Pirate Land Campgrounds, and the state park before veering right onto the start of Ocean Boulevard. A large wooden sign welcoming tourists to Myrtle Beach stood in the V of grass and palm trees.

We took the first right onto Springmaid Boulevard past an enormous sculpture of an octopus made of plastic jugs. The last time I was on this street was the morning when Moody summoned me at what I thought was the behest of Gomez to look at the body of Connor West. I kept this thought to myself. No shoptalk.

We pulled into a lit parking lot. Attendees were climbing

from their vehicles as other cars rolled in. The sun had gone down in the fifteen minutes since we left my driveway, leaving behind a black sky. Venus still glittered and was joined by a bright Jupiter and dimmer Saturn up above out over the ocean.

Since meeting her, I had only seen Gomez out of her work clothes once when I met her and Moody at the Bar-B-Cue House in Surfside to lay out what happened the morning of Paige Whitaker's death. On that occasion, she wore a jogging outfit.

We climbed from the car, and I got my first look at Gina in her dress. My breath caught. Her dress was satin, green, revealing, and hugged all the right places. It matched her eyes.

She looked over at me and said in a stern tone, "Pick your chin up off the ground, Clark."

"Sorry," I muttered. She made no apologies for her appearance, nor did she need to. Her hair was curled and draped over her shoulders. She wore the right amount of makeup. Just enough to cover whatever blemishes she may have, of which there had to be very few.

She pulled two tickets from her handbag, closed it, and allowed it to dangle from her shoulder on a chain. "Let's go."

We walked side by side across the lot to the front stairs. She hooked an arm around my elbow halfway. I wasn't sure what was happening, but I liked it. Autumn was the farthest thought from my mind. I wasn't sure if that was a good or sad thing. Probably good.

Then it hit me what this was. My mouth went dry. The uninhibited laughter, the last-minute makeup touchup as I climbed in the car, the form-fitting dress, our closeness as we climbed the steps to the entrance. This wasn't an invitation to a fashion show, but a date. A date, date. She made a reservation at

Travinia's in Market Common after the event. I hadn't been on a date in twenty years. She had said she needed a date, but I thought she meant the word as a formality. She used the word "platonic" when calling me, but right now, this felt anything but platonic.

We stood in a queue of the well-dressed Myrtle Beach upper class waiting for entry. Nobody was home on the Golden Mile because they were all here. At least, that's what the snarky voice in the back of my mind said. Gomez and I were out of our element. No wonder she didn't want to come alone. I was here for moral support as well, a job which I was ready to perform.

"Detective Gomez!" a voice boomed to our right. We turned to see mayor Sid Rosen angling toward us with his wife in tow.

"Mayor Rosen," Gomez said as he held out his hand for me to shake.

I did, and said, "Mayor Rosen, good to see you here."

"You too, Clark." He turned to Gomez, forgetting to introduce us to his wife. She stood beside him with a bored expression on her face. "I wanted to thank you for the work you did with the John Allen Howard case."

"It was nothing," Gomez said. "It was open and shut. Clark was there that evening and contained the situation."

He regarded me with a skeptical eye. "Yes, I'd heard that. Thank you too."

"No problem," I said. Rosen was a defense attorney before running for mayor. He spent a good deal of time in the courthouse around Autumn, and we had met at various functions before her passing. We used to be on the Myrtle Beach Downtown Development Corporation together before my escapade at OceanScapes caused me to vacate my role.

"Good to see you both here," he said and gestured ahead at

the growing line. "I'll see you inside. Come on, dear."

His nameless wife moved with him, offering a tight smile and wave as she passed. She was a new model, I think.

As Gomez and I moved forward, she said under her breath, "I hate this. Chief Kluttz was supposed to have been here, but she hates these events as much as I do. They're perfunctory. She only does these to help with the police image, but word on the street is that she's on her way out. Her husband is retiring, and they're thinking of moving up north to be near their grandchildren."

"That's news. I thought you said no talk about police work."

She squeezed my arm. "I know, but sometimes there's no way around it."

"Look at it as a compliment to you. If Kluttz wouldn't come, she'd still want to do what was best for the department. I mean, look at you. Putting their best face forward was you."

"Sometimes, Clark, I don't know when you're being sarcastic or nice." She leaned back and regarded me. I held a straight face. "I think you're being sincere."

"Of course. Why wouldn't I be?"

"For the reasons I just mentioned."

"Oh, yeah. Those." I explained, "No, you've been in the news more recently, beyond the two murderers we caught, for good reasons. You helped bust a drug cartel and a human trafficking ring. If I'm Kluttz and ready to ride off into the sunset, I'd want to leave the department in the best shape, and that would include trotting their current MVP out on occasions like this."

If I had said something like that to Autumn, she would have given me a big hug and thank you. Gomez was of a different variety. She punched me lightly on the shoulder. "You're sweet."

We arrived at a podium, where a well-groomed young man wearing a starched white button-up shirt and bow tie was taking tickets behind a host stand. The words "Franklin G. Burroughs - Simeon B. Chapin Art Museum" were engraved in gray concrete above the door. Locals called it the "Chapin Museum" for short.

"Welcome," he said, taking Gomez's proffered tickets.

"Thank you," she and I said at the same time.

We entered through the open doors and into the museum.

As we attempted to get our bearings, a deep voice in an Appalachian accent said to me, "Hey, I recognize you."

I turned to see who spoke. Before us was a tall man, perhaps a tad overweight, with glasses and hair cut close to the scalp. He wore a brown houndstooth jacket and khakis. His wife's head barely came to his broad shoulders. She had bright red hair in an updo and wore a purple dress that accentuated her curves.

They didn't look familiar to me. "Excuse me?"

"You came into Wicked Tuna a couple months ago." He glanced at Gomez and came back to me. "With a different woman. You were wanting to look at the parking lot footage for some reason."

Then it dawned on me. "Wait. Aren't you one of the part owners? Weren't you two there enjoying some adult beverages?"

The man held up a plastic cup filled with rum and Coke. A few droplets splashed over the rim. "That's right."

Gomez and the redhead smiled at each other. At the same time, they said, "Hello."

"Looks like you've been here for a little bit already," I observed.

"We have. I like to be punctual."

"Look," I said, "thanks for allowing Beth to show us the feeds. It helped to solve a crime."

"Oh really? You'll have to tell me about it sometime." He

stuck out a hand. "Caleb."

I shook it. "Clark Thomas. This is Gina Gomez."

"Hello," Gomez said again.

"And I'm Tasha," the red-headed wife said.

"I believe I interviewed you at Wicked Tuna during the Connor West case," Gomez said.

Caleb bobbed his chin and looked her up and down. "Yeah, you did. Didn't recognize you."

"Look, it was nice to meet you," I said, "maybe we'll catch up later."

"Sounds good," Caleb said.

At that, we parted ways. After they moved off to speak to another couple, Gomez leaned close and said, "He was a bit of an oddball. Nice, but an oddball."

I laughed as we continued deeper into the museum.

We didn't make it much farther inside before a woman wearing an evening gown and a white feather boa taken from a Manhattan runway during Fashion Week greeted us. She was tall, rakishly thin, and had short silver hair swooped back on top, with smooth skin and ageless features. It was difficult to guess her age. She could have been as old as my mom or grandmother.

She clasped her hands together in front of her chest. "Why, you're the most handsome couple I've seen yet. Who are you?"

"I'm Detective Gina Gomez with the MBPD. This is my date, Clark Thomas. He owns the Myrtle Beach Reads bookstore up on the Boardwalk."

"Oh yes, I've seen him before on television." She studied Gomez up and down. "And I think I've seen you as well. You sure clean up well. Both of you do. Welcome to the show. I take it Gail didn't want to come?"

"No, she didn't," Gomez answered.

"Tisk, tisk. Sounds about right, but who could blame her? She's leaving. Why bother with this?" She waved a hand in the air to encompass the museum.

"So, you've heard?" Gomez said.

"I have ears everywhere," the woman said. Then to me, "I'm the museum director, Carmela Van Wyk."

"Nice to meet you," I said, shaking her hand. It was bony and weak.

"The pleasure is mine," she said.

"Are you involved with what happens to artwork when it's removed from your museum?"

"I am."

"We might have a mutual acquaintance."

"Oh, who?"

"Cade Howard. The son of the composer, John Allen Howard."

"What happened to him was so tragic," she said. "Why do you think I would know his son?"

The hair stood on the back of my neck. "He told me he's an art broker, and he's arranged for paintings from here to be sold to private buyers."

Her eyebrows narrowed. "No, that doesn't ring a bell."

I got out my phone and pulled up a photo of Cade after a few taps on the screen. I held it up to her. "This is Cade."

Gomez crossed her arms and bent forward, awaiting Carmela's response.

The museum director leaned closer for a better view. "Nope. Never seen him before in my life."

CHAPTER
TWENTY-NINE

We didn't stay for the fashion show. After Carmela said she had never seen Cade, and Gina asked others who worked at the museum who said the same thing, we exited the museum and raced back to her car.

"And you're sure Cade said he's done work with this museum before?" she asked as I strapped on my seatbelt.

"He specifically said he arranged sales with the Chapin Museum."

"Okay, then. I'd take you home and go pick up Moody, but we have no time to waste. We've already wasted enough of it."

"You think this makes Cade a prime suspect?"

"Innocent people don't lie about stuff like this," she said.

"Has anyone been in the Howard residence since that night?"

"We let a contractor come in and repair the leak in the roof. Officer Nichols was there the entire time to make sure he didn't disturb potential evidence."

"Has any of the family been back inside?"

"No, we wouldn't allow anyone even if they asked as we're still processing the scene. We asked the family to keep us informed of their whereabouts during our investigation." She wrapped a hand around her wrist and squeezed. "Cade flew off somewhere on business."

"You let him leave town?"

"I had no choice. He wasn't a suspect. Still isn't, despite what Carmela just told us. He kept us informed of his movements, so I know he's back in town."

"What if I could provide motive, means, and opportunity?"

"How would you do that?"

"I need back inside. Like tonight."

"You can't do that. I can't let you. The house is under police restriction."

"You're letting me come along to chat with Cade."

Her nostrils flared. "True, but this is different. There's no evidence you could tamper with."

"I wouldn't touch anything. I promise. You lead the way."

The lights of passing cars flashed off her body as we zoomed up Farrow Parkway, bound for the 17 Bypass. Our reservation at Travinia would have to wait. Her eyebrows lay heavy above her eyes. "Look, I appreciate what you've done, but I can't do that. I could lose my job."

"Didn't stop you before."

"That wasn't me that invited you to look at Connor West's body. That was Moody acting in what he thought was my best interests."

She had a point. With both the Paige Whitaker and West investigations, Gomez toed the company line and told me to keep my distance. I couldn't help it if circumstances and my natural curiosity got the better of me. Well, I could help the latter part of that, but chose not to.

"Okay, so now what?"

"We talk with Cade. We'll ask him to confirm what he said to you about dealing with Chapin."

"What if Carmela is correct, and he was lying to me?"

"I don't know. I'll have to sort that out."

"You know what I think?"

"No." She took her eyes off the road and locked onto mine. "Tell me."

I did. She pushed the accelerator to the floor.

* * *

If Cade had done it, the enormous question remained: how? He was in the laundry room on the main level when his dad was shot upstairs. Antonio saw him leave that room after hearing Erin scream. The answer lay in the house. I was sure of it. However, if Gomez pressured Cade and got him to confess, then my part was over, and I was along for the ride.

It disappointed part of me when Carmella and her staff said they had no clue who Cade was. Gomez and I were having a nice evening that was just getting started. It thrilled the other part of me to be back on the chase and possibly heading in a direction to catch the real killer.

The terrain got hillier once we entered Little River on 17. Up hills. Down hills. Not something I was used to living in the flatter Myrtle Beach area. Little River lies a few miles to the north of North Myrtle Beach and Cherry Grove. The sleepy fishing town awakens twice a year with the world-famous Blue Crab and Shrimp Festivals in the spring and fall. The events are so big that shuttles come across the river to bring event goers. I've been to them a few times and enjoyed fantastic music, and of course, seafood.

A variety of businesses, restaurants, gift shops, hotels, and golf courses lined both sides of the highway, lit by neon lights. The sun was long gone. Darkness dominated the night. The glow of the lights did little to push it back.

Gomez had plugged Cade's address into her navigation unit. It looked like his place was near where the festivals occur, off Mineola Avenue. We climbed a small hill before hooking a right onto the two-lane street. Gomez took the first left onto Forest Drive. Cade's house was the third one on the right, closer to the Intracoastal Waterway. The Big "M" Casino ship disembarks near here. I've been on it before, not to gamble, but to enjoy a cheap ocean cruise.

Gomez pulled into a driveway large enough for two cars to park. The house itself was not anything to call home about. The headlights from the Camry shined on a drab gray exterior of wooden horizontal siding and dark red shutters around the windows. A light above the front door on a small porch was lit, as was a light in one room on the right side of the house. Open blinds obscured the interior from our angle. A majestic oak tree swayed in the front yard to the left side of the parking area. Fingers of fog floated across the yard, coming from the Waterway.

I couldn't see the Cade I met buying this house, which led me to speculate that this must be a rental. Every other house in this neighborhood had For Sale signs placed in front of them. The property values here had skyrocketed like most neighborhoods in the Grand Strand. These houses were older. When attending the festivals, I met several people who lived nearby. Most of them were retired and had settled here decades ago. The equity they had in these houses must be enormous, with the housing market being what it was. I get calls and letters from realtors on an almost weekly basis, offering to assist in selling my home. My property value had increased as well, as reflected in the most recent property tax adjustment by the county, but I had no desire to sell. I liked where I was.

"Looks like someone is home," I said.

Gomez stared out the windshield. "It does."

"What do you want me to do? Wait here while you talk to him first?"

"No. You might as well come with me now. It will help if you're there while I ask him questions, so he'll be less likely to lie. He will know what he told you and will be forced to tell the truth."

She unbuckled her seatbelt, and I undid mine. We climbed from the car at the same time. The bass of pounding music vibrated from the home. She took charge and led the way up the two steps to the wood porch. A glass storm door fronted a plain wood door. The main door was cracked open, letting a sliver of light and music leak out.

Gomez rang the doorbell and then knocked on the glass. We looked out of place on this street at this time of night. I laughed.

"What's so funny?"

"Me and you." I had to speak louder over the boom, boom of the music.

"What about us?"

"You, looking the way you do in that dress, and me wearing what I am."

She cocked an eyebrow. "How do I look in this dress?"

I tried to keep my eyes locked on hers but failed. "This is going to sound weird coming out of my mouth to another woman, but gorgeous."

"Doesn't sound weird to me." She returned her attention to the door, where no one had responded to the knock or doorbell. "Hmm. Maybe he can't hear me over the music."

"I believe it."

After trying to summon him again and waiting a minute, I reached out and went to grab the latch on the storm door. She smacked my hand. I pulled it away and held it. "Ow!"

"Don't touch. I have a bad feeling about this." She kneeled and fiddled with something around her ankle. She stood, clutching the grip of a police-issue pistol between both hands.

My eyes grew as wide as saucers as my chest pounded in a rhythm as fast as the music emanating from within.

"Get back in the car," she commanded.

Gomez didn't need to tell me twice. I retreated down the steps as she tried the door latch. It opened. She yelled something I couldn't hear into the interior and held the gun pointing down in front of her with outstretched arms. She took a cautious step inside and disappeared.

I wasn't about to get back in the car as she ordered. I eased over to the room with the lit window and peeked in the horizontal blinds. The room within was an art studio of sorts. Tall speakers sat in the corner, blasting music. Four rows of Cade's artwork were lined in sloppy fashion on the floor against the far wall. Each row held different paintings, but each painting in the row was the same as the ones in front and behind. Cabinets containing art supplies lay against the wall next to the interior door. A half-finished painting of Elisha praying over a sick child sat on an easel in front of a window on the opposite side of the room.

The painting would never get completed.

Cade lay face down in a pool of blood on the floor with a bullet hole in the middle of his back.

CHAPTER
THIRTY

Gomez sent me home with Officer Nichols. I'd met her the morning I'd found Paige Whitaker's body. I almost joked that she and I needed to stop meeting like this, but it didn't feel appropriate. Her stern expression behind the wheel in the glow of the dash lights didn't invite small talk. It was the first time I had been in a police cruiser. I hoped it would be the last. At least I rode in the front seat and not in handcuffs in the back.

After she dropped me at my house and sped away, I went inside and changed clothes. This was the second time I had seen a dead body in recent days. Fourth time overall. At least with Cade, I never got too close to it. When Gomez had spotted him on the floor of the art studio, she'd locked me out and called for backup. That didn't sadden me. I had no intention of getting near him. Besides, I saw something in that room that confirmed something I'd suspected about Cade and provided a motive for killing his father. Even with Cade getting shot, that didn't mean he didn't pull the trigger on his dad.

As I tried to assimilate what Cade's murder meant in the grand scheme of this case, I pulled on a dark pair of Nike jogging pants and a light long-sleeve plain black shirt. Reaching into the top of my closet, I pulled down an old black beanie cap and put it on. I glanced in the mirror on my way out the door as I had done earlier and had to laugh at my appearance. It made me look like a robber from an old movie.

That wasn't too far from the case. It was time to break into a house.

* * *

I drove past the Howard house before parking to make sure no one was there. The yellow police tape crisscrossing the front door still stood out on this gloomy night. A night that had started out so well. That's the thing with living in Myrtle Beach. The weather changed from five minutes to the next.

I parked at the same beach access near the Howard mansion where I turned around the previous day to speak to Louise. I picked this one in particular because of the long parking lot from the street to the walkway leading onto the beach. Many of the parking areas along this stretch of the Golden Mile were shallower and only had enough space for a few vehicles to park. You couldn't park at the beach accesses this late at night, so I hoped a random police cruiser wouldn't pass by and see my Jeep parked at the end of the lot. This was one time I was grateful that the boxy vehicle was all black. It would hide well. I hoped.

Where the fog had crept onto Cade's property in Little River to the north, dense fog penetrated the coastline here. If there was ever a night to break into an abandoned house along the beach, it was tonight. My only fear was the security alarm. Would it be armed? I suspected it wouldn't be with the random police people who went in and out. I climbed from the Jeep and looked around. The clock on the dashboard read 1:32. Dense fog obscured the houses to either side of the access. The main street wasn't visible from where I stood, making me optimistic that the Jeep wouldn't get spotted. An onshore breeze blew against my skin and the tall sea oats on the dunes. The briny smell of the ocean was strong tonight. A car horn honked in the distance. Besides the waves crashing onshore, all was silent. My feet scuffled across the wood planks of the entry point before quieting in the sand. The rubber soles of the shoes I wore squeaked with each step as I made my way to the beach.

I hugged the dunes as I made my way past the two houses between the beach access and John Allen's estate. The first house was dark and still. With the power back on in the area, the vacant house next to John Allen's had landscape lighting that lit both sides of the tall building. The windows inside were dark.

I jumped the gate that spanned the path leading from John Allen's estate to the beach and threaded my way around the pool to the steps rising to the back deck. It seemed insane that people would invest so much in security and fencing for the side of the home facing the street and be so lax in protecting the side facing the ocean. Always be aware of an attack from the rear. Sounded like something Sun Tzu would have written in The Art of War, but I hadn't read that since a literature course in college. DeeDee mentioned that John Allen wanted tightened defenses at his new house after having a break-in at his old one in Hollywood. It made no sense.

Enough of the ambient light spilled over to the side facing me to make out details on the house next door. The tornado had ripped most of the siding away, revealing the plastic DuPont house wrap underneath. A hole, way up near the eave of the roof, caught my attention. It was jagged and long, like that of the path gouged by a meteor when it plummets to the ground.

Focus, I told myself, shaking my head.

I climbed the steps to the deck and crossed to the door, stopping beside a heavy planter containing a tall hibiscus. The night darkened its purple blooms. The interior of the house was darker.

Returning my attention back to what I was doing, I tilted the heavy planter back, reaching a hand underneath. I grunted at the effort. My hand felt something cool and flat. I clenched my hand around it and pulled it out. I set the planter back in its position and held up a key.

Erin had given me the blueprint for getting back into this house while she was in her temporary holding cell upstairs. I thanked her for it as I slid the key into the lock on the back door and turned it. If the alarm sounded, I'd run like the wind back to the Jeep, hoping the police response time this time of night would be sluggish.

I took one last look around. No one was visible. Nothing stirred, besides the palm trees in the wind and the water in the pool. The outdoor furniture was still scattered about. Fog blanketed everything.

The knob twisted. I let out a quick, deep breath before pulling the door open. My heart raced. Silence.

I let myself in on tiptoes and closed the door gently behind me. My plan was to replay the shooting from the perspective of each suspect to see if the timing would work. Only a minute passed between the shot and Erin's scream. Whoever shot John Allen would have had to rush back to their position with no one seeing them.

I started in the laundry room where Cade said he was. The younger man was in better shape than me, but I wasn't sure he'd be able to shave many seconds off my time. I walked around to the table in the middle of the laundry room where Cade might have been folding clothes when the tornado struck. Pulling out my phone, I loaded the stopwatch function and started it. I ran from the room as fast as I could to the stairs by the front door. Each step echoed in the cavernous space. I looked out the windows on the front side of the house, expecting to see a phalanx of police cruisers with flashing lights pulled up front trying to get into the gate and arrest me for trespassing. Instead, the driveway and street were as still and quiet as everything else outside tonight.

I pounded up the stairs to the landing and across to the office before stopping in the center.

"Dad, how could you!" I whispered in a harsh tone, trying to reenact something the murderer could have said before pulling the trigger without being too loud. After firing an imaginary shot with my finger gun, I pretended to drop the gun and ran from the room, back down the stairs and into the laundry room, stopping the stopwatch. 3:23.

"Hmm," I said. Too long.

Of everyone there that evening, Cade and Erin were in the best shape. She looked like a jogger. He looked like a gymnast. He was muscular and didn't have an ounce of fat on him. Antonio was fleshy. Preacher was thin. Louise was bony, weak, and was with me. DeeDee didn't look like she'd exercised since the turn of the century.

None of the timings worked. I re-climbed the stairs to the great room and the fireplace. A familiar painting hung there. The night of the dinner party was the first time I had seen it. I saw it again on my video chat with David Weller. A picture I took using my phone of the conversation confirmed it. Then I saw this painting again inside Cade's art studio. A row of them was on the floor, leaning against a wall. A half-finished version had sat on his easel.

This was what I wanted to show Gomez. It was nice to have a suspicion confirmed, but in this case, now it didn't matter.

Now that I thought about it, coming here wasn't necessary tonight. I had a one-track mind focused on finding proof. Well, here it was and now it meant nothing.

"Stupid," I said to myself, returning downstairs to the back door.

The dining room table lay beside the back door. A built-in bench seat on the walls formed an L shape on two sides of the table. The other sides had normal chairs. When Erin gave Chris and me a tour of the house, she mentioned all the hidey holes the architect had built into the home.

That evening, after John Allen's death, as I roved around the house questioning everyone, there was one constant. Cade. He sat on the bench seat nearest to the door. He didn't get up. He didn't move until the police came and forced him to. Chris noted that he had drunk nothing. Now I understood why. Cade didn't want to get up to pee.

I walked around the table, kneeled beside the bench seat, and turned on the flashlight function on my phone. The hinges creaked in protest as I lifted the seat. I gulped and found something I never expected, but it made everything fall into place.

CHAPTER
THIRTY-ONE

I called Gomez and told her I knew who did both killings. She asked how I figured it out. I told her and had her gather the suspects at the Howard Estate the following morning at ten. I fell asleep hoping Erin was doing the same as comfortably as possible in her prison cell.

The next morning, bright-eyed and bushy-tailed, everyone gathered inside the mansion around the kitchen. I included Erin's attorney, Eric Paulicap, in the matter. He'd dressed in another expensive suit and didn't seem as perky as he was the other day in court. I reminded myself that he lived on the West Coast, so my 10 a.m. meeting was like 7 a.m. to him. He needed a cappuccino from the Astra espresso machine. I did too but opted for a bottle of water.

After I'd left here last night and called Gomez, I had gone home and slept for a few hours before getting up at the crack of dawn, brewing a pot of coffee, and preparing what I was about to say. All of that was difficult to accomplish because I couldn't get the image of Gina Gomez in that dress out of my mind. We were having a splendid evening before speaking to Carmella at the art museum.

Gina stood next to me behind the kitchen island,

unfortunately, not in the green dress, but in her normal blue pants suit work uniform. Her hair was bouncy and pulled back into her customary ponytail. It smelled like she had washed it this morning. Moody stood on the other side, sipping coffee from a McDonald's cup.

Before us stood Paulicap with his hands in his pockets. The rest of the dinner attendees, sans Cade, were present. DeeDee and Antonio stood on opposite sides of the kitchen, not making eye contact. Louise sat on a stool on the other side of the island, still wearing her nightgown. Who cared about the niceties of fashion when you were her age and didn't give a hoot? She wore a white wig with curly hair for the occasion. Preacher and Chris huddled together to the side. I heard them talking about cars before I cleared my throat, causing everyone to stop speaking and look at me.

"Good morning, everyone," I said. Well, it was a good morning for everyone except for one person in the room. Their next stop after here was in the back of a police cruiser. More might follow.

DeeDee cast her eyes around the gathering. "Where's Cade?"

I let Gomez handle this part.

"DeeDee," she said, "I'm sorry to inform you that your brother is dead."

Everyone gasped. DeeDee's hands rushed to her mouth as she collapsed in a heap. Antonio rushed over and put his arms around her shoulders.

"What?" Louise shouted, barely holding herself upright.

Gomez pursed her lips. "We found him dead in his home last night with a bullet wound in his back. We're not sure how long he had been like that."

"Who would do that?" Preacher demanded.

She pretended to ignore his question and said, "I was there a good chunk of the night. We've tried talking to his neighbors to see if anyone had heard or seen anything. He lives far enough apart from the surrounding homes that it's possible we'll come up with nothing from that perspective."

The lines under her eyes betrayed a lack of sleep. Of us all, she likely had the least amount of rest. Came with the job. It was my turn to take over. I knew who killed him.

"It's a sad turn of events. It really is," I said, tapping the counter. "The demise of one of the great modern-day composers, and the death of his son, a talented artist in his own right. I've learned that life has many paths. If you find yourself walking down what you think is the wrong one, you might be on the right course, but treading through a treacherous curve in the path before getting to where you want to go. Maybe that's where Cade was at this point in his life. But I'll get to that in a moment."

I had everyone's attention except for DeeDee's. I continued, "John Allen unfortunately gets ill, loses his wits, and all of you, except Erin, tried to figure out how to get his money before the others did. You should be ashamed of yourselves."

DeeDee sat straight and started to say something, but the stern expressions from Gomez and Moody kept her silent.

"This past Monday, I received an invitation from Erin to attend a dinner party at her dad's behest. I learned that he enjoyed having dinner with interesting people, and he'd learned about me solving a few crimes. What she or I didn't know was that he had ulterior motives for inviting me. You kept him confined in this house under an at-home prison sentence. He was sick with Alzheimer's."

"Yes," DeeDee interrupted. "He couldn't take care of himself, and we didn't want the public to see him like that."

"That might be true," I said, "but that didn't mean he didn't have the faculties to put two and two together. Erin told me that there had been two attempts on his life recently. One being his cane. Someone had tampered with it, cutting it so it would break if he put too much weight on it. It did, and he tumbled down the front steps here and had to be taken to the emergency room. Thankfully, the injuries weren't severe. Erin said the cane looked like it had broken cleanly and looked cut. Unfortunately, the cane ended up in the trash and is now somewhere at the landfill in Conway."

"Good heavens," Louise said.

I didn't acknowledge her comment and continued. "There are multiple tools down in the garage that could have made the cut. Everyone in this room had access to them. The police could dust them for prints to see what pops up."

"Hey now," Preacher said. "Antonio, Cade, and I all used those tools. Cade borrowed them for woodworking. Antonio and I used them for the odd job around the house."

"Well," I said, biting a fingernail, "Never mind on that. The fact remains, you had access to them and could have grabbed the cane at any time to tamper with it. Which brings us to the second attempt on his life. He somehow took the wrong medications, or too much of one, and had to make a return trip to the ER. Erin typically managed his pill schedule but said DeeDee and Cade knew it too in case she wasn't around. I don't know who was here the day that happened or who gave him the pills, but it's possible one of you switched them."

"That's something we can ask Erin about," Gomez said. "Who all was here that day."

Moody grunted. I kicked myself for not asking Erin that question.

"Let's get back to John Allen and his condition. You all treated him like an invalid, but I think he was more aware of his surroundings than you gave him credit for or wanted to admit. I believe he invited me here, not because he thought I was an interesting person, but he wanted me to figure out who was trying to kill him."

"Makes sense in retrospect," Antonio said, looking at everyone for agreement. No one joined him.

"I don't think he was as advanced in his disease as you make out. Sure, his doctors might have told him that upon examination, but the old man had the frame of mind to collect evidence and lay it out nice and neat for me to see."

"Evidence? What evidence?" Louise said.

I stroked my chin. "He had arranged documents on his bed that had information about each of you. Documents that painted a picture of everyone trying to take advantage of him." I swung to DeeDee. "He entrusted you with the running of his charity organization. I'm sure you did honorable deeds, but that didn't stop you from selling certain collectible instruments in the underground economy, as you put it, and keeping part of the proceeds for yourself. The IRS was after you, and you knew you faced time in prison for your deeds.

"At first, I thought that could be why DeeDee would kill her dad. Then, I learned it can take a long time to settle an estate the size of John Allen's. By the time she would have gotten any money, she'd be in jail. She might go to jail anyway, and it would serve you right." My eyes narrowed on the eldest sibling. DeeDee withered under my glare. I pressed forward. "However, she didn't kill her dad or brother."

Her shoulders sagged in relief while shooting me a menacing

glare. She had regained her composure after hearing the news about her younger brother. DeeDee was back.

My attention turned to the man beside her next. "Antonio. You had opened a life insurance policy for his charity, but he abruptly canceled it. You told me it was because you couldn't get him the rate you promised. That may be true, but it also means you lose out on a hefty pay day. It's possible you had more business in the works with John Allen, but he relented after his first experience with you. You might have wanted to murder him out of spite or worked with DeeDee to get the job done. She stood to gain a substantial inheritance upon his death. A chunk for herself and another for the charity. Of the three children, she stood to gain the most. His death wouldn't help her in the short run with the feds breathing down her back, but it could help you if you married her."

Antonio and DeeDee looked at each other and took a step apart. This wasn't my place to mention that Antonio had a ring for her in his desk. That was between them. I said, "But Antonio didn't do it either."

"Thank you," he said as though I was the Wizard of Oz granting him a brain.

Next up was Preacher. I swung to him. "You're nothing but a thief."

He placed a hand on the back of his neck and fumbled for the words before he spoke. "What are you talking about?"

"John Allen had a list of cash transactions on his bed with no name on it. By process of elimination, they had to have belonged to you. You yourself told me you had been investing in an offshore account for him. After listening to you describe the fund and how it pays out, I don't think your fund exists. I think it's a small-scale

Ponzi scheme. You took payments from investors promising grand returns and kept the money for yourself."

His voice deepened. "Where's your proof?"

"I don't have any, but I can prove that you're a thief in another way."

He snorted. "Oh, yeah, how's that?"

"When the tornado hit, you and Chris were together in the garage. You disappeared and said you went across to the studio for protection. You left Chris to fend for himself. An altruistic person would have grabbed Chris and went into the safer room. But it wasn't the safety you were after, was it? It was John Allen's hidden safe."

His eyes darted to Gomez and Moody. Officers Nichols and O'Brien were nearby. "Don't know what you're talking about."

"That night, after you and Chris showed me around the garage, I lagged to check out the studio, but it was locked. Unless you did that on your way out, you couldn't have gotten in. There had to be another reason you ditched Chris. I think it was opportunity. Not an opportunity to kill John Allen, but an opportunity to grab a stack of cash. In the hallway between the garage and studio, there's a gold record hanging on the wall. Behind that gold record is a safe. A safe that is still open."

"What's in the safe?" Chris said.

"That's just it. Nothing. Preacher was investing five-hundred dollars at a time of John Allen's money into his bogus fund. Neither of them wanted the money traced, and that amount would keep it below the feds' notice. At least they hoped. Sure, that meant there were a lot of transactions to equal the five-hundred K, but if the returns were large enough, that amount of work was minor. At least to Preacher. My belief is that John Allen had a substantial amount of cash in that safe and Preacher had the combination so he could get his payments at their appointed times. I can't prove that, but a warrant from a judge to search Preacher's home and office might turn up something."

"Might turn up a few surprises," Moody grumbled.

Preacher took a step back away from the uniformed officers and stared at the floor.

"I know Daddy always had stacks of cash on hand for his own reasons, but I never knew where he kept it," DeeDee said.

"For that reason. Preacher didn't kill John Allen. Why kill the goose that lays the golden eggs?" I rested a hand on the counter and rubbed a finger across its smooth surface. "Let's go back to the moment when we heard the gun go off. Preacher and Chris were on the lowest level. Antonio was concealed in the kitchen here." I tapped a finger on the counter where I stood to show his hiding place, then hooked a thumb over my shoulder toward the corner of the house. "Cade was in the laundry room. Louise was upstairs with me in a closet. DeeDee was in a bathroom upstairs, around the corner from the office. Erin was in John Allen's bedroom next door. Those two were the closest to him when the tornado struck."

I paused, unsure how to explain the next part without revealing that I entered the house a few hours ago. "When no one was looking, I used the stopwatch on my phone to time how long it would take to run from each hiding spot to the office and back. It seemed like less than two minutes passed between the shot, the tornado passing through, and Erin's scream upon finding her dad."

I held up a finger. "Here's the thing. No one outside of Erin or DeeDee could have done it. I'm in decent shape, and I couldn't run as fast as I could from any of the positions in less than three minutes, make it back, and not be huffing and puffing at the end. I even added in time to make choice words to John Allen's ghost, which I would have imagined happened when he saw the gun pointed at him. When I found Erin and all of you came after me, none of you looked like you'd exerted that much physical effort.

"When there's no possible way something happened, then it probably didn't. Once I realized that all our perceptions of that evening were wrong, I thought about it from a different perspective."

"Then who did it?" DeeDee asked.

I didn't directly answer her question yet. I had more to go. "I never got to meet John Allen. It's a shame. You see, he was dead before I arrived that evening."

CHAPTER
THIRTY-TWO

"Whoa, whoa," Antonio said. "Back up. What do you mean, he was already dead?"

"Here's a simple question for all of you. Did any of you see him that evening before his murder?"

DeeDee and Antonio shared a puzzled look. Both shook their heads.

Preacher rubbed his chin. "Did I see him? Nope. He was in his office or bedroom the entire time. I wasn't sure where exactly."

"What was happening when you got here?"

"Let's see," he said. "Erin was in her room getting ready. Cade came from the laundry room and answered the door when I rang. Louise, Antonio, and DeeDee were all upstairs getting their drink on."

"Besides Erin, who lives here, who were the first people to arrive that evening?" I asked, already knowing the answer.

"Cade had been here all afternoon," DeeDee said. "Louise was here when Antonio and I arrived. Preacher came after us."

"And you didn't see your dad?"

She gave a slight headshake.

"Thank you," I said.

"That just leaves Cade and Louise," the attorney, Eric, intoned.

I had watched him out of the corner of my eye during my summation. He had spoken to Erin and received the same story I had from her. His hands kept their spot in his pockets as he shifted from leg to leg. Right now, he was smiling.

Moody and Gomez had remained mostly quiet to this point, content to allow me to do my thing. Right now, I felt like my insides were vibrating. Veins were popping out on my arms from a faster heartbeat. There was a lightness in my head from the adrenaline rush. I took a drink of water to slake my dry mouth and recenter.

"Here's how it went down." I stopped and looked straight at one person. "But you know how it happened, don't you, Louise?"

She twirled the diamond stud earring in her right ear between two fingers. Her mouth opened and closed times before rasping, "Whatever do you mean, Clark. I was with you when the gun went off."

"That's true," I said. "You were. You had the perfect alibi, but you were in John Allen's office when you fired the shot that killed him."

"No," she said.

I ignored Louise's protest. "John Allen left behind love letters, handwritten by Louise to him. Letters that Penthouse magazine would have censored."

Preacher and Chris stared at Louise's bony, wrinkly back and curled their lips. DeeDee made a choking sound. Antonio pulled the collar of his shirt up over his mouth. My stomach did a flip-flop at the thought as well. Eric, Gomez, Moody, and the two officers maintained stoic expressions. They had heard worse.

"I checked Louise's background. She's been married three times. Each husband passed away suddenly. There was an investigation into the last one that went nowhere. While there's no proof she killed her husbands, a questionable pattern is there where one might suspect there was some shady dealings."

"I loved each of my husbands," Louise said. "All of us led happy lives together."

"That doesn't mean you didn't try, or succeed, to kill them," I said. "If you did it to them, you had the courage to do it again."

"Where does Cade come into this?" Preacher said.

"He said he was an art broker," I said, holding up a finger, "when, in fact, he was nothing more than an art forger. You were all sitting around the table when he told me one museum he did business with was the Chapin one here in Myrtle Beach."

"He did say that," DeeDee said. "He traveled around the country brokering deals."

"At least that's what he claimed," I said. "Maybe he did at first. DeeDee, you and your sister told me how artistically gifted he was."

"I did," she agreed.

"That may be well and good, but he didn't do business with the Chapin Museum. Last night, Gomez and I met the woman who runs it. She nor her staff had ever seen Cade before."

"What?" DeeDee said. The question contained the type of disappointed venom one can only have when finding out a family member lied to them.

"It's true," Gomez said. "Clark first caught wind of this when he held a video chat with your dad's friend, David Weller."

I pointed at the ceiling. "The painting your dad has above the fireplace is the same one Weller had on the wall behind his desk. Both came from Cade. We went to Cade's house after Gomez and I left the museum last night when we discovered his body in the studio. There were dozens of identical paintings to that one and others inside. He was doing the same paintings over and over and selling them across the country like they were originals."

"That little--" DeeDee said, before Gomez cut her off with a glare.

I said, "The reason I contacted Weller was because he and your dad had been in contact in recent weeks. Weller hated phone calls and preferred video chats, so your dad likely saw the identical painting in his friend's office. John Allen, Alzheimer's and all, figured out what Cade was doing. My guess is that he confronted Cade about it and was going to turn him into the authorities, bringing down the house of cards." I turned to Louise. "Is this ringing any bells?"

She had no answer.

"Cade's near-violent reaction when we found John Allen in his office was nothing but a front." I explained, "He planned this with Louise. She shot John Allen with the silenced gun before everyone arrived, grabbed the gun in his desk, laid it on the floor, ran into his bedroom, and threw her gun down the laundry chute where Cade was folding his clothes. He was wearing mesh shorts during all this, and knew he had to hide the gun and silencer. It would stick out if he kept it in a pocket. He used the cover of the storm to fire the shot and then run into the dining room while everyone ran upstairs. So, he hid it in the storage space below the bench seat. He was the last one to join us in John Allen's office. Afterward, he came downstairs and sat on top of it all night."

Gomez said to Louise, "We're getting a warrant to search your home as we speak."

"Ah, that's why he wasn't drinking any water or alcohol," Chris said. "He didn't want to get up to pee."

"Exactly," I said, leveling a finger at him. "Since they met, Louise had Cade come over and did odd jobs for her. He probably needed the money. At some point, they became friends and hatched this plot together to make what would be the perfect murder. An idea that would benefit you both. Cade, from possibly going to jail for forgery, and Louise, a vindictive, jilted lover. You couldn't have known who would be first in the room. It didn't matter. There would be no prints on the gun. You knew that everyone who was going to be here that night had even the tiniest bit of motive. Whoever touched the gun first could have been the murderer. Your plan was that neither of you could be there first. That way you couldn't have the murder pinned on you."

"In one conversation I had with Louise, she told me she'd figured it would have been DeeDee holding the gun. She did that to throw me off the scent and further confuse the matter." I turned to her. "Bravo on that part. It worked for a time, but the clues were always going to point back to you. You may have gotten away with killing your first three husbands, but not this time."

Gomez placed a hand on my upper arm. "You might have gotten away with it had Clark been here."

I smiled. "The plan was for Louise and Cade to get here before the other guests. Cade used the cover that his washer and dryer were broken to do his laundry here."

"They weren't, by the way," Gomez said. "I tested them last night at his place. They work fine."

I nodded a silent "thank you" at her for confirming my suspicion. "They knew Erin would have to get ready on the other side of the house. That would be their opening. When she did, John Allen was in his office when Louise did the deed and Cade covered her tracks. My guess is that the plan was to kill him with the silenced gun early, and for Cade to fire a shot out the laundry room window later to make it sound like the murder happened at a different time."

I looked at the two detectives. "You'll find a hole gouged out in the outside wall high up on the house next door, where I figure you'll find a bullet matching the one that killed John Allen. Cade meant to fire one shot out the window into the air but hit the house instead. They couldn't have known about the tornado in advance, but it gave him the perfect cover to fire the shot, since everyone in the house was scattered at the time."

Antonio held up a hand. "What if someone discovered him in the office before he'd fired his gun from the laundry room?"

"Great question," I said. "That would work for them, too. It might make the person who found him look guilty, but if not, then you'd still have to figure out who did it. They made sure that someone would get caught with the gun, either with it on the floor or in their hand. Erin found him first and didn't think not to pick the gun up off the floor."

Louise crossed her arms. "You can't prove any of this."

"Oh, but I can," I said. "I'll wager that they'll find your fingerprints all over John Allen's desk. Even if you'd wiped his hidden gun free of prints, unless you were wearing gloves, you would have left prints behind. We'll find your prints in Cade's house too. Won't we? You murdered him to cover your tracks. He let you into his house, maybe to look at his artwork. When he led you into his art studio, you shot him in the back. The music was turned up loud. So loud we could hear it outside the house. Loud enough to cover a gunshot."

She gulped.

I pressed forward. "There's something else too. I think when you shot John Allen, staged the room, and left, he was still alive. He was already there writing music and managed to finish his composition before dying. Erin said he loved puzzles. He was famous for it, leaving codes in the music he composed. His friend Peter Hinkle told me about John Allen writing a composition with his daughter's name hidden in it."

"I remember that," DeeDee said.

I tapped my chin with an index finger. "That got me thinking. Maybe he tried to leave one last one behind, but he couldn't finish his sentence before dying. What were his last words? Remember?"

"Uh." Preacher said, pinching the skin between his eyebrows. "He said something about 'it being in something.' What 'it' was, he didn't say."

"That's right. He said, 'It's in the,' and that was it. I never had a chance to meet the man, but I feel like we would have been good friends. He could have just come out and said who the killer was, but he left one last puzzle to solve." I pulled out my phone and lit the screen to display the picture I had ready. "On a whim, I took a picture of the staff music sheet he was working on at the time of his death. As you can see," I showed the screen to Gomez, "all the musical notes he hand-drew are neat until you get to the last six. There's even a bit of blood streaked across the section, which meant he drew these after Louise shot him."

I held out the screen and motioned for DeeDee and Preacher to come nearer. "You two are the ones who played music with John Allen. Is there a message in the last notes?"

Preacher held out a hand and took the phone from me. I was glad to let him have it. He and DeeDee huddled close and stared at the screen, their eyebrows creased in concentration.

"Oh man," Preacher said after after studying the image.

"What does it say?" Eric asked.

DeeDee looked away from the phone and turned to him, wiping away a tear running down the side of her face. "Louise."

One by one, everyone turned their attention to the old woman hunching on a stool. She tried to defend herself. "Maybe he was writing me a love song."

"That's garbage and you know it. There's more," I said, then moved around the kitchen island and into the dining room. Everyone followed. Moody went around to the stool on which Louise sat to make sure she joined us. "Those who knew John Allen knew he loved puzzles. I was told as much before his death. My conversation with Peter Hinkle revealed that John Allen had put his daughter's name into an arrangement. I have no musical inclination whatsoever, but I learned about musical cryptography a couple of years ago on a local classical station and knew there was something called the 'Sophia Cipher.' It made me wonder if that's what John Allen did here at the end. His last words were cut off, but I'd wager that he was trying to say, 'It's in the music.'"

I cleared my throat and continued. "When Erin gave us a tour of the home, she said there were cubby holes everywhere for hidden storage. One place being the bench seat on one side of the dining room table." I looked at Moody and pointed at the seat. "Cade sat there all night. Detective, can you lift the seat and tell us what's inside?"

"Gladly," Moody muttered, pulling on a pair of evidence gloves.

He lifted the wood seat with a creak, grunted, reached down, and pulled up a sleek black pistol fitted with a silencer.

CHAPTER
THIRTY-THREE

Forensics found Louise and Cade's fingerprints all over the gun. An amateur move in a diabolical plan. Any armchair expert in murder mysteries would tell you to use gloves or wipe for prints.

With a warrant in hand, Gomez and her crew found the weapon that killed Cade, along with a cache of other handguns at Louise's house.

Eric Paulicap shook my hand afterward and handed me a thick business card. Told me to call him if I was ever in Los Angeles or if I ever needed any legal help. I thanked him and gave him mine as well. He went to work and saw that they released his client within hours of Louise being arrested for the murders of John Allen and Cade Howard.

I went home and slept.

* * *

Three mornings later, Margaret and Karen were stocking a new shipment of books in the store. I was behind the coffee counter making myself a café au lait when Erin and Chris walked through the door and came to me. He carried a large, gift-wrapped box under one thick arm. The wrapping paper was illustrations of books.

"Good morning." I smiled.

It was the first time I had seen Erin since her release. She glowed. Without asking, she came around the counter and wrapped me in an enormous hug. The familiar intoxicating scent of her perfume blossomed in the air. Chris set the box on top of the counter with a thump.

"Thank you. Thank you. Thank you. Thank you," she squealed. "Who knows if I would have gotten out of there without you."

She let go and stood back.

"You're quite welcome," I said. "Although your attorney seemed more than capable. I'm sure he would have found the truth."

"Yes," she said, "Eric is exceptionally good at his job."

"I'm sure," I said, eying the box. "What's this?"

She bit her lower lip. "A thank you present."

"You didn't have to," I said. "Just doing what I felt was right."

She slapped my chest. "Don't be Mr. Modest. You saved me. Go on. Open it!"

I reached up and peeled back the wrapping paper to reveal an Astra coffee machine, identical to the one in her kitchen. Emotions caught in my throat. I didn't know what to say.

Margaret and Karen had walked over when they saw the pair walk in. Karen held a hand to her cheek. "Gracious, Clark. It's beautiful."

"I'll say," Margaret agreed.

"Thank you," I said to Erin after a moment.

"No need for that. I'm forever indebted to you."

"Sorry to make this quick," Chris said, "but Erin and I have plans today."

"What sort of plans?" I asked with a cocked eyebrow.

The pair looked at each other and smiled. Chris said, "Don't know. She wanted a day to take her mind off what happened. She'll mourn later."

"Knowing you, Chris," I said, "I'm sure you can come up with something."

He winked at me. "You know it, Laddie."

* * *

Investigations into Preacher's investment brokerage uncovered a complex Ponzi scheme meant to defraud trusting Grand Stranders. They took him into custody the following week.

After looking into Antonio's business, they did not charge him with any wrongdoing, but his image took a hit when a story ran in the Myrtle Beach Sun News with claims of malpractice. He held true to his word and retired early, which he could afford since he and DeeDee called it quits. The feds arrested her for tax evasion. She was currently out on bond, awaiting trial.

Antonio and I stayed connected over the years. Antonio lived a happy life, sailing around the Caribbean, sipping cocktails, chasing women, and even getting into his own escapades such as the ones I've gone through in the past year. C'est la vie.

* * *

Gomez and I never got to finish our date. To my disappointment, she reconciled with her boyfriend. She called me late one evening after I had shut the store down for the night. This was odd because she usually texted me.

"Gomez, what's up?" I answered.

"Clark, I have some bad news."

What could be worse than her telling me she thought someone had killed Autumn? That she was getting married?

"What is it?" Acid churned in my stomach.

"Autumn's phone."

"Did you find anything on it?"

"We didn't."

Great. Another dead end. "Well, thanks for trying, Gomez."

"No, no. That's the thing. We didn't find anything because we can't find the phone."

"Can't find the phone? I don't get it."

She breathed into the phone. "Someone stole it."

To be continued...

All books in the series are available on Amazon, Barnes and Noble, Books-a-Million, and wherever books are sold. Don't see them in your local store or library? Ask the bookseller or librarian to order them for you.

Learn more on his website at calebwygal.com.

ACKNOWLEDGEMENTS

The kernel of this idea came from a conversation several years ago, long before this series was dreamed of, with Michael Hutchens. He told me about a painting he purchased at a local consignment store. Mike is an artist in his own right and has an eye for art. This painting stood out. There is a plaque on the picture frame that lists Antoine Le Nain as the painter. After Michael did his research and went on the Antiques Roadshow, he learned that Le Nain was likely not the painter and that this was a copy of a famous Benjamin West painting that hangs at the Speed Museum in Louisville, KY. West is widely considered as the Father of American Art. It is a complex story that gave me the inspiration for Cade's character.

I want to thank meteorologist James Hopkins for his insights on hurricanes, tropical storms, waterspouts, and their effects on the coast.

Thanks go out to John Radcliff, a fine musician in his own right, who helped me navigate the field of musical cryptography.

As always, my early readers Haley Mellert, Angie Barnhart, Cari Sparks, and Laurie Cook helped to shape the story, along with my editor, Lisa Borne Graves, into its final form.

All mistakes are mine.

ABOUT THE AUTHOR

Caleb is a member of the International Thriller Writers and Southeastern Writers Association, the author of seven novels, social media marketer, woodworker, occasional golfer, reacher of things on high shelves, beach walker, shark tooth finder, and munchkin wrangler.

His two Lucas Caine Adventure novels, *Blackbeard's Lost Treasure* and *The Search for the Fountain of Youth*, were both Semi-Finalists for the Clive Cussler Adventure Awards Competition.

He is currently at work on the next book in the Myrtle Beach Mystery Series.

He lives in Myrtle Beach with his wife and son (the munchkin).

Visit Caleb online at
www.CalebWygal.com

*If you enjoyed this story please
consider reviewing it online and at Goodreads,
and recommending it to family and friends.*